The Earth Bound

Luke Evans

illusio & baqer

Seattle | San Diego | Los Angeles

THE EARTH BOUND

For more information, to inquire about rights to this or other works, or to purchase copies for special educational, business, or sales promotional uses please write to:

The Zharmae Publishing Press, L.L.C.
5638 Lake Murray Blvd, Suite 217
La Mesa, California 91942
www.zharmae.com

FIRST EDITION

Published in Print and Digital formats in the United States of America

The golden Z logo, and the TZPP logo are trademarks of The Zharmae Publishing Press, L.L.C.

ISBN: 978-1-943549-33-7

Table of Contents

Foreword

PART I: The Awakening

PART II: The Rising

Foreword

As artistic director of Charlie's Port, I receive many requests to help budding singers, dancers, actors, writers, politicians, and even evangelists generate peculiar projects. At age fifteen, Luke Evans sent me his first novel. I couldn't put it down.

Charlie's Port is a creative organization named after my late brother and his stuffed basset hound. Charlie carried "Port" everywhere he went as a little boy. It was assumed that the fuzzy dog made it to the attic or basement at some point, but after Charlie took his own life at the age of fourteen, my family could not locate his "Port" anywhere. After searching the supernatural hole my brother left in my core, I obtained an MFA from Brooklyn College and became a children's theatre director.

When you orchestrate hundreds of tiny people with huge personalities, that gift allows you to invite a handful of immense talents to collaborate with you. I now facilitate a book development process with prodigious youth from all over the world. I am impressed with kids who dive into impossible dreams with perfect faith. Especially those who haul a personal struggle and trust me to help tote the load.

Luke Evans was diagnosed with Asperger's Syndrome at a young age, which is a milder variant of Autistic Disorder characterized by significant difficulties in social interaction and nonverbal communication. Aspie's usually have an eccentric childhood with a circumscribed area of interest and are quite particular about their activities. Many of them have tremendous abilities well beyond their years.

The Earth Bound was a tightly written story that felt as if the reader was being riddled with machine guns spraying word bullets. Luke thought his book was complete, but it needed grammatical editing and additional chapters. The book in some areas went on for pages without a paragraph indention. However, such grammatical flaws were easily dismissed. The writer was fifteen. The content was outstanding.

Luke's main character, Daniel Cohen, also lives with Asperger's Syndrome. This lends a unique element to the YA fiction world, as I'm certain that Daniel and his prophetic paintbrush will become a common reference in high school hallways and middle grade art classes. *The Earth Bound* is blessed with all the riveting plots and twisty turns that keep teenagers turning pages, but it has something else that I have yet to find in mainstream YA fiction. Daniel is not just another introverted protagonist who saves the day. He is one who does so with a prominent disability.

Luke's personal experience and stocked library have sprouted a savvy voice in the paranormal literary market. I am delighted to introduce this new author. Serving as an editor and agent for a minor is not an easy task, convincing publishers to accept his manuscript when most reject more than ninety five percent of their submissions. Whether you chose to read *The Earth Bound* because its paranormal element is unique or Daniel is an Aspie or you are just as tired of vampires as the rest of us... brew a fresh pot of coffee.

Mary Claire Branton
Artistic Director, Charlie's Port
Cartersville, GA

The Earth Bound

Part I
The Awakening

Chapter I
Two Friends and a Psychopath

Rainy days are my favorites. They just have a certain calm to them. The sounds of raindrops pattering on the walls. The sight of water dripping down the windows. It makes the world outside look like a watercolor. I like watercolors. I like all colors, but them especially.

"Daniel!" my father yelled from downstairs. "Are you going to school today or what?"

I groaned. *School.* The rainy days would be alright if it weren't for that little issue. I grabbed my backpack and went downstairs to find my dad in the kitchen but froze when I saw what he was doing. Making pancakes. I raised an eyebrow. "Pancakes?" His head swiveled my way. "Yeah. I figured I'd make us some breakfast and drive you to school."

"Uh, I was just gonna grab some toast and drive myself." I was honestly a little weirded out. My dad hadn't offered me pancakes since I was like, eight. At my words, his smile fell a little.

"Well, I just thought that maybe I could drive you."

"I've had my license for over six months now, Dad. I'm perfectly capable of driving myself to school." With that, I grabbed a piece of toast and head out the door. I didn't even notice the disappointed look on his face.

I climbed into the front seat of my black Honda Accord EX and cranked it, but I stopped short when something caught my eye. Looking back at the house, something seemed to shift in the air. It looked vaguely like fog, only much too dark. Almost black. Like a giant shadow. Whatever it was, it was gone the second I blinked, so I decided it must've been a trick of the light or maybe the rain. I fastened my seatbelt and backed out of the driveway.

***

My parents worry a lot. Not that they think anything is wrong with me, even though there is. It's just their nature to fret, I guess, and they have good reason to. While I drove to school, I thought about the last time my dad offered to make me pancakes. When I thought about it, I was actually seven, not eight. I remember because it was the same week the doctor called and told my parents I have Asperger's Syndrome. I had trouble making friends. I never thought before I spoke. I fixated on things. He said that I "would have difficulty communicating with people or conveying emotions or thoughts". I might develop "unusual preoccupations or rituals" and that I would exhibit "eccentric or repetitive behaviors". Not the best week for the Cohen family.

Things were a little awkward at first but got really bad after Mom and Dad had the big fight. Neither was willing to be alone with the other. It would either be hate-filled, fired arguments, or tortured, unbearable silence. Mom would cook dinner and then take a bath or go out; Dad would stay in his study and work; I would stay in my room and draw with my crayons. I always feel better when I'm drawing. I didn't really understand what was happening. How could I? I was seven. All I knew for sure was that something was wrong with me. And no matter how much my parents say that isn't true, or how much Dr. Farrell says that isn't true, that fact hasn't changed. I'm different. I'm a freak.

Anyways, it happened on a Thursday morning. Mom was ready to drive me to school and Dad was late for work. He came barreling into the kitchen with his briefcase, his hair hastily brushed and clothes askew. He froze when he saw us. It was the first time all week we had been alone together. For one terrible minute, no one said anything. Didn't know what *to* say. But I guess my dad figured that someone had to break the silence. The alternative was waiting for the tension to become so high that the three of us spontaneously combusted.

"A–are you two going?" he asked.

"Yes," was my mom's only reply. "Well," I thought my dad was about to melt. I actually had the image of him melting like a Popsicle in my head the entire time. "Well, do you, uh, have to leave now?"

"We should if we don't want to be late." I'm pretty sure that the only thing preventing the pre-mentioned combustion was the subzero look my mom was giving my dad. It would only occur to me later that Dad shouldn't be late for work either.

"Well, maybe we could have some breakfast? I could make some pancakes or something—"

"You think that'll help?" she asked bluntly. My mom likes to cut to the chase. She always says that beating around the bush is cruel to you, the other person, and the bush. "Do you think making some pancakes will make everything okay? Like the fight never happened?"

"Well what do you want me to do?" he asked.

"You know what I want, but you said it was stupid! Said it was 'unnecessary'!" Mom's voice was still icy, but it was melting. Melting because of a fire blazing underneath the frost. "Like actually treating your child like a person is idiot talk." "So I don't treat him like a person then?"

"NO! You've been treating him like...like..."

"Like what? Come on!"

"Like a book. A really long book, and you want to skip to the end! But you can't so you put it on a shelf and pretend like it isn't there!" She was yelling now.

It was me. They were arguing over *me*. They were both getting

3

so angry, and I was so little, and they looked so big.

"So what? You think I'm ignoring him, is that it?"

"Not ignoring him," Mom replied. "Ignoring the problem."

My problem, I think.

"There is no problem!"

Yes, there was.

"How can you say that?"

"There's nothing wrong with him!"

Yes, there was.

"I DIDN'T SAY THERE WAS!" mom yelled.

Yes, she did.

"BUT YOU CAN'T SAY EVERYTHING IS FINE!" she continued.

"All I asked was if you wanted some freaking pancakes!"

I had wanted pancakes.

"Well we can't solve it like that!" she yelled. "Just by sitting down and eating pancakes and ignoring it until it goes away. It's not going to go away, Nathan! You heard what Dr. Farrell said. He lacks awareness of social norms—"

"I don't care what that quack says, there is nothing wrong with my son!"

"Mommy, Daddy!" I yelled. I couldn't breathe. "Please stop!" But it was like they didn't even hear me.

"Of course there's nothing *wrong* with him, but there is a problem! We need to get him help!"

"He doesn't need us to solve anything for him—"

"Yes, he does. He's seven, he can't fix it himself!" I felt tears coming on. It was my fault. They were fighting because I couldn't fix this.

"Please!" I cried. "Please don't fight, I'll do better!" I ran and stood in between them so they would see me. To make them hear me. "I'll do better, I promise! It won't happen again, please stop fighting!"

They finally looked at me and then glared at each other for a moment. Then Mom grabbed me by the hand and said, "Daniel, honey, let's go to school." She pulled me into the garage.

There was never another fight like that. They bickered a little, but other than that, they pretty much raised me in their own ways. It wasn't for a couple of years that I would actually understand what the fight was about, and exactly what my condition meant, but the gist was still the same. I'm a freak. And my dad never offered us pancakes again. Until this morning, that is.

My eyes started to burn. I reached for a napkin from my backpack and realized that the car wasn't moving anymore. A spark of panic ignited. *Oh crap,* I thought. *Did I stop the car in the middle of the road again?* But wait. All the cars around me were stopped too. Was that the sidewalk in front of me? At some point during my flashback, I had made it to the school parking lot. How long had I been sitting there, lost in bitter memories? I got my answer when I heard the sound of the warning bell, signaling that I had five minutes to run to my locker and get to first period. Hastily, I jumped out of my Honda. But just as I closed and locked the door, I stopped cold. Literally.

An ice-cold sensation came over me. I could feel it in the pit of my stomach. Right down to my bones. It filled me with an overwhelming sense of dread, mingled with excitement and anticipation. *Something very important is going to happen soon,* it said. *Something that will change everything.* That's what this feeling was telling me. It was saying that my life was going to change very soon. And it would never, ever be the same.

With that feeling stuck in my gut, running to my locker in the rain, then sprinting half-way across campus to make it to World History on time, wasn't exactly the best way to start out my day. I'm lucky that Mr. Clearwood is pretty lax about his punishments, because most of my other teachers would have sent me to the office for busting through the door at the last minute and falling to the floor. But all Clearwood did was tell me to take my seat. People were chuckling at my face-plant, and my cheeks burned as I stood up.

I hate people laughing at me. I feel enough like a freak already, and having people laugh and tease doesn't help. My stomach swirled as I stood, and I felt my eyes burning. I started to panic. *Don't cry,* I thought. *Don't cry! Dudes don't cry.* I hate people laughing at me, but I despise people seeing me cry. But sometimes I can't help it. *Just sit down in your seat, Daniel!* Everyone was laughing now, and my legs didn't seem capable of moving. *Move, legs! What's your problem?* I looked at the jeering students for the only face I knew wasn't laughing.

"Daniel?" Mr. Clearwood's voice came through the roar. "Take your seat."

What is the matter with you? Can you not hear them? Shut them up! My eyes kept scanning the student's faces until I found who I was looking for. A pair of shocking, silver eyes popped out at me. I knew those eyes all too well. I looked at the boy harboring them. The dark blond, butterscotch-colored hair falling by his ears. The lean build. *Nico,* I mouthed. He was my only hope. I kept my eyes fixed on him. His face was contorted in worry. He knew I was dying up there. This fear was paralyzing, and he knew it. *Please help me,* I thought. *Help me, Nico, please.* My panic was flooding me. Every laugh felt like a punch in the gut. *Please!*

Then my mind was overcome with a calm thought. A peaceful thought. I looked at Nico as it popped into my head.

It's okay, the voice said. It was a powerful voice. My friend voice. I always called it that. *They can't hurt you, just sit down. It's fine.* This voice always came to me when I needed it. Always brought me strength and composure when I needed it most. I took a deep breath and forced my legs to move. *That's it. You're okay. You're almost there.* I collapsed in my seat next to Nico. The class started to settle down, and I so did I. Thanks to Nico. I know I should give myself the credit. My friend voice was technically my thoughts. But the thing is, it always sounded exactly like Nico. We'd been best friends ever since we were nine, when he saved me from total embarrassment on the playground.

"Hey," he said. "You okay?" I turned to look at him and saw

his shockingly silver-gray eyes filled with concern. He seemed to be analyzing me. That's the thing about those eyes. They make you feel like he can see straight through you. His entire body kind of gave off this *I'll be your friend* vibe. From his light skin with rosy undertones, to his inviting smile. Even his clothes looked kind. Warm colors, modest style. To draw him, I would have to incorporate a lot of soft colors. But his eyes gave the whole image a tinge of *lying to me is useless.*

"Yeah," I said. "Yeah, I'm fine."

Nico sighed, like he was hoping I wouldn't say that. "No, you're not." Damn. I should have known better than to lie to him. Sometimes, I swore Nico Marshall could read minds.

"Well, I will be," I said. That one was true. This kind of thing had happened before. I'd be fine. "They're all jerks."

"It's not just them," he said. "Something else is bugging you isn't it?" Nico never failed to surprise.

"It's...it's nothing—"

"Daniel," he cut me off and looked at me with this look he simply loved to throw at me. A look that said *you can tell me now, or I can figure it out myself. Your choice.* He'd given me that look exactly forty-seven times before. I'd never once chosen the latter.

"My...my dad," I began. "He, uh. He offered me pancakes this morning."

Nico raised an eyebrow, but then a dawn of realization came upon his face. "Oh, right." Of course Nico knew about that week long ago. He was my best friend. He knows everything there is to know about me. "Dragged up some bad memories?"

"Yeah," I answered. "But I'll be okay."

"You know it's not your fault, right?"

"Yes, yes, so everyone loves telling me," I muttered.

"Daniel, you can't—"

"Mr. Cohen, Mr. Marshall." Mr. Clearwood's voice broke us out of our conversation as our heads turned to him. "Is there something you'd like to share with us?" We both stood up. *Why does the universe hate me today?* Nico smirked, which confused me a little. "Well?" Clearwood asked. I know I said that he was lax with his punishments, but if you talk while he's trying to teach, he will smack you silly. If the school board would let him. If the school board would let him, I'm pretty sure he would string us up in the middle of the classroom while the other students watched, then let us hang there for a few days as examples of why you should respect your teachers.

I remained silent. I didn't trust myself to speak.

"No, sir," Nico said. As usual, he came to my rescue. "We were just discussing last night's homework." I swear, Nico was the most collected person I knew. "Sorry if we disrupted class."

"Well just keep quiet and listen to the lesson. Next time, it's detention."

"Yes, sir." We both sat down.

"So, what were you saying?" I whispered to him.

"Shh!" he hissed. "Didn't you hear him?" Nico didn't speak for the rest of the class. I couldn't blame him. He had a job. He couldn't afford to miss a day because of detention. So I tried my best to pay attention to the lesson. Not an easy task.

As Mr. Clearwood droned on about Constantine and the Byzantine Empire, I looked out the window next to my desk overlooking the sidewalk next to the building. I caught notice of someone walking in the direction of the attendance building. His back was to me, so I couldn't see his face, but he didn't seem like anyone I recognized from school. His hair was dark brown and fell past his ears, down his neck. There was something strange about him. He walked slowly, like he wasn't really going anywhere, and I felt this strange sense of...familiarity. Like I knew the guy. He also gave off this weird energy. Even through a glass window and brick wall, I felt the heat of his body as if he were standing inches away.

My staring was interrupted by the sound of the bell. Everyone got up and moseyed to their next class. I looked back toward the guy but he was gone. Strange. When I looked down to grab my stuff, I saw that I had a pen in my hand, and on my paper I'd drawn something in the margins. It didn't really look like anything, just this kind of cloud shape. It was dark and seemed to be swirling and coalescing, with little tendrils of darkness snaking out from it. I got a sort of chill from it, but shook it off and crumpled up the paper. Shaking my head, I gathered my things and left. Nico caught up with me in the hall.

"Like I was saying, you can't blame yourself for the way you are. You were born with your condition."

"Yeah, and because of it, I have no friends other than you."

"Oh, come on. Hayley's your friend."

"Hayley's nice to me because she's your girlfriend."

"Not true!"

"If you hadn't started dating, she never would've spoken to me, and you know it."

"Hey," he exclaimed. "What do we say about that whole 'little spot in the background' mindset of yours?"

"It's all in my head," I mocked.

"That's right, and don't be so sarcastic!" The warning bell went off again. "I gotta get to woodshop, I'll catch up with you at lunch."

"Okay," I said. I marveled at the fact that, no matter how crappy my day was, Nico could cheer me right up. But I hated complaining about my parents to him. I didn't really have any right, considering his own home life. See, Nico's mother is sick. She has a really serious brain tumor. She'd been sick for three years before she had this huge stroke that left her brain dead, and she's been on life support for almost five years. Despite the doctor's insistence that it's time to pull the plug, Nico and his dad are adamant about keeping her as is until they find a way to make her better. His dad works all these temp jobs, but with hospital bills, house bills, food, school, and everything, Nico has had to work ever since he was twelve to help get money. Luckily, he's tall and big, so he managed to convince his boss at the coffee shop that he was fifteen. Nico acted fine about it all, like he accepted the situation, but at times I could tell how much it hurt him. Like whenever I went with him to visit her in the hospital, even I couldn't help but notice the pain in his eyes.

It occurred to me that if I didn't get moving, I'd be late for second period, and Nico wouldn't be there to save me. With a sigh, I sprinted to British Literature. Fun.

***

Fun isn't exactly the right word. But I suppose the class could've been worse. I managed to survive physics and Spanish, but all day I couldn't shake the feeling that something was going to happen soon. Something huge. Whatever it was, I tried my best to shake it off by fifth period.

Today was a *special* day. I had to go to the school guidance counselor to talk about my feelings and give a tearful confession of my inner turmoil. But before all of that good fun, I'd have to wait outside Ms. Fairchild's office with the other depressed kids. And of course, I'd sit alone, dying slowly of discomfort until she called me in to finish me off. I walked into the front office and shuffled toward the bench. I stopped short when I saw who was sitting there. Leo Rivers. Only the scariest kid in school.

He moved here that summer, so he'd been going to school for a few months. People feared him from day one. He wears all black, loose-fitting clothes, and his hair is this flat black color that looks like soot. It's unruly, as if he long ago decided that brushing it was too much of a hassle. It falls down almost to his eyes, which (surprise, surprise) are black. Obsidian. Stony, hard, and cold, almost like he has coals for eyes. Everything about him is black, except his skin, which is shockingly pale alabaster. It looks like pure snow against the rest of him. I could draw him easily with only blacks and whites. Tall and gangling, Leo Rivers is a scary dude.

He's been arrested twice for vandalism, is rarely seen without a cigarette in his hand, and teachers have found booze in his locker three times. But the thing about Leo that sends most people running in the opposite direction is the look he always has on his face. As if his face is a big lump of white coal that will blaze like an inferno if hit with a little spark. That's the part that would be difficult to capture on paper. The intensity of his sensitive and dangerous eyes. I would probably go with a charcoal drawing. Ironic? Maybe. But it would capture the whole thing a lot better. Maybe all black and white, but fiery red for the eyes. That would be cool.

Seeing him, my blood ran cold. I really, really didn't want to sit there with him and wait for Ms. Fairchild to call one of us in. I looked to the other bench, and there sat a beautiful girl with wavy, golden hair that came down to her elbows. Her skin was flawless with a peaches and cream complexion, picture perfect teeth, and heavily lined hazel eyes with thick mascara. She was dressed in trendy clothes, like she had just walked off the cover of a fashion magazine. Any drawing of her would probably have her posing like a model. She was certainly slim enough to walk down a runway. Her name is Natalie Duke. The richest and most popular girl at Spirit Ridge High School. She was applying make-up. Then removing it and reapplying.

Who to sit with? Natalie was looking a lot better than Leo. I was less likely to get burned with a cigarette lighter. But what would I say? Silently praying to die seemed like a good option. I would have to sit down at some point. But then another person caught my eye. A girl with bright emerald eyes, an oval shaped face, light-olive skin, and a mane of curly, black hair. More of an athletic physique than Natalie. Strange, considering I'm fairly certain I've never seen her exercise. I don't think I'd ever been so relieved to see Hayley Rutter in my entire life. The second I saw her claim a spot on the bench next to Leo, I muttered "sold" and sat next to her but on the side away from him. "Hey," I said. Her bright green eyes turned my way.

"Hey," Hayley said with a smile. "You too?"

"Yep," I said dryly. "Can't tell you how glad I am you came in."

"Because your alternatives are Spirit Ridge Barbie or

Frankenstein's felon?"

I chuckled and smiled sheepishly. Natalie and Leo looked at each other in disgust.

"Oh come on, you can say it."

"Okay, fine," I said uncomfortably. "That's the basic idea." That's Hayley for you. She won't hesitate to tell you how she feels right in front of your face. And she will force you to do the same. The only thing she'd never say to me is why we're friends. She would never admit it to save her life, but she only talks to me because she's madly in love with Nico. Otherwise, she never would've taken notice of my existence.

"Man, I hate guidance counselors," she said. "They bring us in here and they talk to us like broken toys that they've been hired to fix. I mean, I once walked into a guidance counselor's office, and she said she was going to 'work on me'. Work on me! What am I? A Buick? Like she was going to fix my 'emotional problems' with power tools. I had to hold myself back from punching that little..."

We talked like that for a while. Or, she talked, and I nodded along, smiling and laughing when appropriate. Being around Hayley is slightly similar to living the Fourth of July every day. Always noise and excitement, and every chance someone might get a third degree burn. Her color scheme consists of black leather jackets with some kind of party color underneath, almost always with a profane or dirty slogan on it. To her, the school dress code consists mainly of fashion tips, not actual rules. Fashion tips she prudently ignores.

To draw her, there would probably be sparks flying in the background with a lot of sharp accents. It would give off this air of *I will do whatever I want*. We kept talking until Leo was called. I turned to Hayley, expecting some comment about Fairchild coming out with no eyebrows, but her expression had turned grave and she was staring at the door.

"Hey. Hayley, are you okay?"

She snapped out of her trance and looked at me. "Yeah. Fine." But she definitely didn't sound fine. Then she did something I did not expect. She glanced at Natalie, whose face was serious too. They exchanged a knowing look, and all of a sudden, the air shifted. Like there was this invisible barrier between Hayley and me that connected her to Natalie. Something passed between them. Something that worried them both and kept me on the outside. Just like always.

A wave of bitter resentment filled me. Daniel Cohen, always just outside the group. Forever out of the loop. Never anybody's first choice. *NO!* I thought. *Stop it! No self-pity.* I hated feeling sorry for myself. *Shut up and deal.* That was my motto. Bottle it up somewhere deep inside where no one can ever find it. Natalie nodded, and Hayley turned away and started rubbing her temples.

"Sure you're alright?" I asked, concerned now.

"Yeah, I'm...I'm o—" she grabbed her head and groaned.

"Hayley?" Panic was rising. I'd seen Hayley have migraines before. It was a problem and it really worried me.

"My head," she moaned.

"Come on, head in the knees, you're alright, it'll be okay." I tried my best to sound soothing. She pulled up her knees and buried her head in them. Then she was still. Natalie was rapidly by her side, her hand on Hayley's arm, hazel eyes full of worry. We waited while Haley didn't move a muscle. My panic was making it hard to breathe. *Will she be okay?* I couldn't stop wondering. Did she need medicine, or would the migraine pass? Should we get somebody? A nurse maybe?

Suddenly, there was a cry from inside. Leo came charging out of Ms. Fairchild's office, the coals in his eyes on fire. Natalie and I shrank away from him. I tried to pull Hayley away, but she jerked abruptly and jumped to her feet. She stood facing Leo, her face completely unafraid, eyes daring him to make a move. Ms. Fairchild emerged, holding a bunch of blackened, smoldering papers. My heart stopped. *Did Leo set them on fire?* How could Hayley stand there facing him? He took a step toward her, and I did something very stupid. I jumped out of my chair and stood next to her, staring right at Leo.

He seemed put off by this.

"What the hell are you doing?" he asked, looking at me with narrowed eyes, raking me over. I couldn't say I wasn't scared. For some reason I wasn't backing away.

"Daniel, sit down," Hayley said. I still couldn't seem to find my voice, so I shook my head. The fire in Leo's eyes surged, but it was momentarily overpowered by something else that I couldn't identify. As for Natalie, her concern for Hayley seemed to stop just short of standing with her against a pyro. But Leo saw that Hayley and I weren't backing down. Slowly, he pushed through us. We watched him storm down the hallway and slam the main office door hard behind him. I looked at Ms. Fairchild and the smoking papers. I didn't realize until later that Leo didn't have a lighter in his hand.

Chapter II
Spirit Ridge

My appointment with Ms. Fairchild was cancelled due to the little incident with Leo. "Are you sure you're okay?" I asked Hayley as we left.

"I'm fine, it was just a headache. What about you? You looked like you might pass out."

"Well, we can't all be fearless like you." She chuckled. Most girls giggled, but Hayley would sooner die than giggle.

"You sure your head's okay?"

"It's *fine*, Daniel," she said before rushing down the stairs and into the science hall where Nico should have been. No doubt going to tell him what had just happened, and I was left alone.

Not that I minded being alone. Sometimes I sought out alone time. I liked being able to walk around with my thoughts. I couldn't believe how Leo had looked facing Hayley and me. So angry. I didn't know a human being could look so angry. I half-expected his ears to start spewing steam. But what bothered me even more was how Hayley and Natalie looked at each other before Hayley's migraine hit.

I hate it when people act like they know something I don't. It makes me feel cut-off. Unwanted. Unwelcome. Besides, as far as I knew, Natalie and Hayley weren't even friends. Natalie definitely didn't seem like the type of girl Hayley would hang out with. I mean, Hayley lived in the worst part of town with two little brothers and a single mother. Natalie was a rich girl who lived in Wind Eye Hills, the high-end, upper class neighborhood, with her aristocratic parents and a team of nannies. Sure, they'd known each other since Pre-K, but this was Spirit Ridge. Everyone knew each other. That didn't make them best friends. But from the concern in Natalie's eyes when Hayley's head was in her knees, you'd think they were sisters. I didn't understand. Not that that was a new thing for me. It was so frustrating. I had all of these emotions rattling around inside but I had no idea how to get them out. I feel like that all the time.

There was only one thing that made me feel better. I left the main building when the idea hit me. Next period didn't start for another fifteen minutes. *What should I do to occupy this free time?* I was supposed to skip psychology to see Fairchild, so I could have gone back there, but I had seen enough psychos for a day and didn't feel like wandering around school with my thoughts for a quarter of an hour. It was fifth period. Which meant that Mr. Wright, the art teacher, was out to lunch. Which meant that the art room was empty. And Mr. Wright rarely remembers to lock the door. I could practically hear the sketchpad calling my name. A wicked grin spread across my face as I ran to the arts building. I crept through the hall until I reached the art room. I turned the handle. *Yes!* It was unlocked. I slipped into the room, but when I shut the door, I heard a shriek. I whirled around and my heart stopped.

There was a girl I didn't recognize. She was absolutely gorgeous. Sun-bronzed skin, almond-shaped brown eyes of the deepest chocolate. They were warm and soft and beautiful. She was tall and curvy and had straight, sleek, jet-black hair that fell down her heart-shaped face and over one shoulder. I immediately wanted to draw her, but I would never be able to. Anything I would attempt would be an insult. It would be like trying to capture the air of a goddess. As I stared at her like an idiot, she stood still, holding a small painting and clutching a piece of paper. She looked very startled.

"Um, hi," she said. All of a sudden, I felt very aware of myself. My palms were sweaty and my tongue had quickly become very dry.

I didn't know what to do and my heart was pounding so hard it was a wonder she couldn't hear it.

"Uh, I...uh..."

"I'm Annabelle. What's your name?"

My name. I should tell her my name. What's my name again? I tried very hard to make my mouth form words, but nothing came. My throat was so dry; I felt like I might vomit. And yet through that, I somehow marveled at how beautiful her voice was. It was like music falling through soft velvet. It made my head swim. And my heart pound harder, if that was even possible.

"Are you okay?" she asked. I had to speak. I had to say something. I didn't want her to think I was a freak. Not her. Say something. Anything! "Well, I'm, uh...I'm just gonna..." she moved toward the door in discomfort.

NO! Don't let her leave. I didn't want her to leave. Not yet. The room wouldn't be beautiful without her. And she would leave thinking I was an idiot. I have no idea how, but I managed to force it out. "Wait!" She stopped at the door and looked back. "My name." Doing good so far. She looked at me expectantly. I remembered I should probably finish that sentence. "It's, um, Daniel. Daniel Cohen."

"Well, nice to meet you, Daniel Cohen. I'm Annabelle Martin." She smiled. I thought I might faint. Her smile was beyond incredible. "So, um, what are you doing here?" Oh no. More words? "I came to draw."

"Oh, really?" she said, raising an eyebrow. It occurred to me that that was probably pretty obvious.

"I mean, I'm free. I mean, not free as in, I'm not seeing anyone, which I'm not! I mean...oh kill me." She giggled. I literally thought I might keel over, dead. "I meant I have a free period, and I wanted to come and draw for a while."

"Ah," she said.

"Um, I don't know you." She raised an eyebrow again. "I mean, I don't recognize you! I mean...what I meant was...oh God."

17

I took a deep breath. "Are you new here?"

"Yes," she said. "I just moved here."

"Why would anyone move *to* Spirit Ridge?" I blurted out. She laughed at that. Oh my God. I had made her laugh. It was enough to make me smile. Man, she has the greatest laugh.

"I know it's kinda small, but, it's nice. Homey."

"Talking to someone who's lived his entire life here," I said. "So, um, where are you from? You know, originally?"

"No offense Daniel, but I just met you, and you've said like ten sentences to me, so I'd rather not tell you my life's story just yet."

"Oh," my heart fell a little. "Okay then."

"I'll see you later?" Then she left.

Immediately, the room felt duller, and I felt like falling to the ground. What had just happened? I forgot why I had even gone there. I obviously hadn't known she was there. I must've been there for a reason. To do something. All my mind seemed to want to think about was her. Draw. I had gone there to draw. Did she say she'd see me later? She actually planned on speaking to me after that? I did make her laugh. And I suppose it could've gone worse. At least I said more than what I was thinking, which was simply, *you're pretty.* For the first time I actually spoke to a girl who wasn't a friend, my mom, or someone trying to copy off my homework, and it actually went well. She definitely didn't seem to hate me.

Whoa there! I thought. *You talked to the girl for under a minute. For most of it you were stuttering and mumbling, and the rest of it you spent with your foot in your mouth.* She'd never go for me. I mean, I couldn't even have a decent conversation with her, and it's not like I'm the most handsome guy in school.

I mean, I'm not ugly, just very, very average. Sure, I'm tall. Five eleven, in fact. But I never feel tall. I normally feel about five feet, and I slouch. Plus, I'm thin and bony, so my height exaggerates it and makes me look scrawny. My hair is plain brown that curls slightly at my neck, and my skin tone is medium. My eyes are certainly not average, though. They are this shockingly pale, bright blue color. Opalescent blue. Closer to white than blue, really, managing this strange mix of brightness. As if they don't stand out strongly enough already against my dark hair, my darker lashes and eyebrows make the contrast even sharper, so they look almost luminescent. My mother calls them piercing blue, but I call them frightening. Human eyes are really not supposed to be this color. There's nothing about me that could possibly appeal to a girl like that.

I turned to leave, then saw that she had left the painting she had been holding. I picked it up. It was a house. A beautiful beach house. The back view of a two-story beach house painted a light mauve. The roof was wooden. Mahogany by the look of it. It had sliding glass doors and a staircase leading down from the back deck into the bright, clean sand. The sun was shining on the sand, making the tiny little crystals in it sparkle. The sky was the most gorgeous shade of baby blue without a single cloud. The brush strokes were smooth and delicate. The accents were soft and soothing, giving it the feel of a home. The black seashells in the sand made the sparkling crystals pop. It was simply amazing. I knew it was someone's home, someone who had spent many hours sitting on that back deck listening to the sound of waves crashing against the shore. I could practically hear the sound of people laughing, little kids running, maybe even a dog barking. I could see happiness there, so much comfort and love. But also a strong wistfulness. A longing for that home. My eye roamed up to a window. A second story window with the drapes closed. I heard screams echoing from inside, filled with terror and seeming to resonate from inside the painting itself. There was a dark past to this painting. Memories of happiness mingled with fear. I wondered if Annabelle had lived there. There was no signature, but a few parts were still wet, meaning she may have been in here to finish it. I ran my hand along the sand. She had used textured paint to simulate the gritty sand and seashells. I gasped at the realization. *She painted this.* I'm not sure how I knew. I just did. I knew it was hers. The same way I knew that she lived here.

I checked my watch. Four minutes left until next period. I used those four minutes to dry the painting by holding it over the kiln. Little trick I picked up in class. When the bell rang, the painting was dry, so I put it in my backpack and left.

***

"You took the painting?"

"So I could give it back to her," I told Nico, my voice taking on the tone of someone teaching a child that two plus two equals four. We were at Nico's house with Hayley watching a movie.

"Don't get smart," Nico warned.

"Hello," Hayley said. "Earth-to-Nico. Daniel took the painting for obvious reasons. He gives it back to this Annabelle chick, instant excuse to talk to her, and she's all grateful. They bond over their mutual love of art, and *BOOM!*" She snapped her fingers for emphasis. "They're rolling around naked on canvas."

I laughed. "Yeah, that was the general idea," I said, my voice dripping with sarcasm.

"Called it," she said, raising a hand in the air triumphantly. Nico laughed and put his arm around her, smiling at her affectionately.

"Look guys, I just wanted to return the painting."

Nico looked me in the eyes. "Seriously? You're not even a little attracted?"

I squirmed under the gaze of his warm silver eyes. "N–n–no."

"Liar," he said with a smirk.

"Look, what does it even matter?" I asked, grabbing a handful of popcorn.

"Why wouldn't it matter, Daniel? You're a catch," Nico said.

"Yeah, sure. The ladies are all over me."

"You're a smart-ass, you know that right?"

"And you're a jack-ass, you know *that* right?" They both laughed.

"See?" Hayley said. "If you were as relaxed around other people as you are around us, you'd be beating back the ladies with a stick."

"Well I'm not," I said curtly. Nico gave Hayley a nudge and a look of disapproval, and her playful smile vanished.

"I'm sorry," she said. "I didn't mean it like that."

"It's-it's fine," I muttered. "I'm okay."

"She just meant Annabelle would be all over you if she knew the real you," Nico said.

"Yeah, sure she would."

Nico rolled his eyes. "Daniel—"

"Can we just watch the movie please?" Nico was always good at understanding when I really, really didn't want to talk, so he shut up. I guess Hayley took that as a sign that she should shut up too.

We watched the movie for a while. It was some old, slasher flick with a lot of blood. Hayley picked it out. I joked that Nico only agreed so that Hayley would bury her face in his chest at the scary parts. Not that there was even a slight chance of that happening. Just as the psycho killer was about to cut open some screaming blonde girl, Hayley's cell phone went off. She groaned before looking at the caller ID, but when she saw the name on the screen, her face turned deadly serious. I tried to look at the name, but she turned the phone away and looked straight at Nico. She said nothing, just stared into his eyes, emerald to silver. A dark shadow fell over his face that I had never seen before. It kind of scared me.

"Are you guys okay?" I asked. Nico turned my way, and Hayley looked surprised, like she had forgotten I was there.

"Yeah, sure," Nico said. "Hey, uh, I completely forgot. My dad will be home soon, and he wanted to have dinner, just the two of us, so—"

"We're gonna have to go!" Hayley exclaimed.

"Right," he said. "So, uh, you know...bye."

"Uh, okay," I said. He rushed me downstairs and practically pushed me out the door. "What about Hayley?" He looked at her, and I could practically see the *whoops!* on his face.

"Uh, she can stay a little while longer," putting an arm around her waist in a manner that suggested they would *not* be watching another movie. She did the same, so I took a hint. I turned to leave and started toward my car. I got in and cranked the engine, but instead of driving home, I sat there for a second. Hayley had tried to hide the name on her caller ID, but I had caught a glimpse. It was Leo Rivers.

***

I couldn't figure out why Hayley would talk to Leo. Maybe he wanted to tell her off for standing up to him today. If that were the case, would he also come after me? I had stood with Hayley. I didn't sit down or back away. I didn't feel like going home yet. My parents probably wouldn't be expecting me for another good hour and a half. I had only been at Nico's for like thirty minutes. I knew exactly where I wanted to go.

I did a U-turn through the town square. Not that there was much town. Spirit Ridge was a small place. The kind of town that big city dwellers call "quaint", and the people who actually live here call "prison". Almost every kid in town dreamed of leaving someday, living in New York, or Los Angeles, or even some European wonderland like Venice or Paris. But hardly anyone ever made it. Most end up marrying someone they've known since childhood and having kids that would know your friend's kids through childhood. That's just how it works here. I thought about that for a while as I drove. *I bet Hayley and Nico will end up together*, I thought. Those two had been together for two years, and I had never seen a better match. True, Hayley is upbeat and wild, while Nico was calm and collected, but opposites really did attract in this situation. Hayley is the only person that could get Nico fired up, and Nico is probably the only person capable of taming her. Truly a match made in...well, Spirit Ridge. And matches made in Spirit Ridge always ended up in 'till death do us part' and all that.

I turned the corner where clusters of buildings become few and far between, soon reaching a wide clearing in the woods, in the center of which is an old warehouse, long since abandoned that weeds and brush have grown around it. I never noticed the place until my parents had another big fight a few years ago. I had gone out for some fresh air and discovered the dilapidated gem. The place is a dump. The bricks are chipped, the paint faded and cracked. The huge letters on the window have faded away, leaving white marks where they used to be. The rafters are falling and hanging by splinters, which are the only pieces of wood not rotted. Inside, cobwebs rest in every corner, and a thick layer of dust covers the floors and walls, hiding paint stains of all colors. On the broken sign reads "Alexander Gallery" in fancy cursive writing. It's perfect in every way.

I got out of the car and admired the rickety sign. I opened the doors to my art studio and was instantly bombarded by the scent of acrylic paint. It made me a little dizzy, but it made me smile. When I walked in and shut the door, an intense nirvana came over me. My shoulders relaxed and I breathed out a sigh of relief. It felt like I had taken a fifty-pound weight and dropped it at the door. I felt safe. Like nothing could hurt me. Leo, Nico and Hayley, Mom and Dad, Ms. Fairchild, Annabelle, my condition. All of that was outside. I was safe and secure as long as I stayed in there. Nobody knew about it but me. Not even Nico. It was my place. All mine.

Using my phone as a light, I found the matchbook and candles I kept around and cheerfully lit them. As soon as the room was sufficiently illuminated, I walked to an easel, took out my assortment of pens and pencils, situated my large sketchpad, and flipped open to a blank page. I checked my watch. Nine o'clock. One hour left. I picked up a pen and pressed it lightly to the pad. Immediately, my hand disconnected from my brain and started moving of its own accord. This was all I did there. I didn't think about it. I just drew. Just zoned out and drew. I watched as the pen moved across the sheet, drawing lines and curves that flowed together, creating shapes that came together to create a scene. It felt like all the emotions, all the anxiety, all the fear and doubt that ran through me during the day, poured itself out onto the page. Paper was more empathetic than words. It could say what I was feeling way better than I could. I could draw whatever I wanted and nobody could judge me for it. Paper didn't judge me. Paper understood me. I let myself draw. I let myself go. And the entire world fell away.

Chapter III
The Hand Possessed

I stayed at my studio longer than planned. It was an hour past my curfew when I blew out the last candle. My parents had already called—twice each. It's not like I intended to stay until eleven o'clock. When I started drawing, I lost myself. I didn't hear either of my mom's calls, or my dad's first one. As I unlocked my car, something *snapped* nearby. I turned toward the sound and saw nothing but woods. I felt a strange sensation, like I was being watched, but I didn't see anyone. My mind said it was probably just an animal, but a gut feeling told me that it was something else. But what?

When I got home, I pulled up as quietly as I could, praying my parents had fallen asleep. Should've known better. The light in the living room window clicked on the minute I cut the engine. I leaned back in the seat and groaned. I wondered if it would be Mom or Dad grounding me. Surely they wouldn't chastise me together. I took the keys out of the ignition and went to face my death. As I unlocked the door and stepped inside, I thought it would probably be Mom. *After this morning, there's no way it's Dad.* I was right. My mom was sitting in the den, waiting for me.

"Where have you been?"

"Mom, I know my curfew was ten, but—"

"Do you have any idea how worried I've been?"

"I know, I'm sorry, the, uh, movie lasted longer than we thought. The TV broke, and we, um, ordered a pizza, and the guy was late." I know what you're thinking, and yes; my excuses are always that weak.

"The school called," mom said. "I know about what happened with Leo Rivers." This took me aback.

"Oh," I said. "That." I stared at the floor.

"Daniel, why wouldn't you tell me? And why would you challenge him like that?"

"I had to!" I exclaimed. "He tried to hurt Ms. Fairchild, and he was going to hurt Hayley."

"So the solution is to let him hurt you?"

"I thought you guys wanted me to stand up to bullies."

"Bullies, yes. But not criminals!"

"So I should've sat on my ass and let Hayley get burned?!"

"DANIEL!" she screamed. I immediately regretted this. Bad things happen when I curse in front of my mother.

"I'm sorry," I said, looking straight at her. Honestly, I look almost nothing like my mom. We have about the same medium complexion, but that's about it. The bright blue eyes, the truffle brown hair, the facial structure; all of that was my dad. "I just didn't want Hayley to get hurt." "Daniel, I'm proud that you stood up for your friend. But what if Leo had hurt you? You should've told Hayley to back down."

I snorted. "Hayley Rutter? Back down? Dream on." She glared, and I knew it was time for submission. "I'm sorry," I said. "It won't happen again. I promise."

"Okay," she said reluctantly. As long as she gets an apology and a promise of repent, my mom's happy. She let me go up to my room where I showered, brushed my teeth, put on pajamas, and got in bed.

Just as I drifted into sleep, the door cracked open, spilling light into the room. "Dad?" I muttered groggily.

"Hey," he said.

"If you're here to get on to me about Leo too, can it please wait until morning?"

"It's not. I wanted to talk about this morning." I was wide-awake now.

"What do you mean?" I asked apprehensively.

"Just wanna see if you're okay."

"Yeah," I said. "Fine." I silently wondered how many times I had said that today. Dad sighed.

"You know I love you, right?" he asked.

"Yeah, of course," I said. "I love you, too."

"I know I've been a little hard lately, with your condition." I really didn't want to have this conversation. "But it's only because I know you're going to have a lot to face. Some stuff you're going to have to face on your own." Now I didn't understand.

"On my *own*?" I repeated.

"Yes," he said. "You have special gifts, Daniel." I was confused.

"I don't understand." *What gifts?* He looked at me sympathetically.

"You will," he said, and got up to leave. I was going to call him back, but something made me stop. I just let him go, leaving me lying in the dark.

***

"Then he said, 'you will', and left." I was telling Nico about what had happened with my dad. We were in Spanish, and Señor Garcia was blathering on about conjugating, yadda-yadda-yadda. At least that's what I was getting from it.

"That's weird," Nico said. "What do you think he meant?"

"Dunno," I answered. "Thinking he was a little drunk." Nico grinned. "It's the first time in a while since he even mentioned my..." I stopped. "Condition," I finished.

"You can say the word, you know," he said. "It's not like it's dirty."

"Nico." He didn't say another word about it. The thing was, what my dad told me lined up perfectly with the cold sensation I had felt the day before. Whatever was happening, it had something to do with these gifts my dad was telling me about. I was sure of it.

As I walked toward the front office for my appointment with Ms. Fairchild, I heard a locker slam nearby. I whirled around, and my heart stopped when I saw who had slammed it. Leo Rivers. He towered at the end of the hallway, obsidian eyes giving me a death stare. Two black daggers. Coals sharpened into knives pointing straight at me, cutting clean through me like warm butter. Without saying a word, he took out a lighter and lit a cigarette. He took longer than necessary, making sure to let me see the blue of the flame. He put the lighter away, gave me another glare, and walked away.

He hadn't said a word, but that look conveyed everything. Standing up to him had been a mistake. I had challenged him, and he was telling me that I had better mind my own business. *Or else.* With just a look, he had threatened me. I had just been threatened. I had never been threatened before. I let that sink in for a minute. Something became perfectly clear to me. I had to stay away from Leo. No matter what.

***

I came into Fairchild's office a little late.

"I'm sorry, I got held up." It wasn't a lie. I was held up by standing in the hallway in the exact same spot for ten minutes. Processing what had happened. But there wasn't a chance in hell I was about to tell a counselor about it. I wasn't a snitch. Plus Leo would surely have my blood.

"It's alright," she said. "Have a seat, Daniel." I sat down across from her. Ms. Fairchild was a medium-height woman. She had rosy skin, with short, strawberry blonde hair, and compassionate aquamarine eyes. Or at least the make-up she was wearing made them appear aquamarine. It was a simple enough trick. Add that with her sensible, grandma clothes, and she was pretty much designed to make people think, *what a nice lady. I can tell her all my deepest, darkest secrets.*

"So, um…" I began. "What am I doing here, then?"

"We're here to talk about issues you've been having with your Asperger's." I flinched a little at the word.

"Think my 'issues' have been a lot less severe this year."

"Well, yes, but we're just trying to see if it's a true progression." Translation: she wanted to know if I was faking it. Which I was, but there was no way I was going to let her know that. She opened the folder in front of her, and examined the papers inside. "Now, you were diagnosed when you were seven. Is that right?" I nodded. "What happened then?"

"It's in the file," I said.

"Yes, but I want you to tell me." I was *so* hating this woman.

"I, uh…I…" supremely hated telling this story, "was at an art tent at a crafts fair with my parents. And I, uh, told a woman that her painting was poorly shaded and boring."

"Why?"

"Because it was," I said simply.

"Ah," she said, as if this made perfect sense. "Go on."

"So, I took out my crayons and started to color over it. My parents had to pay for it, and when we got home, I had no idea what I had done that was so bad. My mom had me tested." She started writing this down. Obviously, I understood now why it had been wrong, but that painting had still sucked. It was amazingly uncreative and derivative of Monet's work, plus the "artist" had placed the accents in all the wrong places.

"So you like art?" she asked.

"Sure," I answered.

"Daniel, you know Aspies often have special interests that they fixate on."

"I know."

"Do you think that art is your special interest?"

"I guess. Drawing, really," I added when she gave me a *yes, and* look.

29

"Mmm. So when you criticized this painting, you weren't thinking."

"Of course not."

"You acted on impulse."

"Yes."

"But there hasn't been much of that lately." I thought of my disastrous conversation with Annabelle. I'm pretty sure I didn't actually plan on saying that I was single.

"No, not really," I lied.

She bent down to write something else in her notes. I rolled my eyes at the top of her head while she wasn't looking. I really wanted to leave. When she straightened, I nearly jumped out of my seat. Her eyes had turned completely black. There were no irises, no whites, just entirely black. The compassionate, caring image vanished and was replaced by something sinister and cruel and unnatural. I stared in horror at what I was seeing, at those fathomless black pits of eyes and felt like I was seeing something not at all human.

"Daniel?" she said.

I blinked and her eyes went back to aquamarine, the sweet, understanding grandmother image back in place, and she was staring at me with a furrowed brow.

"I–I'm sorry, what?" I said, flustered by the frightening sight.

"I said, why do you think that is?"

"Um," I thought, trying to convince myself it had just been a trick of the light. I had spoken my mind a lot before. I used to be even worse than Hayley. I had absolutely no filter. No impulse control. If it went through my head, it instantly came out my mouth. No matter who it hurt or embarrassed. "Hey Mrs. Torres, I like your wig." "Hey mom, this meatloaf tastes like doggy butt." "Hey Millie, I can see your boobs." "Hey Justin, my butt itches." "Hey Nico, I'm sorry your mom's a vegetable."

People would laugh at me. Or look at me like I was a freak. Or just avoid talking to me. I was always either alienated or ridiculed. Always one of them. Eventually, I learned that it was better not to even trust myself to speak. If I spoke, I would just end up saying something wrong.

"Well?" Fairchild asked. I snapped my head up, having lost myself in memories.

"Just grew out of it, I guess," I muttered.

"Did you? Or did you just go further in?" We were both silent.

***

"Did you?"

"You're a jerk, Nico," I answered. We were in art class, the one class I actually enjoyed. We were partnered up to make a clay pot.

"Seriously," he said. "For so long you were Mr. Impulsive. But after a while, you became Mr. Shy. How'd that happen?"

"I don't know," I said defensively. "People change?"

"Try again," he said.

"Learn from your mistakes."

"Not quite."

"Shut the hell up and hand me the chisel?"

"Don't think that's it either," he said with a smirk. I reached over and grabbed it myself. We worked for a few minutes, but then the door creaked open and I looked up to see who was there. My heart skipped a beat when I saw who it was. *Did the room just get brighter?* It was Annabelle, looking a little sheepish as she walked in to meet Mr. Wright.

"Little late, aren't you?" he asked.

"Sorry," she said. "I'm still trying to learn my way around." I nudged Nico and nodded my head at her. He turned to look at her and then looked back at me.

"Is that her?" he asked. I nodded. He turned back to get a better look. "Well you weren't lying about her looks." I hit him with some dusted clay.

"Hey!"

"Hayley Rutter," I reminded. "Name ring a bell?"

31

"I was supporting you."

I rolled my eyes.

"It's okay," Mr. Wright said to her. "We're making clay pots, you'll need a partner." Nico's head snapped toward me, and he was smiling like he had just had an idea.

"What?" He grinned and then doubled over, moaning. "Nico?! Are you okay?"

"My stomach," he moaned. "My stomach is killing me."

"Mr. Wright!" I yelled. His head turned toward me and he came running over when he saw Nico. "He says his stomach is hurting."

"Nico, are you okay?" he asked. Nico shook his head.

"I think I ate a bad taco at lunch."

"Do you need to go to the nurse? Or the bathroom?"

"What about our pot?" Oh my God. He wasn't.

"Uh...Annabelle!" She looked startled. "Come here, you'll be Daniel's partner. They can finish it."

"Well...okay," Nico said. "I guess that's alright." Mr. Wright walked him out and Annabelle came to stand next to me. As Nico was leaving, he turned back to me and winked.

"Hey again," Annabelle said.

"Hey," I said. "Fancy meeting you here."

She giggled.

"Is your friend gonna be okay?" she asked.

"Uh, something tells me he'll be fine," I responded.

"Good," she said. We were both quiet for a moment. "So, uh, you wanna get me up to speed on the assignment?"

"Oh, right," I said. I had to get better at this. "Well, the basic idea is to...well, make a clay pot." "That's it?" she sounded a little disappointed.

"Well, we can make a face in it if we want."

"Well, what you've got so far looks like a clay ash tray." She wasn't wrong. I may love art, but I'm really better with a pencil or a paintbrush. 3-D isn't my thing.

"You know something about this?" I asked.

"Step aside," she said. "Let the master work." I moved aside and let her at it. She cracked her knuckles and stretched her neck like pro-boxers do in movies. I chuckled. Then she went to work on the clay. Within seconds she had smoothed the surface and started to lay down groundwork for it.

"Wow," I said.

"Well, what did you think 'master' meant?"

"Not that."

"Well, what about you? Aren't you an artist? You were sneaking into an art room yesterday."

"So were you," I muttered.

"Fair enough," she said. "But you said you came to draw, right?"

"And does this," I held up the chisel, "look like a pencil?"

"Touché," she said with another giggle.

"But apparently, you're like the jack of all trades."

"I wouldn't say that," she said.

"What would you say?" I blurted out. Holy crap. I was talking to her. I was actually talking to her. I was talking to her and I wasn't mumbling or stuttering or blabbering. We kept talking while we worked. Or *she* worked, and I handed her tools. I felt like Nico when we partnered up in a painting assignment. It felt so good to actually talk to a girl like that. It felt great. And we made a pretty awesome clay pot. It had an intricate design etched into the handles and holes in the side. When we presented it to the class, the teacher let us turn off the lights and put a candle in it, which cast these really cool lights on the walls. Annabelle had a real gift. Toward the end of class we were still talking with ease. Quite a record for me.

"So you've lived here your entire life?" she asked.

"Pretty much," I answered. "Ever since I was born. Most people here have lived here their whole lives."

"So I'm pretty much like an alien to you guys?"

"No, actually it's more like the mainlanders invading the island tribe." She laughed.

"So you're going to roast me over a fire?"

"Of course. The bonfire's tonight. It's gonna be the party of the year. Only, you'll be the one from the beach." She stopped laughing and stared at me in confusion. "What?" I asked.

"How did you know I was from the beach?" she asked.

"Didn't you tell me?" I said.

"No," she said, seeming a bit put off. "I never told you that."

I racked my memory, but she was right. She hadn't told me. I had seen the painting, and it seemed like she had painted her home. But she had never told me. It was the painting.

"How did you know that?" she asked, seeming frightened by my silence.

"I—" I tried hastily to explain myself. "I—I saw it, the purple house and it was sunny, and you loved it! With the little boy and the dog, and—"

"How do you know about my dog?!" she shrieked, sounding truly scared now. "How do you know about my little brother, how do you know I lived in a purple house?"

"No, it's not what you think." *The painting* I thought. *Get the painting from your bag and explain it to her.* But right then was when the bell chose to ring. Annabelle grabbed her backpack and ran out the door before I could say a word.

I knew this would happen. I knew it. I let go. I started to trust myself to talk to someone other than Nico or Hayley (who weren't allowed to judge me) and this is what happens. I screw up. Now Annabelle thought I was some sort of freaky stalker, instead of someone who happened to pick up a painting she left. I felt sick to my stomach. My head was spinning. My chest hurt. She would never speak to me again. We had actually talked. I had actually made a new friend. A beautiful, funny, cool friend who actually seemed to like me, and I blew it. Classic Daniel. Of course I'd blow it. Why had I been so stupid? I should've just let her work and stayed silent. Or told Mr. Wright that Nico was faking. Of course, then he would think Nico was trying to skip class, and Nico would get sent to detention, and Nico could not afford detention when he had work right after school. I shouldn't have even pointed Annabelle out to Nico. Then he never would've tried to help me, I never would've gotten comfortable, and she wouldn't hate me. I was walking through the hallway, sulking, feeling like crap, when Nico came up.

"So, how'd it go?" he asked.

I looked up at him, and a pint of resentment welled up inside. He should've minded his own business. He should've stayed in class and stayed out of it.

"Well?"

"You suck," I said. Nico looked taken aback.

"What?" he asked.

"Why did you do that? Why couldn't you stay out of it?"

"I was trying to help you," he said, staying calm. God, why is he so damn calm all the time?

"Well, you didn't! I ended up talking to her for almost the entire class." Nico was quiet, like he expected me to say more.

"So? That's *good* isn't it?"

"No! That guarantees that I'll blow it!"

"How did you blow it?"

"I accidentally let slip that I knew she was from the beach."

Again, he looked like he wasn't following. "So?"

"So, she never told me that! I only gathered it from the painting. Now she thinks I'm stalking her!" Nico finally looked like he understood.

"Oh," he said. "Daniel, I'm so sorry—"

"Why couldn't you just leave it alone? Why did you have to try and do that?"

"I wanted to help you," he said, his voice so calm, it was making me mad. "I didn't know that would happen."

"You should've!" "How would I know?"

"BECAUSE YOU SHOULD'VE KNOWN I WOULD MESS IT UP!" I yelled.

"Daniel!" he said. Somehow he managed to raise his voice

without actually yelling or sounding angry, or frustrated, or anything. I stopped as my friend voice filled my head. *Everything will be fine. It's fine.* Slowly, my anger ebbed away. What was I doing? Nico was my best friend. He had been trying to help. Nico would never hurt me intentionally.

"I-I'm sorry," I said.

"It's okay," he said. "It's not your fault."

"Hey," I said after a second. "If I skip calculus, will you cover for me?"

"Yeah, sure," he said.

"Thanks." I started to walk away.

"Where are you going?" he asked.

I waited a moment. "I just need to be alone." He nodded and let me go. I went out to the student parking lot and started up the Honda. I needed to get out of there. I needed to leave my problems. I needed to feel safe.

***

When I got to the studio, I ran in and practically slammed the door. I would have, if I didn't know that doing so could've possibly brought down the building. I went straight to an easel and opened it to the drawing I had started the night before. I picked up a pen, but something felt wrong. I didn't want to keep going on this one. I wanted to start a new one. I tore the drawing out and flipped to a blank sheet.

Without warning, an image flooded my mind. The funny thing was, I couldn't make it out. I knew that if I drew it, it would be clear. I took the pen and started running it across the sheet. Something felt weird. Different. But somehow, not wrong. I knew I needed this image on the paper. It needed to be there. I had to get it out of my head. I had to see it. My head was pounding, like the image wanted to be freed. It wanted to be on the sheet, I desperately needed it to be there. I started drawing faster. My hand took on a sense of urgency. I had to finish. I had to finish it right then. My hand moved faster and faster, racing across the blank white square, filling it with color. I knew I had to keep going. I could *not* stop until it was finished. As I drew, I felt a tingle go from my head, down my neck, and through my arm into my hand. Like I was taking the unclear image and pouring it out onto the canvas so that I could see it. A feeling of anticipation filled me as I approached the finish. It was almost done. I would see it in just a minute. I would see it, and everything would be right again. A little splash of color here. One more line there...*there!*

It was finished. At once, the sense of urgency vanished. My head stopped pounding. I took a step back to look at the drawing and was surprised by what I saw. It was a staircase. A pure white staircase dripping with blood. I cringed when I saw the blood. It was a deep, dark scarlet, and it seemed to be streaming from the top stair. Hanging over the ledge of the step, was a hand. A human hand, hanging limp and frail. It was so pale, it was alabaster, close to the white of the stairs below it. The stairs she had died on. She was dead. I had drawn a dead woman with blood streaming down the steps. I wasn't even sure how I knew she was a woman. It was just a gut feeling.

Wait a minute. Why was I concerned about her gender? I had drawn a dead person. Why would I do that? Why would I draw something so morbid, so...disturbing. Why had I needed to see it so badly? But the most frightening part of the drawing wasn't even the dead woman or the blood. It was what was above her. Darkness. There was a hole, like a large window, or a door, and it seemed to be pouring out darkness as if it were sunlight. Pitch-black darkness. I wasn't sure why it was so frightening, but it was. It looked menacing, and looking into it, I had a powerful sensation that I was suffocating. The darkness was pressing hard on me. Squeezing me. I couldn't breathe. It was like it was coming out of the drawing just to drain the life out of me. It was...evil.

That was the only word for it. Evil. Looking into it, I knew it was what true evil looks like. I didn't understand. Why was this image in my head? Why had it been so vague? Why did I want it drawn so badly? What did it mean? I only knew one thing for sure; this was it. That feeling I had had. The one that said something was about to happen. This was it. I wasn't sure exactly how. But this was it. Another cold feeling came over me. It reverberated throughout my entire being. *I am different now. Everything is different now.*

Chapter IV
Art is Pain

Normally when I go to my art studio, I draw abstract designs, or something beautiful I encounter (meaning that the drawing I started the night before was, of course, Annabelle), but I didn't often draw someone dead on a staircase, with the essence of evil looming above them. That was a new one. I couldn't quite figure out why I had done it as I walked to my car. It was probably some image I had seen in a book or something. Seems like something some messed up Renaissance artist would paint. But that didn't explain why I had wanted to draw it so badly. Didn't explain that powerful feeling of...something like...like a beginning. Like I had waited a long time for something, and here it was. I didn't know what to make of it.

It was five o'clock. I was driving home. School had been out for an hour and a half. I really hoped Nico had come up with a good enough excuse for our calculus teacher as to why I wasn't in class. It struck me that this was the first time I ever left the studio not feeling better. I mean, I wasn't thinking about how Annabelle was terrified of me, or how I had lost my cool at Nico. But now I was worried about my own mental health. Only people with deep, deep psychological issues draw dead people for no reason, right?

Was I crazy? I wasn't crazy. Then again, crazy people never think they're crazy. But I wasn't crazy. I remembered seeing something online about scientists trying to find a link between Asperger's and psychosis. Were people with my condition crazy? I knew a lot of serial killers had it. But was it really a cause-effect situation? No. I was not crazy. There were a number of classes I was taking with textbooks I could've seen that picture in. Psychology, Art, Literature. Plus I do watch a lot of horror movies. It's not like I was a psycho, or I was into necrophilia or anything. I didn't even like cemeteries. I had only ever been to a funeral once. I had seen a picture somewhere. That was the only explanation.

On my way home, I drove by the local café, where Nico worked, and stopped to get myself some coffee. I know it sounds like caffeine probably wasn't the best thing for me at that point, but for some reason coffee calms my nerves. Familiar faces were perched at the round, shiny, metallic tables with laptops and iPads, some with ear buds, listening to music or watching YouTube. The ones actually having coffee were seated along the row of neon colored, backless chairs in front of the polished countertop. I approached the cash register, not needing to look at the multi-colored menu posted overhead.

"I'll take an Americano with extra cream, extra foam, and four shots of espresso, to go," I said to the barista.

"Four shots?" she asked.

"Yes, please," I said. She shrugged and went to make the order. I was counting out my money when something in the corner caught my eye. I looked up and saw a guy standing in the corner, apart from everyone. Nobody was paying him any attention. He just stood there, with his back to everyone. Even though he was facing away from me, I felt like I could feel his eyes on me, drilling into me. The sight stirred something in my memory. I had seen him the other day in World History. The guy who had caught my attention out the window. *Who was he?* Nobody seemed to notice him. The sight of him left me in a trance, incapable of moving. Again, I felt that strange sense of power coming off of him, like he was right next to me.

"Hey, Daniel." I snapped out of my trance and spun on my heel to see Hayley.

"Oh," I said, relieved. "Hayley."

"Little nervous?" she asked.

I chuckled…well, nervously. "Yeah, a little." I looked back to where the guy had been, but he was gone. I furrowed my brow, figuring he might have left or gone to the bathroom.

"Something wrong?" Hayley asked.

"No. Nothing."

"Nico told me what happened with Annabelle."

"Oh," I said. "Well, um…I don't really wanna…"

"Yeah, I know," she said, waving my discomfort off as if it were trivial. Which, to her, it probably was. "I'm just seeing if you're okay."

"I will be," I said. "Once I get some caffeine in me." She raised her eyebrow, clearly confused. "Caffeine calms my nerves."

"Ah," she said. "Mine too."

"Really?"

"Why do you think I love it so much?" I smiled. Hayley did love her coffee. "So what are you going to do?"

"About what?"

"Annabelle." I was silent for a moment, mostly out of shock, because she had so abruptly brought the topic back up.

"I thought I said I didn't want to talk about it."

"You did," she said. "But the thing is, I don't care. You're gonna." I was astounded at how casually she said it. Like it wasn't possibly the rudest thing ever said. Although, I had spoken way ruder to her.

"Well, it's not like there's anything I can do."

"Oh, come on. That's quitter talk."

"Well she thinks I'm a stalker, so I'm not really seeing any outs."

"How about explaining that you're not a stalker?" she said sarcastically.

"And she'll believe me. What stalker admits he's a stalker?"

"One without any proof he's not. Like a painting of a girl's childhood home that they can use to explain their knowledge." I stopped short. The painting. In all the anger and sadness and confusion I had forgotten about the thing that had caused it.

"The painting," I said slowly. "Show her that I found the painting."

"And, just like that, you're back in the running." I nodded slowly, but then shook my head quickly.

"No," I said. "Even if I convince her I'm not a stalker, what's going to make her see me as anything more than a friend?"

"Maybe friends is a good start. And maybe she already does." I was silent for a long moment.

"Here's your coffee." I jerked my head up. The woman at the counter was back, holding a steaming Styrofoam cup of coffee. I took it and paid her.

"Thanks, I'll see you later, Hayley," I said hastily.

"Daniel, wait," but I was already out the door. Hayley could be really annoying sometimes. I know she was trying to help, but she didn't know where to stop. She just couldn't see where the line was. I suppose the same could be said for me, but at least I had the sense to just not talk. She rambled on and on until someone got hurt, or Nico made her shut up.

As I drove, I wondered what exactly had made me so mad. That she had tried to help me? Or that she had gone too far? Maybe I didn't like Hayley trying so hard to help me when Nico wasn't around. She wasn't *really* my friend. I was fine with Nico there, because she was trying to earn brownie points. But when it was just the two of us, it seemed...fake. Because that's what it was. Fake. It was her trying to stay in my best friend's good graces. She didn't actually care.

The talk with Hayley stuck in my mind all day. She had invaded my privacy when I told her I didn't want to talk. Maybe the worst part was that it was so hypocritical. She knew what it was like to not want to talk about something. Her father had abandoned her, her mom, and her brothers when she was eleven, and she hated it when people tried to talk about it. She should understand. But it didn't mean she was entirely wrong. About the painting, not about

Annabelle actually liking me. If I returned the painting, she would realize that I wasn't some creep who had looked into her past or spied on her or anything. All I had to do was give her back the painting.

***

There was a door. I had no idea where it had come from, but there it was, standing in front of me. A grand oak door painted pure white with a gilded doorknob that looked like it was made of gold. I had the feeling I should open it. My hand itched to grab hold of that doorknob. To pull it open and bask in what was inside. Something was inside. Something that wanted me to see it. But was it really something that I wanted to see? I knew it was something that I should see, but what if I didn't want to? It was really my choice. Open the door, or don't open the door. Simple, right? No.

Something told me it wasn't at all simple. If I didn't open the door, then I didn't open the door. But maybe I was meant to see what was inside. Maybe it was my responsibility, my duty to open it. But if I didn't want to, then why should I have to? Did I want to? I took a step toward it. This feeling of anticipation welled up inside. Oh yes. I wanted to open the door. I took two steps toward it, more excited now. It was waiting for me.

As I took another step closer, the handle caught my eye. It had some sort of design etched into it. I looked closer, somehow knowing that seeing the design would make it clear. Whether or not I should open the door. I would see everything clearly once I saw the design on that doorknob. I was getting close enough to make it out...then there was a cry. I whipped around but couldn't see anything. Just darkness. Everything around me was dark. All except for this door. It was bright. Almost glowing. Like a lighthouse, standing still. A beacon for me to follow.

"DANIEL!" It was calling me. It wanted me to open it. "COME ON DANIEL!"

"I'm coming," I said. Just let me look at this doorknob and then I'll see what's behind you...

"DANIEL!" I shot up out of my bed, sunlight streaming in through the window. My mom was calling me from downstairs. It had just been a dream. I was honestly a little disappointed. I wanted to see what was behind that door. But still, some nagging thought at the back of my head said it was for the best. I didn't need to see it. I shouldn't see it. I was a little confused as I got out of bed and got dressed. I had wanted to open that door. But it was good that I hadn't. Wasn't it? Yes. That door was better left closed. *What am I thinking?* I thought. *It doesn't matter. It was only a dream. Nothing more. There is no door, so it doesn't make a difference whether or not I opened it.* But it had made a difference.

I brushed my teeth and went downstairs, still thinking about the door. I couldn't get it out of my head.

"Morning pillow head," my mom said. "What had you so deaf?"

I paused for a moment. "Just a dream." I wasn't quite sure why I wasn't telling her the whole story. It didn't seem right. Somehow, I felt like it was connected to the drawing of the dead woman on the stairs.

"Want some breakfast?"

"Nah, I'll grab something at school. The breakfast there is actually tolerable now." My mom grinned. I was heading toward the kitchen when there was a ring at the front doorbell. "I'll get it." I went to the door and thought I might explode. Annabelle was standing there, looking apprehensive. It was a moment before I could speak.

"Annabelle," I said.

"Hi," she said hesitantly. "Look, I...I came here because I don't understand what happened yesterday, and I want to."

"Oh," I said. "Okay. Um, how did you find my house?"

"Asked the first person I saw."

Of course, I thought. *It's Spirit Ridge.*

"Look, I have no idea how you knew I was from the beach. I didn't tell anybody where I came from except the principal and the guidance counselor. And I didn't tell them I had a dog. Or a brother."

I couldn't muster a syllable. She folded her arms.

"Stalking is a felony, you know?"

I was speechless. She actually wanted me to explain. Was she giving me the chance to explain what had happened? Maybe she wasn't completely convinced I was a psycho.

"Just, hold on one second," I said, as I dashed upstairs.

"Hey, wait a minute!"

But I was already up in my room. The painting of the beach house was still on the easel where I had left it. I grabbed it and rocketed back down the stairs. She was still there, thank god.

"Look," I showed her the painting. Immediately, her face morphed into one of shock. She didn't speak for a moment, but when she did, she sounded even more scared.

"How did you get this?" she asked.

Oh god. Are you kidding me? Probably should've mentioned how I got it. Mentally, I was face-palming myself.

"Did you steal this?"

"*No!*" I said, maybe too angrily. I wasn't angry at her. Just at my own pitiful communication skills. "You left it in the art room the other day, and I assumed that it was your home. As for your brother and dog...heard it through the grapevine." Eh. What's a little creative storytelling? "I was gonna give it back to you during art, but then you got scared of me and ran away." She looked at me as if trying to decide whether or not to believe me. Slowly, the fear and anger in her face dissipated.

"You promise?" she asked.

"I swear on my life." She was quiet for a moment, but then looked deeply chagrined.

"O-okay"

"Okay," I said. It felt that simple. She believed me. She actually believed me. She believed that I wasn't a stalker, or a creep, or a psycho. "So you believe me?"

"I guess so," she said. "And now I've accused my only friend here of being a stalker."

I was a little startled at the word "friend".

"Well, luckily we're pretty tough here, so I won't hold it against you," I said. She smiled.

"Okay, great."

"So, we're good?"

She laughed. "Shouldn't I be asking you that?"

"We're good," was my only reply.

"Good," she said. "Well, uh..."

"I've gotta get to, you know, school."

"Yeah me too."

"Did you drive here?"

"Yeah, and my car is in the driveway, probably blocking you in, so I'd better go." I watched her walk back to her car with the painting, and couldn't help but marvel at my good luck. She believed me. She believes I'm sane, normal, and considers me her only friend in town. But, I kind of felt a little sad at the word "friend". Not that I ever thought she could look at me as more than that. I mean, I wasn't that handsome, and she was just...no. She wouldn't be interested in me. I should take the slot as that shy, nervous friend that you can't help but love. I was about to go to my car, when I heard Annabelle shout. I ran over to her, where she was parked in the driveway.

"Something wrong?" I asked. She slammed her steering wheel and threw her hands up in exasperation.

"My car won't start."

"Are you out of gas, or—"

"Nope. It's just a piece of junk is all." She got out of the car angrily.

"Well," I said. "What do you think is wrong?"

"I don't know, but I need to get to school somehow. Class starts in," she looked at her phone, "*thirty* minutes."

"Well, um," I couldn't believe I was about to do this. "Maybe...I could give you a ride."

"Could you? I mean I don't want to ask anything of you, especially after I accused you of stalking me."

I smiled. "It's really no problem, I mean, you did have good reason for that accusation."

"Well, thanks, Daniel," she said. We walked over to my Honda. I opened the passenger side door for her, and went around to the driver's side. This day had gotten off to an amazing beginning. I started the car and maneuvered out of the driveway. It occurred to me then that I should probably talk to her.

"Um, the painting," I said. "It's really good."

"Oh, thanks."

"The seashells in the sand really make the crystals stand out, and I like how you used textured paint to simulate the sand." She looked at me like I had just spoken in tongues. "I—I'm sorry."

"No, it's," she said slowly. "I—I've never heard someone compliment my paintings like that."

"Well, I've been into art since I was a little kid. I also like how you can tell that it's a home. The accents are relaxing and the brushstrokes were gentle, like...a labor of love. That's how I could tell it was your house." She looked impressed, and that gave me this deep sense of satisfaction. "So, where did you live? Obviously on a beach, but from that I could guess you lived in Australia." She laughed.

"Destin," she said. "It's in Florida."

"Wait, so not only did you actually move *to* Spirit Ridge, but you moved here *from* a place called Destin?" She laughed again. We talked easily for the rest of the drive as she told me about her home in Destin. I was surprised by how easy it was to talk to her once I actually started getting words out. She lived with her mom and dad and little brother. Her parents had to move to Spirit Ridge on business, and she had to leave her friends in Florida. I felt kind of bad for her on that one. It was hard enough for me to make friends with people I'd known my whole life. I think moving that far away, for me, would be complete social suicide.

I liked hearing about Annabelle. She's been into painting and sculpting and art since she was a little girl too, and when they moved away, she painted her house so she would always have something to remember it by. I was a little disappointed when we got to the school. I sort of slowed down a little, and deliberately re-parked a few times, so it would last longer. Just having her in my car. The smell of her— like strawberries—suffusing through the air. I wanted to stay there forever. That's why I was more than disappointed when she got out of the car.

"Thanks for the ride," she said. "It was fun."

"No problem." I got out and went over to her. "Uh, what are you gonna do with that?" I asked, pointing at the painting.

"I'll just leave it in my locker," she said. She hesitated before saying, "Thanks for picking it up."

"You're welcome," I said. "Um, can I see the painting for a second?" I'm not sure why, but I wanted to touch it. Thank it.

"Sure," she said, and handed it to me. Our fingers brushed as she passed it to me, and I felt a surge of electricity. Intense, powerful, and incredible, it shot through my entire body; stemming from that one spot where my skin touched hers. It was unbelievable. I couldn't move. I looked up into her eyes. Her deep, brown eyes the color of melting chocolate. And I felt the feeling go deeper, straight down to my core. It touched every part of me, just because she touched that one part of me. Her eyes seemed to be locked on mine. Neither of us moved, and I stood there staring into those eyes, falling into them, lost in them.

All of a sudden, someone running past slammed into me. I was thrown backwards, torn away from her gaze. Sounds of the real world came back to me. I heard screaming. People were scared of something. There had been a scream in the science building, and people were rushing to see what it was. I looked back at Annabelle, and we both ran to see what was going on. We shouldered through the endless crowd of people, trying to see what they were all looking at. For some reason, I needed to know. Something deep inside of me needed to know. I felt like I had in my dream. Like I needed to see it. I had to open the door. As I came to the front of the crowd, I saw people crying. Some people were wrapped in their friends for comfort, others standing in shock, or awe.

As I pushed past the last person, I saw it. But it couldn't be. How could it possibly be? The stairs had never been that white. They were gray. But the tile had been taken out for repairs. All you could see was the white cement underneath. And the blood. Streaming down from the top step, where a pale white hand hung over. *Just like in my drawing,* I thought. *But no! It can't be.* I took a step up, past the crowd, then another. I don't know what I thought I would see, but as I stepped up the sixth step, I saw her face. Her alabaster face, with blood coming out of her mouth, nose, ears, and eyes, her strawberry blonde hair drenched in it, and soft eye shadow to make her aqua eyes look compassionate and sympathetic. But those eyes didn't look like that anymore. They looked like pale, baby blue marbles. Blank. Unseeing.

Ms. Fairchild. And she was dead.

I heard voices that were more mature come into the cacophony of screams and panics. A teacher came up the stairs and shouldered past me. I looked above her and saw it. A great window right above her. Sunlight was streaming in, but I knew what was supposed to be there. Darkness. Terrible, suffocating darkness that had reached out to kill her. The same darkness I had drawn just yesterday. Another ice-cold feeling of dread settled in. It chilled me to my core and I knew exactly what it meant.

That darkness. It's coming. It's coming for me.

Chapter V
Nowhere Is Safe

School let out for the day. Didn't seem like anyone was going to focus on the square root of Pi after seeing Ms. Fairchild on the stairs. Me especially. Seeing her, so broken and pale, I had stood there on that same step until I felt a hand on my arm. I turned to see Nico's gray eyes filled with worry. He didn't say anything, but I let him lead me away from the stairs. We walked through the halls, and out into the parking lot. He led me to my car and got into the driver's seat.

"Hayley's following us in my car." I nodded. I got in the passenger side, trying hard not to think about what had just happened. I was silent for half the ride, trying to think about anything but the fact that I had drawn someone's death. *Damn*, I thought. There it was. I thought about it. But how could I help it? They had found her exactly the way I had drawn her. What did that mean? Was it possible that I...killed her? I didn't know when she died. Probably during the night, when I was asleep. But what if I wasn't? What if I killed her in my sleep? I read somewhere that that can happen.

But I *was* asleep. I had that dream with the door. And my parents would have noticed if I had left the house. And who said anything about her being killed? She could've fallen down the top staircase and stopped at the landing. If she hit her head hard enough, that would explain all of the blood. But that still didn't explain how I had drawn her. But wait. What if I didn't? There was no face in my drawing. I had drawn her hand hanging over the ledge, but it didn't actually show anyone's face. It probably wasn't even Fairchild. How could it be? People didn't actually predict a death before it happened.

Maybe none of it was connected. That was possible. Right? Of course. It was nothing more than a moment of weirdness when I had drawn a dead woman- person! I didn't know it was a woman. And it was nothing but a coincidence that that moment of weirdness happened the day before a woman died. There was nothing weird to any of it. But that still didn't explain why I was so sure that something bad was going to happen.

Nico and Hayley dropped me off at my house, where my parents immediately swarmed in with "Do you want to talk?" and "Do you need a hug?" Together. They were doing it together. But I didn't even take notice of that. I flew straight through the both of them, ran upstairs, and went into my room. I had absolutely no idea what to do. Normally, when I felt this stressed or this freaked out, I would draw. But I was way too scared to draw. Too scared of drawing something else like Ms. Fairchild, or the darkness looming above her. I couldn't stop the unshakable sense of paranoia that told me the darkness was all too real. It hadn't been there when they found her, but I knew it was something. Something real, terrifying, and very, very deadly. Something evil.

"Daniel?" I turned to see my mom standing in the door.

"I'm not really in the mood to talk, mom."

"Are you ever?" she asked. I didn't smile. "Are you okay?"

"Yes, I'm fine," I said curtly.

"Are you sure?" she asked.

"Why does everyone always ask me that?" I yelled. "All I ever hear is, 'Daniel, are you okay?' 'Are you sure?' 'You sure you're okay, Daniel?' Everybody is always so worried about if I'm okay! Did it ever occur to all of you that I. Am. Fine?!" I know it sounded really harsh, but I really was sick of hearing that. I was sick of being pitied.

"You're not," she said, a touch of anger in her voice, but controlling it. "You saw a woman die today, and you are in shock."

"You have no idea," I whispered exasperatedly.

"You need to talk about it," she said.

"I didn't see her die, okay! I saw her, and she was already dead, I was nowhere near her when she died!" I wanted it so badly to be true. Please let it be true.

"You need to talk—"

"I saw her," I said. "She was dead. I talked. Bye."

"Daniel!"

"Mom please," I said. "I want to be alone."

"Okay," she said after a moment, then turned to leave. I fell back on my pillows, wishing desperately that I knew what was happening.

***

The door was there again. The pure white door and golden knob with the obscure design etched into it. The one I had wanted to see so badly. Again, I could feel that it wanted me to open it, and I felt like I should. But this time I was scared. I didn't want to open it anymore. Something terrible would happen if I did. Someone would die. I wouldn't do it. I turned away from the door, but behind me, I saw the darkness coming toward me. Black as midnight, it was creeping slowly in my direction, thick, shadowy tendrils moving forward to ensnare me, squeeze me, choke me. Kill me.

I looked back to the door. The pure white of it seemed even brighter in the darkness. If I stayed outside the door, that darkness would get me. But if I opened that door, someone would die. I was certain of it. But the door offered shelter, protection. Safety. But it also offered death, sorrow, and pain. I looked back and forth between the door and the darkness as it inched its way closer. I had to make a choice. Stay here and let the darkness kill me, or open the door and embrace what was on the other side, letting someone else die. I didn't know what to do. My heart was racing, and sweat was dripping down my neck. I had to make a choice. I had to decide. Please wake up. Please just wake up.

I shot out of my bed, fully clothed. I had fallen asleep when I had lain down. I didn't realize how tired I was. Even though it was only.... I looked at my phone to check the time and saw that it was the very thing that had woken me. It was ringing. I looked at the caller ID, but it was from an unknown number. I debated for a moment whether I should let it ring or risk hearing some salesman lecture me on how if I didn't switch insurance agencies my car would be destroyed in a fiery explosion, but I clicked "answer" and put it to my ear.

"Hello?"

"Daniel?" came a voice that quickly had me wide-awake.

"A–Annabelle?" I said. *Is this happening?* I thought. *Am I still dreaming?*

"Hi," she said.

"Hi. H–how did you get my number?" Why was I asking that? What did it matter?!

"Some girl came up to me and gave it to me. Said she was a friend of yours."

Some girl? Who would...wait. "Curly black hair?" Bright green eyes with a wicked gleam?

"Yeah," she said.

"Hayley," I said.

"Who?"

"Nico's girlfriend. Nico, being the friend who got sick in the art room."

"Oh, okay," she said.

"I swear that I did not ask her to give it to you, but, Hayley is kind of allergic to minding her own business." She laughed at that. "So, what made you decide to call?"

"I just wanted to check on you. You seemed pretty shaken up this morning."

"Yeah, well, there were probably people worse off than me. It's just that she was the school guidance counselor, and I saw her yesterday." I paused for a second. "And telling you that I had to go see the guidance counselor probably doesn't help the whole, 'I'm not a psycho' story." She laughed again. I smiled.

"It's fine," she said. "I actually had an appointment with her tomorrow."

"Right," I said sarcastically.

"Well, why not?" she asked. "New girl, small town, everyone knows each other, maybe I could use some help."

"It's not that, it's that tomorrow is Saturday," I said. She was silent for a second.

"And the award for worst liar goes to…" I laughed now. "But that doesn't mean I don't need any help."

"Maybe," I said. She didn't talk for a second, like she was expecting me to say something. Was I supposed to say something? What did she want me to say? "Um, maybe…"

"Yeah?"

"Maybe I could help you." Was that right?

"Okay. You want to hang out tomorrow?" Oh my God. Was this happening? I must still be dreaming. But even if I were, why not indulge it? I had a crappy enough day. I was about to say yes, when all of a sudden I remembered what had happened. Someone had died. Someone I had talked to the previous day. Right after I drew a remarkably exact death scene. But it was silly to think that the same thing would happen again if I hung out with Annabelle. Right? No way that would happen again. But I still felt like the darkness had killed Ms. Fairchild and was out there somewhere. After that dream, it felt close to me. What if I went to hang out with Annabelle tomorrow, and something happened to her? What if she ended up on those stairs next? I don't think I would be able to live with myself.

"Daniel?" she asked.

"Uh, I'm not sure if I'm free tomorrow." Each word felt like I was cutting myself.

"Oh, well okay. What about Sunday?"

"I just really don't feel up to it, Annabelle. You know,

considering..."

"Oh, right," she said. "I'm really sorry." *You're sorry?* I thought. *I'm the one who is currently screwing myself with my words.*

"It's fine," I said. "Maybe another time."

"Okay," she said. "Bye." I hung up the phone and let out this huge breath of air, I hadn't known I was holding in. That was definitely the *single* hardest thing I have *ever* done. I couldn't believe I had turned Annabelle down. Annabelle Martin. How could I do that? Off of some stupid delusion. I hadn't caused Ms. Fairchild's death or predicted it. It was coincidental. I wanted so badly to call her and take it all back and hang out with her on Saturday. Hang out. I couldn't say...date. She hadn't asked me out. Had she? No. I was her only friend here. She said that herself. She just wanted someone to help her get her bearings in town. But still. To get to be with her, possibly all day. The idea made my head swim. And I had sacrificed it because of some stupid idea and a stupid dream.

I looked down at the time on my phone. It was five o'clock. I had slept that long? I couldn't go to Nico's; he would be at work by now. I couldn't go to the studio, which made me feel even sicker. The darkness I had drawn infected it, made it feel dirty. Menacing. Without warning, I felt exposed. Naked. I had no safe place anymore. I always had that little getaway, where I could go when I didn't know where else to go. Now it was gone, because of one drawing. Nowhere was safe anymore.

Chapter VI
The Wrath of God

Saturday didn't seem to have the same feeling it normally did. The feeling of relaxation and freedom. No school, nowhere I had to go, nothing I had to do. But the many things I wasn't doing included being with Annabelle. Instead, I decided to spend the day at Nico's. His boss had given him the day off after hearing what happened to Ms. Fairchild. Obviously, Nico hadn't told him himself. He never missed a day of work if he could help it. He had to keep getting his paychecks so he could help his dad pay the bills. Otherwise, he would be living in "The Pit" with Hayley. Not that there was anything wrong with how Hayley lived.

I knocked on the front door. While I waited, I looked at the empty streets. After the news of Ms. Fairchild's death had spread, the entire neighborhood hunkered in fear. Not that they could be blamed. At least it was a pretty day. Hardly a cloud in the sky, and a breeze that brought with it the smell of nearby oak trees. It seemed like Mother Nature could give less of a damn who had died.

"Daniel." I turned to see Mr. Marshall standing inside, the door open in front of him. "Hello."

"Hi, Mr. Marshall," I greeted him. "Is Nico here?"

"Uh, no," he said hesitantly. "He took off this morning."

"Oh. Well do you know where he went?"

"Yeah," he said, raising his eyebrows at me. "He went to see her."

He didn't need to say anything else. I understood perfectly what he meant. "Ah. Thanks, Mr. Marshall. I'll see you later."

He nodded as I retreated down the sidewalk. I needed to get to where Nico was. I drove through the town square and hung a right down James Street, making my way to Spirit Ridge Memorial Hospital. I went straight to the building adjacent to the main building; the long-term care facility where Nico's mother was situated, since the actual hospital wasn't equipped to handle coma patients for long periods.

I walked through the automatic doors and exchanged hellos with Mary, the receptionist. She didn't even ask me where I was going. She knew me well enough from the countless times I had accompanied Nico.

"You know where he is," she simply said.

I nodded at her and went down the hall. I stopped in my tracks, lightning quick. Something was in front of me. A kind of fog or shadow, drifting toward me. It swirled and coalesced as if it were alive. Then, just as quick as it had come, it was gone. I froze for a moment, unnerved, but then I shook it off and continued to Mrs. Marshall's room. The door was wide open, and when I peeked inside I saw Nico sitting in a chair holding his mother's hand.

Hesitantly, I knocked on the open door. Nico's head swiveled around to look at me.

"Hey," he said, his voice somewhat thick. I decided to ignore that.

"Hey," I replied. "I went to your house and your dad told me you were here, so…"

"Ah," he said, standing up and brushing a few strands of hair out of his face. "Sorry. I probably should've called you, after what you saw yesterday."

"You saw it too," I stated.

"Yeah but you were the one to have talked to her the day before she died."

"True," I conceded. "Which is why I was thinking we could hang out today. You know. Do what we always do when we feel like shit."

Nico chuckled and grinned at me. "Yeah sure, let's go." He started out of the room, almost too quickly, but I couldn't miss the glint of pain in his eyes when he looked back at his mother's blonde hair, her body motionless.

***

A horror movie marathon may seem inappropriate after what had happened, but with Nico and me, they had significance. I've liked horror movies since I was a kid. When I was like ten years old, I had this really bad experience. I went to the zoo with Nico and his dad, and we wanted to see the giraffes, because I had always pictured riding a giraffe. I asked Mr. Marshall if I could, but he said no, it was too dangerous. Impulsive little me snuck into the habitat while he took Nico to the bathroom, and I tried to climb up on a giraffe to ride it. Of course, that didn't go over too well with the giraffe. Mostly because I tried to grab its tail to pull myself up. But when Mr. Marshall heard me screaming, he freaked out, but I was already on the giraffe's back, and I kept climbing, so the zookeepers had to raise a ladder to get me, and use a sedative on the giraffe, grabbing me just before it went down. My parents never let Mr. Marshall take me anywhere again, and I could only play with Nico when one of them was supervising until I was at least thirteen.

But the experience had shaken me up too. So a few weeks later, on my birthday, Nico managed to sneak into my house while my parents were out. He had stolen some horror movies from his dad, and we watched them just to terrify me. The idea was to make the experience at the zoo pale in comparison. Nico had always been pretty smart about that. Ever since then, whenever something bad happened to either of us, we got together and watched bloody, spine-chilling horror movies, and silently said, "Hey, at least we're not them."

We were currently watching some newer movie—a lot more

blood and gore than suspense. I liked suspense better. It was a lot scarier than just watching some dude's guts fall out. Nico, however, was way more into slasher flicks. We finished the movie with the girl walking away believing she had killed and buried the bad guy, only for the audience to see his hand burst out of the dirt.

"Are you kidding me?" I said. "So cliché." Nico laughed.

"You want a drink?" he asked.

"Sure," I said. "Dr. Pepper."

"I know." I smiled. Of course he knew. I always drank Dr. Pepper when I watched a horror movie. Something about watching people be killed or maimed that made me want Dr. Pepper. I don't know. I'm weird.

I got up to pop in the next movie, which I had picked out. Something with a demon child that infiltrates an orphanage. Suddenly, a glint of light in the corner of my eye caught my attention. I turned toward it and saw something shining in the desk drawer by Nico's bed. I leaned forward to look, and saw a small crystal gleaming from the drawer. I can't explain it, but I felt drawn to it. It was a simple white stone, a bit jagged, but had smooth sides. It was beautiful. The light seemed to refract through it, shattering into a million colors. I reached out to touch it. My fingers brushed the cool edge and this surge of pressure went through my fingers, extending through my entire body, mingling with the cold feeling. Colors and images flooded my mind, but I couldn't see any of them. It was like there was this veil blocking them, so I could only make out blurry shapes. My hand was itching for a pen. *No,* I thought. This was exactly what I had felt before I drew the dead woman, only much more intense. My head was screaming, pounding, hammering, the images fighting against the confines of my skull, struggling to get free. My hand needed to free them. Only my hand could free them. It was like the images were wrapped up in a shrouded prison, where the only opening led into my arm.

I reached into my pocket, where I always kept a pencil. My hand was in my backpack, and I was pulling out my sketchpad. *NO!* I dropped the pencil. *Not again.* I would not do this. I wouldn't draw. The pain in my head would stop as soon as the images vanished. I staggered back to the couch and lowered myself down. I waited for Nico to return. Eventually he walked in, holding a can of Dr. Pepper.

"Hey," he said.

"H-hi," I forced out through the pain.

"Something wrong?" he asked.

"Nope," I said. "Let's watch the movie." I hit the play button and downed my drink, gripping the edge of my cushion, silently willing the images to go away. But they weren't. They kept pounding on the inside of my skull, throwing punch after punch to my brain in an attempt to get free. They were relentless. Didn't they know I wasn't going to do this? But the pain was so terrible. It felt like any second, my head could split open just to spill the images out. I couldn't stand it. I had to make it stop.

"Can I get another drink?!" I half-asked, half-yelled to Nico.

"Uh, sure," he said, and got up to go get another one. He looked back at me, but I just nodded. The second he was gone, I dove for my sketchpad. I opened it up to a blank page, grabbed the pencil off the floor, and started drawing. I could feel the pressure leaving my head, traveling through my arm and into the paper. The pain began to subside as I drew. I didn't know what I was drawing, and I really didn't care, I just wanted the pain to stop. I kept drawing, the lead making lines all across the page, shading and shadowing until it was complete. I breathed a sigh of relief when it was done, as I pulled the pencil away from the paper, the pain in my head completely gone. It was a moment before I looked down at the page. I was kind of scared to look. I didn't know what I might see, but I knew I didn't have much time before Nico came back. Luckily, his freezer took some jiggling to get open.

Slowly, I looked down at the picture, and I couldn't have been more relieved. Nobody was dead. No blood, no darkness. But it was something else. The door. The one from my dreams. Only this time, it was cracked open, and there was someone standing in front of it.

The drawing was pencil, so I couldn't tell the color of the hair, but it looked like a guy. He was tall and lean and wiry. His hair came down to the nape of his neck. I couldn't see his face, but I knew who it was. I knew him well enough to know, even if I couldn't see his face. It was...

"Hey."

I looked up. "...Nico."

"Yeah?" he said.

"Oh, uh, nothing," I said. It was *him*. I was sure of it. But what could Nico have to do with the door I kept seeing in my dreams.

"What's that?" he asked, gesturing to the drawing. I snapped the sketchpad shut.

"Nothing," I said, maybe a little too sharply. "Come on, what is it?"

"Nico!" I yelled. He looked a little startled. "It's nothing."

"Okay," he said. I wasn't ready for Nico to see that. Not that he would be able to tell that it was him. He'd never seen the back of himself. But he might wonder who it was. Or why I had drawn it. And I'd like to figure that out before I told him.

Nico and I watched horror movies for the rest of the day, but I couldn't stop wondering about that crystal I had found. It had mesmerized me. That surge of power I had felt when I touched it. It had triggered those images. I was sure of it. It had also caused that cold feeling to hit. Those feelings were becoming more and more frequent. I really wished I knew what they were, or what they meant, but I couldn't figure it out. They were always accompanied by these shockingly accurate vibes, almost like... premonitions. *Something big will happen to change your life. Annabelle painted this. This drawing will change everything.* All of those had turned out to be correct. But what did it mean? I didn't get it. I wanted to. I felt like the answer was close, and it apparently had something to do with Nico. I saw him near the door that apparently wanted me to open it. But what did any of it mean?

I left Nico's at about nine, after we had run out of DVDs and ordered more. Nico's house was close enough to mine that I could walk instead of drive. As I was walking by this really creepy old house, I heard something fall inside the house. I turned toward it, and I swore I saw something shift in the window. That was kind of weird. As far as I knew, nobody lived in that house. It had been vacant for years. I don't think anyone even wants to live there. It's three stories tall, with windows on each floor, and these really long hallways. It has a railed stairway going up to it, and honestly, it looks like something out of a horror movie I had just watched. Some old fifties crap about vampires. I wondered who was in there. Probably some kid who was bored. Sometimes kids will dare each other to go into the house for ten minutes, or go in and bring something back from the basement. Sometimes even to spend the night. Small town like this, kids get bored, and they have to find ways to entertain themselves. I remember once, Hayley convinced Nico and me to play Truth or Dare, daring me to go in. I got through the front door before spotting the one thing all haunted houses needed. A big portrait of the former owner, situated right above the burned out fire place, whose eyes seemed to follow me through the room. I bolted.

Every town has a haunted house. The Whitmore House is ours. Everyone fears it. There are legends that some guy killed himself in the house. Other legends say that some family of witches lived there, and now it's haunted by their evil spirits. People love to pass the time by coming up with new versions and spreading it around town. You'd have a hard time finding two people who heard the exact same version. Looking up at the window where I saw the movement, I got the feeling that I should keep going. So I kept walking until I got home.

***

The next day was Sunday. My parents and I went to church. I loved going to church ever since I was diagnosed. It was the only time that my parents took me anywhere, together. Even now, with everything that was going on, I was excited. I put on my "Sunday Best" which was a button-up shirt tucked into khakis, and went downstairs to join my parents. My dad was standing there with his usual brown sweater and black sports coat. My mom was in the doorway, wearing her blue church dress. I couldn't stifle my happiness at the sight and went downstairs.

We drove to Holy Spirit Methodist Church, the quaintest church in town. It's a pretty simple place. One story, but tall enough to be two because of the high ceilings of the sanctuary. It has big red doors that lead into an atrium where we wait until the sanctuary opens. There are buildings on either side leading to the places where people go to Sunday school. It's not that big, which means it floods with people.

I hopped out of the car, and my parents and shouldered through the mob. I've always been good at ducking through crowds. I'm thin and I'm quick. I slowed down for my parents, though. I didn't really want to leave them alone. They would fight if I did. As I ducked in between an old married couple, I found myself colliding face-first with someone. I have no idea how I didn't see him, all I know is that the next thing I knew I was on the ground, with one of the youth pastors trying to help me up.

"I'm so sorry!" he kept saying as he helped me right myself. He brushed the dirt off my shirt, even though there was none, and I took a step back.

"It's fine, really." I looked at the guy I had bulldozed. He was about my height, but you could tell he was at least ten years older than me. Still, he was young for a youth pastor. His mahogany brown hair was meticulously combed, not a single strand out of place, and his clothes looked freshly ironed. It was possible he even used one of those lint rollers that no one ever used. If I were to draw him, I thought, he'd probably be standing rigidly straight, with his arms folded neatly in front of him, hands clenched over a copy of the Bible. Kind of like he was now. I knew I had seen him around church before, but I couldn't quite remember his name.

"Craig," he clarified, giving me a nod.

"I know," I lied, not wanting to admit I hadn't known his name. "Daniel."

"Daniel," he said, nodding. Seems like he didn't know me either. Shocker. "Like the prophet."

"I...never really thought about that." I had a perfectly normal name, so I had always assumed my parents had just liked it. It wasn't bad.

"Say," Craig said. "Isn't your dad Nathan Cohen?"

"Um, yeah," I answered. "Yeah, he is." Craig smiled, and opened his mouth to say something else, but it was cut off by a more familiar voice.

"Hey, Daniel!" I turned and saw Nico and Hayley coming in my direction.

"Oh, sorry, those are my friends," I turned back to Craig, but he was gone. Shrugging, I walked over to Nico and Hayley.

"Hey," I said. "Got something to tell me Hayley?"

"You're welcome," she said with a smirk. I rolled my eyes. "Did she call?"

"Yes, and I totally blew it. Again."

"What?" Nico said. "What happened?"

"I'll tell you later," I muttered as my parents caught up.

"Hi Nico, Hayley," said my mom. "How's it going?"

"Good," Nico said. "Considering, you know..." My head snapped toward him. I really didn't want to talk about Fairchild. Nico seemed to pick up on that and quickly shifted gears. "...that...we...have to go back to school tomorrow." *Thank you,* I thought. He smiled.

"Yeah, it's so sad what happened to Ms. Fairchild," she said. *Crap,* I thought. *You don't give up, do you, Mom?*

"Yeah," Nico said. "But, uh..." He was silent for a moment. Just in time, they opened the doors to the sanctuary and everyone started filing in. "We'd better go on in," he said, and pulled Hayley in with him. She groaned. Hayley wasn't the biggest fan of church. Not that she didn't believe, she just thought it was boring.

"You sit there and listen to a guy talk," she would say. "How's it different from school?" She only came for Nico, and to get away from her house. My parents and I went into the sanctuary. It looked like a normal sanctuary. Long, narrow, with rows of pews on either side, a huge wooden cross hanging on the wall, great stained glass windows depicting various biblical settings. I used to marvel at those windows throughout the whole service when I was a kid. How someone could make something so beautiful out of glass, I could never understand.

We took our seats in our normal pew as the pastor began his sermon. However blunt Hayley was, she wasn't wrong about the actual service. Not that it wasn't interesting, just that eventually, listening to our ancient pastor belt out some spiritual stuff about repenting our sins got old. I looked over at Hayley and Nico, wondering if they were thinking the same, but Hayley had her head in her hands. I shot up into a straight position, suddenly alert. Another migraine? Nico had his hands on her shoulder, but he didn't seem concerned. He seemed somewhat exasperated. He was saying her name, and he seemed to say something like, "stop it".

Stop having a migraine? What was he talking about? What was wrong with him? I was about to lean over to see what was happening, when I heard my friend voice. *Don't*, it said. *Leave them be. It's not your business.* I sat down and looked up to the pastor, but I couldn't really focus on him, so instead I looked at the screen where the choir's lyrics had been, and where now, there were colors swirling around. I tried to watch the colors, keeping track of them, following their movements across the screen. Watching them mix and move, and separate and swirl. I saw new colors join, blending into the old ones, creating shapes and pictures. *Like a painting,* I thought. But the pictures were blurry. I couldn't make them out. I squinted, trying to see them, but then my heart skipped a beat as I realized what was happening.

I wrenched my eyes away from the screen, but too late. Once

again, images flashed mercilessly against the inside of my skull, unclear, but powerful. The pain was excruciating, but I would not give into them this time. The images could rot in there, because I would never let them out. If necessary, I would never touch a pencil or brush ever again. These images would stay locked away in my mind forever. I would take them to the grave. If there was one thing in this world I knew how to do, it was keep things bottled up. Defiantly, I gripped the edge of the pew, determined to stay there until service was dismissed. I tried my best to ignore the pain, waiting for it to go away, but it only seemed to be getting worse. It felt like someone had stuck one of those air pumps into my head and was seeing how much air a cranium could take. I felt like I could black out. Still, I gripped the seat harder, so hard I could hear the wood creaking. I could feel tears springing to my eyes. The edges of my vision were beginning to go dark from the pain. My mind was falling to shambles. I fought desperately against the urge to draw. I wouldn't do it. The pain was so terrible. *I can't.* If I could stop myself from screaming, I could stop from drawing. *I won't.* My head was splitting open. *I don't want to!* I didn't want to! *I HAVE TO!*

Just like that, I snapped. I wasn't thinking about blocking the pain, or ending the pain. I was no longer thinking. I was out of my seat and out the door before anyone knew what happened. I was no longer in control. My legs ran through the hallway of their own accord, stumbling through the blinding pain. I didn't know where I was going. All I was doing was what the agony was commanding me to do. I turned the corner into another hallway and felt a mad rush of emotions. Freedom and excitement, mingled in with worry, all covering up resentment, anger, sadness, and bitterness. Then it was gone. I whipped around and saw Hayley in the hallway.

"Daniel?" she looked confused and disoriented. Then she was gone. Literally. She just vanished into thin air. But I didn't even have time to wonder, because the pain came rushing back, and I was running again. I crashed through double doors and into the nursery. Toys scattered across the floor, and there were tiny easels with finger paintings on them. I jumped to one of the easels and my hand grabbed the canvas. I had a brush in my hand, and with no thought, I started painting. The pain poured out of my head, charging so hard through my fingers and onto the canvas, it's a wonder it didn't break the easel. I was painting furiously, letting the images explode out of me in this huge tidal wave. I knew it was wrong, but I didn't care. The pain had been too intense, the relief too great. I let it all fall out until the last drop of color was on the canvas. I pulled my arm away and looked down. I knew when I looked, my relief would vanish. I knew that it wouldn't be like before. I would see something terrible. I could hear people running outside, toward the room. I had to look. I had to see. I had to get rid of it in time, but before that, I had to look. I tore my gaze away from the floor, and brought it up to the painting.

Chapter VII
Light It Up

Fire. That's what I saw when I looked at my painting. Flames leaping across the canvas, bright, hot tongues touching everything around it. It had spread so far that I couldn't even see where the scene was. It was a harsh, terrible fire. I could practically feel the heat coming off in waves, like the fire was actually leaping out at me, determined to burn me. But I did see a shape. Deep within, wrapped up in the merciless blaze. A human shape. *No,* I thought. *Please, not again.*

The voices outside snapped me out of my trance. I had to get rid of this thing. Nobody could see it. Hastily, I grabbed it and... what? What could I do with it? I had to do something. They were coming. They would be in here any second. I looked at the wet paint, and... wet paint. I took the canvas over to the bathroom sink where the toddlers washed their dirty little selves, held the painting under the faucet, and turned on the water. It hit the canvas, and immediately, the paint was washed away. I watched it mingle with the water, and watched the multi-colored liquid swirl around the sink before falling through the drain.

Flustered, I splashed some clean water on my face and flushed the toilet just as I heard the door open. I groaned, trying to sound convincing, doubled over, hoping I had learned something from Nico's performance the other day, and stumbled out into the room. The first person I saw when I looked up was the town pharmacist, Mr. Carries. Mr. Carries wasn't too pretty, so that wasn't the most pleasing first sight. But then I saw my parents file in behind him, followed by Nico and Hayley, and a few other people.

"Sorry, everybody," I said. "Just had a little stomach problem. I'm alright." Nico came to help me upright, while my mom started wiping away the pretend sweat. I looked up at my dad and found him looking at me really strangely. I brought my eyes up to his, the exact same opalescent blue eyes as mine, and saw them filled with this look of...finality. Like he had waited a long time for something, and it was standing right in front of him. Another premonition shot through me. *He knows something.* But I didn't need it. *I know.* I told it. *I know.*

My parents took me home after my little episode. On the way, I had time to wonder exactly what had happened. I had no idea why I kept making these things, but I did know that I had painted another death. Just like I had drawn Ms. Fairchild's death. And it was pretty clear that all blocking the pain would get me was blinding agony. I also wondered what that little encounter with Hayley was. She had materialized right in front of my eyes when I had the rush of emotion in the church hallway, only to vanish into thin air. It's possible she ducked out to get Nico or my parents. But she had seemed so confused, as if she was every bit as surprised by her sudden appearance as I was. Maybe the pain had me so messed up I was seeing things. But that didn't explain why the pain had momentarily ceased. Not to mention...my dad.

That look in his eyes when they found me seemed like he knew something I didn't. Like what the hell was happening to me. When we got home, my mom basically forced some antacid down my throat, despite my protests. Although, I couldn't really protest too hard without admitting that there was nothing wrong with my stomach. I took refuge in my room but knew I wouldn't be alone there for long. I sat on my bed for a few minutes until he came in.

"Hey, dad," I said.

"Hey," he answered. "Feeling alright?"

"Okay," I said. We were both silent for an excruciatingly long second.

"So what happened?" he asked. I shrugged.

"Gastro-intestinal distress?" I didn't know how to confront my dad. *Should I even confront him?* Or should I be discreet? I decided on discreet. "What else would it be?"

"Daniel...you know you can talk to me about anything right?"

"Of course," I said, which any kid knows translates to *No, but I'm going to let you think so.*

"Anything," he said. "Even if you think I won't understand." What was he getting at?

"L-like what?" I asked.

"Like...changes." Somehow, I didn't think he was talking about the birds and the bees.

"What kind of changes?" I got the feeling he knew exactly what I meant. Now it was a question of whether or not he would tell me. I waited for him to answer.

"You'll see," he said. My shoulders fell and I let out a breath. I felt a surge of anger.

"Bye, dad," I said harshly. *How dare you not tell me! I have a right to know what is happening. I need answers.* My dad knew what was happening to me; I saw it in his eyes when he left. He may not know about the paintings, but he would be able to explain them, and he wasn't telling me anything. And it probably involved Nico, if my drawing was right. And Hayley, but she probably wouldn't be much help. That left Nico. The one person in my life who was always honest with me. Nico was my only hope.

***

The next day we went back to school. I was actually surprised by how few people seemed on edge. Most people were gossiping about Ms. Fairchild's death. Only a few kids seemed genuinely upset, and most were the "bottom-of-the-food-chain" kids who went to see her three times a week. As I walked through the halls, I saw people whispering to each other. Not the normal giggle-and-snicker whispering, but the kind of whispering they only did when something big happened. The kind with gasps and wows and the occasional, "Oh my gaaaawwwwsh!"

I hate gossip. Ms. Fairchild deserved better than that. She'd been a little annoying, sure, but she had cared about her students. That much you could tell. But I couldn't think about them. I was looking for Nico. I knew he had something to do with why I had made those paintings, and I had to know what it was. All the while, I was on the tip of my toes, looking for any signs of a fire. A lighter, a match, something. But I saw nothing. The smokers weren't even smoking under the stairs like normal, and it wasn't even hot. At the thought of fire, my mind went to Leo. I was sure he had been in that crowd of people swarming the steps Friday, but his face had been totally expressionless, as normal. I wouldn't put it past Leo to set fire to a building. Even if it had a person in it.

As I walked through the science hall, I spotted something that could definitely qualify as strange. I saw Natalie at her locker, surrounded by her usual clique of fashionably dressed, lip glossed Barbie dolls. They all stood in their usual positions, draped across the lockers with Natalie in the center. She might as well have been standing on a pedestal with the rest of them doing some kind of worship dance around her. None of that was at all out of the ordinary, until Hayley came busting through the ring of girls.

She pushed her way through to the center, accompanied by the sound of "hey!" and "weirdo!" She came up to Natalie and started to say something, but Natalie just got flustered and hastily said something back at her. I couldn't hear what was being said, but it made all the other girls shriek in giggles, and made Hayley roll her eyes. Hayley said something else and Natalie tried to just shoo her away, but as I know all too well, Hayley Rutter is stubborn. After a moment, Natalie took her by the arm and led her away, rolling her eyes very exaggeratedly at her girlfriends as if this were a great inconvenience for her. I realized that if I kept standing there, they would probably see me, so I ducked behind a nearby open locker.

Peering through the slits in the doors, I couldn't hear what Natalie and Hayley were talking about, but I could somewhat read their lips.

Hayley was saying something adamantly about a person, though I couldn't make out the name. Natalie was saying something like "crazy" and "not possible", but Hayley seemed very certain. After a moment, Natalie snapped at her what seemed like "Get lost", and Hayley said something angrily before storming away. I buried my head in the locker as she passed by, praying that she wouldn't recognize me. She clearly didn't, and when I pulled back, Natalie was walking back to her friends, shaking her head at Hayley's retreating figure and twirled her finger at her ear in a cuckoo gesture. I didn't understand at all what I had just seen as I pulled away from the locker.

Quickly, I walked away from the locker before its owner could come back and find me there. I went downstairs, having all but given up hope on finding Nico, for it was as if he was hiding from me, when I saw a flash of shiny, jet-black hair.

"Annabelle," I called before I could stop myself. She turned in my direction and smiling, she came up to me.

"Hey," she said. "Listen, I'm sorry about Friday. You had just seen somebody you knew...and me there, throwing myself at you..."

"No, it's fine," I said. "I actually kind of regretted saying no so quickly."

"Really?" she asked.

"Truth is," I said. "Maybe I could use a distraction. I'd like to take you up on that...hang out... thing." God, I was bad at this. But she laughed.

"Alright," she said. "How about after school?"

"Great," I said. I couldn't stop smiling. It wasn't a whole Saturday, but hey, beggars can't be choosers. "Sounds great." She beamed at me. It was then that the warning bell chose to go off. I silently cursed the school schedules.

"I've got to go," she stated.

"Yeah, me too." Reluctantly, I headed toward World History. I would have to talk to Nico under the drone of Mr. Clearwood. Sudden movement appeared out the window. Someone was walking away from the old gym. I didn't get a good look at him, but he was walking away pretty fast. *Go to class,* I told myself. *Go to class. It's probably a substitute teacher.*

Oh yeah? said another voice. *Then why is he heading* away *from the school? Why's he going so fast? Why is he in a building that hasn't been used in years?*

I don't know, but—

No buts! Go

No, I thought.

Go, my inner voice said.

No.

Go.

No!

GO!

I growled in frustration and went out the door to the building. *What am I doing?* I thought, as I stalked across the grass. I shoved open the rusty, creaky metal doors, and walked in. It was a typical gym. Basketball goals at each end, bleachers on the sides, manual scoreboards on the walls. But ever since they built the new gym, this one hadn't been used in many years. There was an inch-thick layer of dust over everything, and the windows were all boarded up, so it was too dark to see anything.

I took out my phone and turned on the flashlight app. I didn't know what I was looking for. I just knew I was looking for something. My legs took me to the left bleachers. I looked underneath but didn't see anything. I raised the light higher but still didn't see anything. *Great,* I thought. *This was pointless. Now I'm late for class with no reason.* I was about to walk away and start thinking of a good enough excuse when I got a glimmer in the corner of my eye. The light from my phone reflected off a pool of liquid. I took an uneasy step toward it and saw that it was scarlet red. My stomach dropped. Blood. Lots of it. And it was fresh. I took another step, frightened. I raised the phone higher, and the wide beam fell upon a face. My blood stopped in my veins. The face was pale and lifeless, the eyes blank and dark. It was a girl with long, black hair scattered across her ivory face. There were multiple colors streaked into it. Blue, purple, green, red, and she wore all black. I knew her. Her name was Angie Morgan. I knew this girl. And she was dead. And I had found her.

But something else was wrong. This wasn't my painting. There was no fire. Where was the fire? There was supposed to be a fire. Maybe this had nothing to do with my painting. *Why was I thinking about my painting?* A girl was dead. Quickly, I brought my phone down and dialed 911, but out of nowhere, the darkness was pierced by something bright. I felt heat on my back. I whipped around and saw Angie's body had suddenly caught fire. It was blazing and spreading to the wooden bleachers. The fire was bright, nearly white, and it had such a harsh look to it that it hurt my eyes. This was the fire from my painting. I backed away and started running but slipped in the pool of blood and my stomach fell on an iron support. I felt the wind go out of me, and I struggled to get a breath but inhaled smoke. I coughed as the smoke seared my lungs; I couldn't breathe; it was too hot. I struggled to my feet and stumbled. It was difficult to walk with smoke around me, the fire spreading quickly across the bleachers, showering me with ash and embers. I made my way out from under the bleachers and started for the exit.

My throat felt so dehydrated from the smoke. I needed water. I needed air. I needed to get out of there. I fell against the wall and used it to keep myself steady, pulling myself desperately toward the exit. My eyes were starting to burn from the smoke. I didn't understand how the fire could spread that fast, and I honestly didn't care; all I knew was that I had to get out. I got to the doors and put my hands against it to leave, but I immediately jerked them back, a scream of pain wrenching itself from my throat. The metal was white-hot. The pain was searing. My hand, my eyes, my throat, my stomach, my lungs. All of it hurt, and the fire had somehow spread across the gym to the other bleachers and the ceiling, as if it were alive.

I knew I had to escape, but the door wouldn't let me leave. The metal was too hot. I fell to the floor, my mind scrambling for a way out. I tried to pull my shirt up to my mouth and nose to avoid breathing in more smoke, but my clothes were infused with it. Everything smelled like smoke, and the heat was unbearable. It was like the air itself was on fire now. I wasn't even sure the door could be pushed open anymore. It was stuck and too damn hot. I wasn't going to get out. Whatever that darkness had done, it was about to take me too. Everything was going fuzzy, and I couldn't feel any air inside of me. The light and heat and smoke overloaded my brain and I couldn't think. I couldn't see or hear or think of anything. Just the fire.

But then the sound of crackling fire and wood was pierced by a tremendous screech. I felt the door behind me wrench open and a blast of cooler air hit my back. I fell backwards through the open door. When I felt the sunlight hit my eyes, I was seized by this deep, primal, all-consuming urge to survive. Muscles aching, lungs burning, I began to drag myself across the threshold and over the hard concrete. Inch by inch, I crawled my way out into the grass until the heat of the fire behind me was just a glowing warmth. My limbs collapsed underneath, my body hit the ground, and everything went black.

Chapter VIII
Little White Lies

When I woke up, I was lying in a bed. My entire body felt heavy and yet soft. My eyelids felt sticky when I tried to open them, and I had to blink a couple of times to see clearly. When I could, I saw my parents sitting on either side of my bed. My mom pounced the second I woke up.

"Oh my god, are you okay? How do you feel? Are you in any pain?"

"Mom?" My voice came out scratchy and harsh and my throat stung.

"Oh my god, baby, are you alright? Do you hurt anywhere? Talk to me."

"Wha–" My voice cracked as I tried to get the word out and dissolved into a fit of coughing.

"Whoa, whoa, take it easy buddy," my dad said. "You inhaled a lot of smoke in there."

"Smoke?" I asked.

"The fire."

I tried to think, but my head felt fuzzy. It felt like my brain was stuffed full of cotton balls.

"I can't—" I tried to talk but it just dissolved into coughs again.

"Sh," my mom put her hands on my shoulders and tried to push me back into the bed. "It's okay baby. They just gave you something for the pain. Try and sleep."

"But..." I tried to remember. There was something important I needed to tell her. Something very important. But I couldn't remember. I tried to argue with my mom's insistent hands pushing me back down on the pillows, but before I knew it my brain was being swallowed up by the soft blackness of sleep. "Fire...Angie..." And then I was gone.

***

"Sorry he's not awake yet."

"How long has he been out?"

"A couple of hours. The doctors say he should be waking up soon though. I'm Nico. You're Annabelle, right?"

"Yeah, um...just...just tell him I stopped by, I guess."

"Wait. Do you wanna sit with him for a while? Maybe wait for him to wake up?"

"Um...just tell him I stopped by."

***

"Are you sure he's okay?"

"Nico, the doctors said he'd be fine."

"He's been out for a long time."

"It's only been a few hours. He *was* just in a fire after all. Do you think he did this to him?"

"Well who else could it have been?"

"This is getting out of hand. What are we gonna do?"

"I don't know."

"Look—"

"Sh! Is he waking up?"

"Daniel?"

***

My whole body felt like I'd been run over by a steamroller.

Which probably wasn't a far cry from what happened. My stomach, my legs, my arms, everything felt stiff as I slid open my eyes to the glare of the fluorescent hospital lights. I had to blink once or twice for my eyes to adjust. Once they did, I got a real grip on my surroundings. I was still lying in a hospital bed, only this time my parents weren't there. Instead, Nico sat in the chair next to my bed, and Hayley stood by the foot of the bed, leaning on the wall with one leg propped up against it.

"Daniel!" Nico said as soon as I opened my eyes. He immediately stood up and leaned over me to see if I was okay. "How are you feeling? Are you alright?"

"Nico..." I tried to sit up, but a sharp pain in my gut sent a cry out of my mouth before I could stop it.

"Whoa," Hayley said, moving to the end of the bed. "Easy there, tiger. The doctor says you bruised yourself up pretty good in there."

Nico eased me back down onto the pillows and the pain in my gut subsided to a dull throb.

"God I feel like crap."

"Well I'd expect so," Hayley remarked. "Escaping a horrible fiery death will do that to you."

"Hayley," Nico shot her a look and she resigned to picking at a loose thread in my blanket. "The doctor said you're gonna be sore for a while."

"Understatement," I muttered quietly. My voice still sounded gruff and scratchy, and my throat felt incredibly parched. I opened my mouth to ask if there is any water, but before I could even say anything, Nico handed me a cold glass. I looked at him for a moment before taking the glass, my hand closing gratefully around the cool moist surface. I realized that my hand was bandaged and underneath it felt warm and dry. A memory came to mind. A burning door. My hand pressed against searing hot metal. Me trying to escape.

"The fire," I muttered. "The gym."

Nico and Hayley both just nodded grimly.

"What happened?"

"You tell us," Hayley answered. "We just found you unconscious outside the burning gym." She looked at Nico and smirked. "Nico here was the first one to see you out there."

"I'm sure I wasn't the first one to see him," Nico insisted. "Just the first one in the class."

"Well thanks all the same," I said to him with a grin. "How long have I been here?"

"A while," Nico said. "You've been in and out for hours."

"Probably something to do with all the pain killers they pumped into you," Hayley said. That explained that slow, fuzzy feelings I had before with my parents. Wait...my parents.

"Where are my parents?"

"They're outside talking to the doctor," Nico replied. "They finally let us in to sit with you. We would've been here before but they wouldn't let us in. Immediately family only."

For some reason that idea seemed strange to me. As far as I was concerned, Nico was family.

"Are they saying when I can go home?"

The two of them exchanged a strange sort of look. I wasn't sure what it was but it was suspicious. "What? What's wrong?"

"Well..." Nico began. "Daniel, you got banged up pretty bad in that fire. I mean burns, bruising, smoke inhalation. The paramedics had to rush you to the hospital."

"Nico."

"You're gonna have to stay here for a couple of days."

"What?!" I exclaimed. A couple of days? "That's not necessary, I feel—" As I raised my voice, it cracked again and I went into another coughing fit.

"Daniel!" Nico took the glass of water and brought it to my lips. I gulped it down like a fish, and once my throat no longer felt like it was going to split in two, I took another stab at talking.

"I don't need to stay here for days. I just need to go."

"Well, no offense to your medical expertise," Hayley said. "But

I think we'd better leave that decision up to the professionals."

"You don't understand," I argued, trying to pull myself into a sitting position. "I need to leave."

"No," Nico pushed me back down onto the pillows. "You need to rest."

"No, Nico, there's something–" I stopped, trying to remember why it was that I needed to leave. Something happened. Something important.

"Whatever it is, I'm sure it can wait."

"No, it's...dammit I can't remember."

"It's okay," he said soothingly. "You have meds in your system. Just relax."

"No." I had to tell somebody something. *Dammit, what was it?* Before I could think of what it was, the door opened and my father walked in. When he saw that I was awake, he was across the room to me in seconds.

"You're awake. How are you feeling?" He turned to Nico. "Is he alright?"

"I'm fine, Dad," I answered. "I'm also not deaf."

"Sorry," he attempted a smile, but his face seemed grim.

"Is something wrong, Mr. Cohen?" Hayley asked.

"What? Oh no, it's just..."

"What?" I asked. "Dad. What's wrong?"

He stared at me grimly for another moment before he looked down and opened his mouth. "They found someone else in the gym. A girl. Angie Morgan."

"Oh my god..." Hayley said. His words sparked something in the back of my brain. A dark room, underneath the bleachers, so much blood...

"Angie," I muttered. That was it. That's what I needed to tell them. "Oh my god, Angie!"

"Daniel...when you woke up earlier, before you went down again, you said something. You said her name."

"I saw her. She–she was in the gym."

"Oh god Daniel," Nico said. "What was she doing there, did she say?"

"No, no you don't get it. I found her. She was...she was already dead when the fire started."

A heavy silence fell over the room. Nobody spoke. They just stood where they were, taking it in. Nobody needed explaining. There was a murderer out there. And he'd just taken another victim. And he set that fire to try and cover it up. But none of them had seen what I saw. As much as I would've liked to deny it, nothing ignited that fire. There were no matches, no loose wires, no nothing. It sprang to life out of nothing. Angie's body spontaneously erupted in flame with no cause. And I had no idea what that meant. For any of us.

***

My dad left to tell the police what I had just told him, and Nico went for ice cream, leaving me alone with Hayley. She just stood in the corner leaning against the wall and picking at her fingernails. I'd never liked being alone with Hayley. It always felt awkward, especially then. Normally, I could leave if I wanted to.

"So," she said, breaking the standing silence. "You found Angie."

"Yeah," I answered simply.

"Where?" she asked. I raised an eyebrow at her. "I mean obviously, in the gym, but like where?"

"Why does it matter?"

She just shrugged. "Guess it doesn't." She was silent for another excruciatingly long moment. "Was she bloody?"

"What?!"

"You know, did she look like Fairchild did when she was found. Do you think the same person killed them?"

"I–I don't know. Probably."

She nodded thoughtfully.

"Why do you care?" I asked.

She shrugged again. "Just curious, I guess."

"But—"

"So your girlfriend was here."

"W–what? What are you–Annabelle?"

"Damn Daniel," she said with a smirk. "How many girlfriends do you have?"

"None. She's not my girlfriend," I said quickly. Then after a moment, "She was here?"

"Uh huh. She heard about your little roast and she rushed over to wait with baited breath for you to wake."

"Hayley," I said dryly.

"Fine," she conceded. "But she did drop by. And she seemed worried. Oh!" She walked across the room to a chair where her backpack sat and fished around for a moment before pulling out a sheet of paper folded into a square. "She left this for you. I may have peaked." She handed me the square and I unfolded it.

It was a note, just a few words scribbled on it in neat, beautiful handwriting.

Hope you're alright. Sorry we couldn't hang out.
-Annabelle

It was nothing fancy but still brought a smile to my lips.

"Aw," Hayley said. "I know. Sweet isn't it?"

"Screw you," I mumbled, but I held onto the note in my non-bandaged hand.

After a while, Nico came back with some ice cream. Visitors rotated in amongst my parents, Nico, Hayley, and a couple of people from around town who wanted to check in. The police also spoke to me briefly about how I had found Angie. I told them as much detail as I could, omitting the fact about the fire springing to life out of nowhere. Instead I made it seem like Angie had a cigarette in her hand when she was attacked that started the fire. It felt weird lying to the police but it's not like they would've believed me anyway.

Once the police left, Dr. Lester came back in and insisted I get some rest. I closed my eyes, expecting to be much too wired for sleep. Instead, I found myself drifting away into a world of dreams.

***

I spent the entirety of the next day in the hospital. I tried to tell the doctors that I felt much better and was fine to go home, but they just spouted out some medical mumbo jumbo about smoke damage and bruised abdomen, and blah ba dee blah blah, so I was relegated to roaming around the hospital in a wheelchair. Turns out exploring the trauma center of Spirit Ridge Memorial isn't as interesting as one would think.

Nico helped me ward off boredom by bringing movies, but all the gut-wrenching horror in the world couldn't stop me from going stir-crazy. I needed to get out of there. Partly because the hospital food tasted like cardboard smeared with expired gravy, but mostly because I needed to find out what happened to Angie in that gym. While Nico and I were watching a particularly gory piece that involved a psycho killer who wore the scalps of his victims as hats, I tried to find a way to pull it up to see what I could find out, but to my surprise, Nico beat me to the punch.

"So have the police been back here today?" he asked while a nosey cop in the movie was getting scalped.

"No, not since yesterday. Why?"

"They haven't asked you anything else about Angie?"

"No," I said suspiciously. "Nothing. Why? Have they talked to you?"

"No," he said. "I was just curious. Wanted to know how they're going on catching the guy who did this."

I nodded. "So you haven't heard anything about it?"

"Nope. But I'm sure they'll catch him."

"Yeah," I said, thinking about the way Angie's body had just spontaneously caught fire. "What do you think happened?"

He just shrugged. "I don't know. Same thing that happened to Fairchild. It's terrible isn't it?"

"Yeah...yeah it is. And you've got...no theories on who it is?"

He turned to look at me with raised eyebrow as if to ask if I was kidding. "If I had any theories, don't you think I would've shared?"

"Right. So nothing, then?"

"Nope. Nothing."

"Okay," I said hesitantly. I couldn't believe it. Nico was lying to me. Seriously lying. I'd known him long enough to know that. But he had never lied to me before. Nico was the only one in my life who had never lied to me. But he was doing it now. *What was I supposed to do?* Call him out? I probably should've, but something about the idea of calling my best friend a liar made me twisted up inside.

"Hey boys!" Nico and I turned our heads to see Hayley walking in the room carrying a bag of what appeared to be microwaveable popcorn. "I come bearing gifts! So why don't you point me towards the microwave and we can do this up right."

"I think there's one down the hall," I said.

"On it," she said. "Nico, walk with me?"

"Yeah," he said hopping up immediately and following her out of the room.

I stayed where I was for a moment, just staring out after him. *Why are you lying to me?*

***

"He's not ready," a whispering voice whizzed past me, and then it was gone.

"He's not ready, he's not ready." The voices were like gnats. They were fast and fleeting, and seemed to zip right by my ear, but when I turned to look for a source, it was gone.

"He's in danger, isn't he? Please, let me help him."

It sounded like multiple voices talking at once, though not in unison. They overlapped and echoed. I didn't even know where I was. It felt like nowhere, and at the same time, everywhere. I was high in the sky, yet deep below the earth. I was in a great expanse, a never-ending void, and also in the smallest bubble of air. Wherever I was, the voices seemed to resonate through every crevice. Like they were coming from within the fabric of the air itself.

"Please. Someone out there wants to hurt my son, you have to let me protect him." This voice sounded different. Normal. Familiar, even. Very familiar. Yet I couldn't pinpoint an exact source.

"Find his own path...path...path. It is his destiny."

"But he's just a boy! He can't handle this!"

"Faith...faith...faith..." the voices said. "You must have faith."

"But—"

"Faith," they repeated. "Faith."

"Okay...okay. Faith. I have faith. But is there anything I can do? Anything at all?"

There was a long silence, but it was like I could feel noise. Like I could sense the voices conferring with each other, but I couldn't actually hear them.

"Guide," the voices answered. "Conceal...and guide..."

I jerked awake back in my hospital bed, the voices from my dream still echoing in my head. I had no idea what that was, but like so many of the dreams I'd had lately, it felt incredibly real.

I looked to my side at the clock that sat on the bedside table and saw that it was twelve twenty four in the morning. I also saw my father sitting in the chair next to me. He was slumped over, head on his shoulder, snoring. He'd had to work all day and couldn't spend much time at the hospital, so he insisted on staying overnight, no matter how much I protested.

I tried to lay my head down and go back to sleep but couldn't. Not after that dream. I felt electrified, yet uneasy. Either way, there wasn't a chance in hell of me getting any sleep. I decided that maybe a walk would do me good. Ignoring the stiff pain in my abdomen, I pulled myself up and got onto my feet. I still didn't feel a hundred percent, but I felt fine enough to walk without that stupid wheelchair.

Carefully holding my bruised stomach, I left to roam the hallways. They seemed almost cavernous at night. Something about that seemed eerie, but it also seemed kind of calm. Like for the first time that day, I was alone. All day people had been in and out of my room, be it my parent, my friends, some doctor. I wasn't allowed a moment to myself. But in those empty halls, it felt like the whole world was sleeping, and I was the only one awake. It was just me.

As I wandered aimlessly, I thought about what I was going to do when they released me. My mom and dad would want to take me home, but what would be waiting for me? More bed rest? More people talking to me like an invalid? *Thanks, but no thanks.* Besides, I needed to find out more about the fire and Angie's murder, however the hell I was going to do that. And I probably wouldn't be able to do that from home. But what else was I supposed to do?

A sound behind me sent me spinning. I expected to see a nurse telling me to go back to my room. But I didn't see anything. The hallway was just as deserted as the moment before. Except something felt different. The emptiness was ominous. I felt a chill go down the back of my neck that had nothing to do with the breezy hospital gown. When I breathed, I swore I could see my breath materialize in the air.

Rubbing my arms, I decided to go back and give sleep another try, but the minute I took a step forward, I was running. My feet pounding against the polished linoleum floors, racing down the hallway. I didn't know why but I had to get away from something. Something terrible and horrifying and I had to get away. My breath hitched in my throat and stung my smoke-damaged throat but I plowed on, turning down one corridor after another.

Where is he, dammit, where is he? What has he done with him? Where is he?!

What am I running from? What is happening to me?

I didn't know, and part of me didn't care, but I needed to know.

When I turned yet another corner, I looked back but saw only darkness. Then it was gone. Like flipping off a light switch, that sense of terror, of needing to get away, was gone. I was left alone, my body aching.

***

I stood in front of my bed at one thirty in the afternoon. The doctor insisted on keeping me for a while longer to make sure that I wasn't going to collapse from smoke damage and die on the way home or something. Normally that would have been really annoying, but at least Nico and Hayley could be there. Following two consecutive murders on school grounds, the board thought it best to suspend all classes under further notice. Although I couldn't help but look at Nico smiling at me and resent that he was one of the ones keeping the truth from me.

"And you're feeling alright?" The doctor questioned one last time.

"Yeah, I feel fine," I said. *For the umpteenth time.* "Can I go now?"

"Well," he said, looking over my discharge papers. "Everything is in order. Just remember to drink plenty of water and take it easy."

"He will," my mom said. "We'll make sure of it."

The doctor nodded and took one last look at my papers before leaving.

"Man," Hayley said. "Why doesn't he just chain you up and lock you in the room?"

"I'm still not entirely sure that you should go home," mom said. "But he's the professional."

"Mom, I'm fine," I stressed.

"Listen to him, Grace," my dad said. "I'm sure it'll be fine once we get him home and we can look after him ourselves."

She nodded reluctantly. "Yeah alright." It seemed to comfort her a bit, which made what I was about to say even worse.

"No. I don't want to go home."

My parents looked at me like I'd just spoken Latin.

"What are you talking about?" Mom asked. "You've been complaining for days about being here, I thought you wanted to leave."

"I do want to leave, I just...I don't want to go home."

"But—" she spluttered, clearly shocked by this sudden turnaround. Dad however, just looked at me as analytically as a scientist observing something particularly interesting.

"Where do you want to go?" he asked me.

I looked down for a minute before looking at Nico, praying that he picked up on what I was asking. He held my gaze for a moment before turning to my parents.

"He can stay at my place," he said. My mom looked at him like *he* had just spoken Latin.

"He needs to go home."

"Mom, stop. I *want* to go to Nico's."

"Y–you were just in a *fire*! You need to come home with us."

"Grace, let him go," my dad said. My mom turned her glare on him.

"What is wrong with you?" She was becoming hysterical and stood up to face him.

My dad put his hands on her shoulders. "Grace. Stop. He's fine. If he wants to go with Nico, let him go with Nico."

"What has gotten into everybody?!" My mom wasn't going to let up. I wanted to know that too, though for different reasons. I was already moving towards the door with Nico. "Daniel! Where are you going?"

"I'm going to Nico's, I told you."

The look of plain hurt on her face was almost too much to bear. "Daniel, please..."

"Grace! Leave him alone!" All eyes were on my parents. My mom threw up her hands and flew out of the room. I locked eyes with my dad. I hardly recognized him anymore.

"Come on, Nico," I said. I stumbled briefly on my way out but kept walking. I knew I probably hurt my mom, and I hated it, but I needed to do this. Nico had answers; that much I was sure of. So did my dad, but I was getting nowhere with him. He wasn't going to tell me the truth. Nobody was. But I had to find answers. And I had to do it on my own.

Chapter IX
Things People Hide

The houses in Spirit Ridge look like something you might see in a New Yorker's small town fantasy. As we drove, I stared out the window. All of them look homey and cozy, half of them with porch swings. You can't look in any direction without seeing at least a dozen trees. Tall oak trees and evergreens, that always seem to be bright viridian, no matter what time of year it is. The sky is blue with only a few clouds, and there are playgrounds behind every house. Of course, we were rolling through the good neighborhoods. Where the middle class people live. Nobody sees the bad parts unless they live there. Weering Heights (though everyone just calls it "The Pit") is where the broke people, like Hayley, or the delinquents, like Leo, live. That is where people get sick, fights break out, all the houses smell like smoke, and some are covered in graffiti. And then there is Wind Eye Hills, the neighborhood where every house has a pool, a hot tub, a grand foyer, and a maid. That's where people like Natalie live.

"Here we are," Nico said, snapping me out of my trance. We got out of the car and went in. It was about two o'clock. "My dad is still at work, so it's just us."

"Okay."

"Want a drink or something?"

"I'm good." I looked at him, into the familiar face of my best friend. The same face that had smiled as he scared the crap out of me with horror movies, and that was angry when he defended me against bullies, or filled with concern when I was embarrassed. All I could think was *why are you lying to me? Why are you* lying *to me?* But I nodded and for a few hours, we contented ourselves with playing video games.

But Nico seemed to have this nervous edge to him, almost like guilt. He spoke almost apologetically, like he wanted to apologize, but didn't want to let me know there was anything to apologize for. But I knew there was. But he couldn't say anything, so he settled for letting me win at Halo, even though I wasn't really trying. I was about to blow him to pieces for the seventh time, when his phone went off. He checked the caller ID, then put it down. "I'll be right back," he said.

"Saved by the bell," I said.

"What?" he asked.

"The game," I said, gesturing to the frozen screen. "I was about to kill you. Again." Luckily, I knew how to joke when I was pissed or depressed. Plastering a phony smile onto my face and saying I'm fine is my specialty.

"Oh," he said. "Right." He headed out of the room and I waited a second before standing up to take a look around the room, hoping to find...I don't know what. Anything. Something odd or out of the ordinary that might tell me what Nico had to do with the murders. A deep part of me felt dirty for suspecting him of having any part in this, but what else was I supposed to believe? I knew for a fact that he lied to me about knowing anything about Angie. I didn't really have much choice.

My eyes fell on a drawer. The drawer where I had seen the strange stone. I wondered if it was still there. Without conscious thought, my feet took me towards the drawer. It was like this magnetic pull drawing me in. I reached my hand out to open the drawer.

"Daniel?"

I turned to see that Nico had come back. My arm fell to my side and that strange pull disappeared. "Yeah?"

"That was my boss," he said, raising his cellphone. "He wants me at work right away. One of the guys at work is sick so I have to cover his shift."

"Oh," I said, biting back a curse. I had been counting on having until at least four until Nico had to leave. "Um, okay."

"I'll be back in about four or five hours, but I doubt you want to stay here for that long."

I hesitated for a moment. "Actually, would you mind?" He looked at me with his eyebrow raised. "I'd really rather not deal with my parents right now." He looked me over with those cool gray eyes, and I felt like I was in an X-ray machine. But I held my ground, pulling my eyes up to his, trying to graft a pleading look onto my face. Just a guy asking his friend for a place to hide out for a little while. I let that thought fill my head until I almost believed it. Nico let out a sigh, almost like relief.

"Sure," he said with a warm smile before leaving. I waited until I heard him walk out the front door, crank his car, and pull out of the driveway. Then I jumped up and ran down to Nico's bedroom. I felt a stab of shame at what I was doing. *Searching my best friend's room?* It felt like I was betraying his trust. But all I had to do was think about Nico looking me straight in the eye and lying to me, and that shame turned to anger. I needed to know what happened in that gym. Nico knew, and he wouldn't tell me. I was betraying him? He had betrayed *me.* So had my dad, and Hayley. Nobody would tell me the truth. Did they not think I deserved it? Or did they just not care?

"Shut up and deal," I chanted under my breath as I pulled open one of the drawers on his desk. It was mostly clutter. Old, crumpled up papers, parking tickets, bills, and I think I spotted a fake ID. Not for what you'd think. He forged it to fool his boss into thinking he was fifteen so he could work. Most of the same was in the rest of his drawers. I looked through the drawers on his nightstand and saw nothing, but when I pulled back up my eyes fell on a picture that sat on top of it. The picture was of Nico when he was young, maybe five or six. He sat on a park bench, beaming up at a woman with dark blonde hair and one hand on his head, beaming back down at him. Nico's mother. The way she stared adoringly down at him and the way he smiled at her gave my heart a twinge. The Marshalls really had been a very happy family until Mrs. Marshall had her stroke. It really sucked that they had to go through that.

I shook my head to snap myself out of it. *Focus.* I searched the bookshelf, under his bed, in his closet. I couldn't find anything. I didn't really know what I was looking for; I only knew I wasn't finding it. I racked by brain trying to think where Nico would hide— whatever. I knew Nico better than anyone, or at least I thought I did. Nevertheless, if anyone could figure this out, it was *me*. Where would he hide something he wanted kept secret? In plain sight? No. That wasn't Nico. He would keep it hidden somewhere he wouldn't forget about. Someplace secure, where nobody could see it, and only he could get it. Because *that* was Nico. Careful, but not paranoid, so it might not be over-protected. Somewhere you couldn't know about unless he told you, but not over-complicated. Somewhere simple. As I turned, I nearly jumped through the roof. Someone else was in the room with me. *He* was in the room with me. The guy I had seen outside school and in the coffee house. He stood in the middle of the room, again with his back to me, staring down at the floor.

"Who are you?" I asked. "What are you doing here?" He didn't move, but kept staring at that spot. Again, I felt that startling sense of familiarity, like an incessant teasing at the back of my mind saying *I should know this guy.* And again I got the sense that even though his back was to me, he was staring directly at me. Wait, how had he even gotten in here? I looked behind me, but the door was still closed. When I looked back, of course, he had disappeared. I looked down at the spot he had been staring at.

"Of course," I whispered. I dropped to my knees on the floor, pressing against the floorboards. A memory came back to me of when Nico and I were about eleven or twelve.

"You wanna see something?" he had asked. I looked up at him and saw that he was grinning.

"What?" His grin widened and he ran over to a spot on the floorboard. He put his ear to the floor and pressed them until he seemed to have heard what he was looking for. Still grinning, he jammed his fingers into the space between two floorboards and started pulling. He worked his fingers until I worried he would hurt himself, but eventually, the board gave. It came up from the floor and Nico pulled it aside, looking mischievously at me.

"The floorboard broke a couple months ago," he said. "My dad tried to fix it himself, but you can get it up if you really try."

"Cool!" I said, scrambling over to sit next to him. He reached into the floor and came up holding chocolate bars. He handed one to me, and opened one for himself. As we dug into our chocolate, Nico smiled knowingly at me. I had loved knowing about this. It made me feel like I was in on something, even if it was something so small and insignificant. But it was significant to me, and Nico knew that. That's why he had showed me. Because he knew it would make me feel included. I tried not to think about that as I worked the floorboard. Eventually, it gave way and came loose from the floor, and I pulled it aside. The space underneath was about two feet deep. But there were no chocolate bars in there this time.

I saw the top of a small metal square. A safe. My heart jumped. I reached down for it before realizing two things: The safe was too wide to get out through the hole, and I didn't know the combination. I groaned, thinking if I knew the combination, I could reach the dial from here and pull out whatever was inside. I could guess, but it might take forever. For all I knew, it could've been a completely random order of digits. But Nico wasn't the type to put something so important in there unless he was sure the numbers would stick in his head. I thought for a moment, and an idea formed in my head. I had learned things about objects by touching them before. I had brushed Annabelle's painting and known she had painted it. Maybe…

"Please let this work," I muttered as I grabbed a blank sheet of paper from his drawer and a pen. I reached down and lightly touched the top of the safe. Immediately, a premonition settled in, the cold sensation stemming from the smooth, metal roof of the safe spread through my whole body. The hand with the pen in it immediately moved. I don't remember moving it myself, but when I looked at the page, four numbers were scrawled across it: 07, 26, 20, and 05. I leaned down to put in the combination before stopping to look at the numbers again. 07, 26, 20, 05. July 26, 2005? The day Nico's mother had her stroke. I looked back at the photo on Nico's nightstand of him and his mom. Despite my anger at Nico, I felt a pang of sympathy for him. With that jumping around in me, I put the combination into the safe, felt a click, and the door swung open.

I felt around inside and found mostly papers. I grabbed them and pulled them out, wondering why papers could be so important to keep them in a safe under the floor that only your best friend knows about. What was written on the papers was nonsense. It was a bunch of pages ripped out of books, but I didn't understand a word of the content. There were some papers that Nico had written on himself. However, I didn't get a chance to look, because at that moment, I heard the garage door opening downstairs. Nico was back. Hastily, I put the book pages back in the safe, but kept the page that Nico had written on. I swung the safe door shut, turned the lock away from the last number, and then put the board and the carpet back in place. Hastily, I went back to the living room, stuffed the paper into my backpack, and headed for the door. Just as I grabbed hold, the door swung open, and I saw Nico's father standing there.

"Daniel," he said. "Hey, what are you doing here?"

"Hi, Mr. Marshall," I said. "I was just leaving."

"Hey," he said as I walked past him. "I heard about the fire. Are you all right?"

"I'm fine," I said through gritted teeth. I really was sick of people asking me that.

***

The second I got into my house, I swerved to avoid my mom,

ran up to my room, and locked the door. I dropped my backpack onto the bed and pulled out the paper. It was short. There were five terms scribbled onto the page. The first was *telepathy*. As in, mind reading? I wondered why Nico could possibly be writing stuff like that. But then, I remembered that look he would always give me. The one that told me that if I didn't tell him what was going on with me, he would find out anyways. Like he could read my mind. He'd always seemed to be able to read my mind. I looked at the second: *telekinesis*. Wasn't that the power to move things with your mind? I was confused, but for some reason I was getting more and more anxious. Almost sweating now, I looked at the third term: *empathy*. I think that was the ability to feel what other people were feeling. Nothing came to mind on that one, so I looked to the fourth, but I didn't really understand it: *astral projection*. I was puzzled for a moment, but then I remembered something from some horror movie I had watched once. Astral projection was the power to leave your body and wander around as a spirit. I remembered Hayley appearing in the hallway at church. Then she was gone. Like a ghost.

My heart pounded, and I could feel something stirring inside me. Right in my core, something was recognizing all of this. Like pieces of a puzzle clicking together, all coming into place. It was making sense, but I couldn't figure out how. I looked down to the fifth term: *pyrokinesis*. I had never heard the word in my life. It didn't even sound like a word, but somehow I recognized it. Images of fire came to mind. It was the power to start fires with your mind. I didn't know how I knew that. Maybe the prefix, "pyro", but I didn't think so. It was something else.

I thought of the gym. How Angie's body had seemed to erupt in flames, with no apparent cause. Then another memory came up. Ms. Fairchild running out of her office with smoldering papers, Leo walking out in a rage. But no lighter. How had he lit those papers on fire without a lighter? Everything felt like it was coming together. I felt a sense of dawning, but it was only emotional. Mentally, I couldn't find the connection. It felt like there was a barrier. Like I didn't really want to know. But nevertheless, a sixth term came into my mind. It wasn't on the paper, but I somehow knew it should be. *Precognition.* The power to see the future.

The word came out of nowhere, accompanied by the ice-cold pressure in my spine that was becoming so familiar to me. I didn't know why it suddenly came into my mind, but it came strong and powerful, echoing through my skull like a shout. I had no idea why it was there…and yet I did. But I couldn't. It just wasn't possible. All at once, the confusion was replaced by exhaustion. Overpowering exhaustion. My knees felt weak, and I could feel myself slipping away. My knees buckled underneath. I was asleep before I even hit the bed.

Chapter X
A Good Fire

In my dream, I saw Nico standing in a worn down bedroom. The bed had a wrought iron frame that was rusted and old. The sheets had a thousand moth holes in them, along with the drapes on the window. The walls were coated in dust, and the paint was faded and chipped. Hayley was there too, along with Natalie, and they appeared to be arguing.

"I know what I heard!" Nico yelled at Natalie. That was weird. Nico never yelled.

"You must've gotten it wrong, you said yourself that hearing him was 'problematic'!"

"Well it would line up with what happened in the church, and why Daniel was at the front of the crowd, and the one who found both bodies," Hayley said.

"So what are you saying? He's one of us?"

"It's possible!" Nico said. "He certainly seems to think so."

"Well, he's wrong! Besides how would he know? He doesn't even know anything about us."

"He could!" Hayley shouted. "He saw me at the church, he heard you and Nico with the vase, and he saw Leo attack Fairchild!"

"All of those were explained, you know how good they are at that," Natalie said.

"That's not the point," Nico said. "We need to know for sure, because he definitely knows that I lied to him and that is not okay! He's my best friend." Hayley put a hand on his arm.

"Oh boo-hoo!" Natalie scoffed. "Is your little bromance in jeopardy?" Hayley snapped her head toward her.

"Easy talk for someone who has to buy all their friends."

"Well at least I can afford to," Natalie snapped back.

"Hey!" Nico yelled. "That's enough. I know what I heard in the car. Daniel knew I was lying to him, so whether he's one of us or not, he definitely knows something." Out of nowhere, there came a blood-curdling wail from the adjacent room. Natalie was at the door in a second, throwing it open and running out. The dream shifted, the ancient room disappearing. A new scene formed.

It was my room. The sky outside was dark and gray, like it was going to rain. There was a seven-year old boy sitting on my bed. His hair was dark and thin, he hadn't cut it in months, so it came down past his ears. He had big blue eyes, both pale and bright at the same time; he was me, when I was seven. He was wishing it would rain. He loved rainy days. He was sitting on his bed with a sketchpad and some crayons, coloring. He was drawing a picture of a phone, buzzing like it was ringing. It was a split scene, like on TV, where one half of the screen shows you, and the other half shows who's on the other end of the phone. But all that was waiting on the other end was tears.

The scene shifted again.

The little boy was there, only this time he wasn't in his bedroom. He stood in the dark, musty basement of his house. He was searching through boxes for a coloring set but couldn't find it. As he turned to a different box, he saw something on the wall.

He moved toward the back wall, where some kind of mural was painted. It looked like a tree, branches extending every which way, only the branches had faces and names on them. He didn't recognize any of the names or faces, until his eyes landed on a couple he did. One of them was a picture of his grandpa, and under it: Andrew Rhett Cohen, 1932–2001. The branch extended to a picture of the boy's father: Nathaniel David Cohen, 1970–. Beyond that was a picture of the boy himself: Daniel Jacob Cohen, 1998–.

The boy stared up at the massive tree in awe and wonder. He didn't know any of the faces beyond those three, but he felt that they were all familiar, though he didn't know why. Maybe he'd seen their pictures before. Maybe it was something to do with the fact that they all bore the exact same bright opalescent blue eyes as him.

His eyes roamed to a specific face. He didn't recognize it, but it looked a lot like him. The same brown hair, same eyes, same skin, pretty much the same facial structure. The name below it read: Keenan Elias Cohen, 1782–1803. He didn't know why, but he felt drawn to that particular face. It was a strange magnetic pull, like something in that face pulled at something in his very core.

"Daniel?"

The boy looked up at the top of the stairs and saw his dad coming downstairs.

"Daddy, what's this?"

He came down and when he saw what his son was looking at, he smiled.

"That," he said as he went over to lay a hand on his son's head, "is us, Daniel. Our family."

"That's me," the boy said, pointing to his picture. "And that's you, and grandpa, but I don't know the rest of them."

"Well that's because they're not around anymore. They went to heaven a long time before you were born. But you know, they still watch over us. They're watching over us right now."

"Really? Are they angels?"

"Kind of," he said, smiling lovingly down at the boy. He crouched down and looked him in the eyes. "You see, the Cohen's are a special family. We're all special, every single one of us."

"Everyone?" The boy looked up at the tree. "Mommy's not up there. Is mommy special?"

His father smiled a smile that made his eyes brighter, made his features melt. "Your mom is very special. But she's not like us. You see, you and I have Cohen blood." He clapped his son on the arm, where his veins were. "And that's a powerful thing. We all have a part of them," he pointed up at the names and faces on the wall. "Each one of us has something special. And we have that something special inside of us. Greatness runs in our family, Daniel."

"What do you mean?" the boy asked.

"I mean...someday you're gonna do great things."

"How do you know?" the boy asked.

The father grinned. "A little birdie told me." He winked and the boy laughed. The father ruffled the boy's hair affectionately as the scene shifted again.

That little boy was there again, only this time he was walking up to his parents' bedroom. He could hear voices from inside. His mom and dad. My mom and dad.

"I talked to Dr. Farrell today, he said that we could take Daniel down to his office tomorrow."

"Yeah," dad said. "Hey, I've been thinking...I don't think we should take Daniel to him."

"What? Well do you have a better idea?"

"I think we should handle this on our own." Mom was silent for a moment, seeming not to know what to say to that.

"What are you talking about? He needs professional help."

"Look, he's our son, so we should handle this ourselves. Plus...you know I don't think that sitting on some couch and talking to a stranger is the way to help him."

"That's crazy! Dr. Farrell is trained to help people with his condition, he's experienced, he's been helping Aspies overcome their condition for years. Daniel needs this."

"I don't think so," he said. "I think he needs to learn how to handle it on his own."

"*On his own?!* He's seven years old, Nathan. *Seven.* He needs his parents to help him through this. Just because you don't feel like dealing with a problem—"

"What is that supposed to mean?"

"Look, Nathan," her voice turned gentle. If I'd been awake, I would've flinched. I hadn't heard my mom talk to my dad with that kind of tone in years. "I talked to Dr. Farrell and he told me it's very common for Asperger's to be inherited. Often...often father-to-son." Now it was his turn to fall silent.

"You think this is my fault. That I gave it to him."

"That's not what I said, Nathan."

"You think that he has this because of me?" "It's not your fault, Nathan, it's nobody's fault. But it's happening so we have to figure out a way to fix it."

"Look, he's my son. I know what's best for him, and he does not need this. His life will be hard enough, he does not need all of this making it worse on him."

"He's my son too, Nathan, and I'm trying to make it *easier*, not harder. On both of you."

"Well this won't help!" Abruptly, the door opened, and the little boy tried to run before his dad saw him eavesdropping.

The scene shifted again.

Now the little boy sat back on the bed, still coloring, but now he was sad. It was raining outside, but it didn't calm him like it usually did. The picture he was coloring was a picture of a man and a woman fighting, screaming at each other, while a little boy sat in the middle, crying. And below them, in the middle, was a stack of pancakes.

Then my dad was in my room, standing over my bed, where I lay asleep. I was older now, probably sixteen. It couldn't have been too long ago. Weeks, maybe even days ago. It was kind of surreal seeing myself sleep. Dad approached the bed, laying a gentle hand on my head.

"Hey there, buddy," he whispered. "Things have been pretty rough for you, huh? Well I'm sorry, but it's about to get a lot worse." I had never seen this look in my dad's eyes before. His expression held this sad, helplessness in it, like someone looking at a stray puppy they wanted to help. "They told me about it. They didn't tell me everything, only that bad things are gonna happen, and you're gonna be in the middle of it, and I'm not gonna be able to do anything about it. I wish I could help you but...you've just got to figure it out on your own. That's our curse. I'm sorry buddy. Just know that I love you, and I swear I will help you however I can. But this is your fight." He bent his head down and placed a kiss on my forehead "Good luck."

The door stood there, shining bright white against the black. As always, I stood just in front of it, a few steps away. Something spoke inside of me to open it. I turned around to see the darkness getting closer. Panic rose in my chest. I knew I had to get to that door. My body had put me to sleep so I could see it. I took a step toward the door, then another, when a cold feeling touched me. Not like a premonition, but a much more sinister cold. It felt like death itself had caressed my back. I knew the darkness was catching up to me. I felt it getting closer as the shadowy claw that had touched me began to snake around my body. I couldn't move, I was so afraid. My voice was caught in my throat. My heart was ice. But I knew I had to get to the door. I had to open it this time.

I pushed through the fear that had clutched me and took another step toward the door. I ignored the darkness following behind, and took one step after another until I was at the door. A sense of anxiety overtook me. Only death and despair would come from opening that door. But I had wanted to open it. I looked down and saw the shadows coiling around my feet; they were going to get me. That was why. I had to open the door or darkness would take me. But I couldn't open the door. Not yet. I had to do something first. I bent down to look at the design crafted into the golden knob. It was an eye. Wide open. Not like the Illuminati, but something...kinder. More natural. Good. That eye could see anything it wanted to see. All it had to do was look. All *I* had to do was look.

I was in my bed again. I bolted upright, sweat pouring down my face. I looked out my window and saw that night had fallen. I marveled at what I had just seen. All of it had seemed so…tangible…powerful…so…real. But it couldn't have been. *Could it?* How could I have known where Nico, Hayley, and Natalie were at that moment? And that little boy. I was sure it was me, sitting up in my room coloring as a child. That, I easily could've remembered, but both the drawings seemed to predict future events. The doctor calling with my diagnosis. My parents arguing, me crying, pancakes…

I jumped off the bed, a million thoughts whirring in my head. I had to know what was going on. I had doubted my knowledge, and sleep had come to give me those dreams. I was sure of that.

Who killed Angie and Fairchild? Who started the fire? How had the fire started? What were those dreams about? Why would Nico have a sheet of paper with five words written on it in a safe under his floor? Who was he talking about with Natalie? How had I painted those deaths? How had I known the combination to Nico's safe? What did my dad know? What was the darkness I kept seeing? Why did Nico lie? What do he and Hayley have to do with Natalie? Or Leo? Aside from Nico and Hayley, what do any of them have to do with one another? *What didn't I know?*

I shook my head vigorously. Too many questions, not enough answers. It was time to be straightforward with everybody and *demand* answers. People knew what was going on with me. And like it or not, they were going to tell me.

I spent the next three hours searching the Internet for everything I could find about each and every term on that paper. Most of what I got was research performed by obsessed quacks who gave "scientific" explanations. Some were voodoo websites that gave incomprehensible, mystical explanations that you'd probably have to grow up with gypsies to understand. The rest were either science fiction or role-playing games for people with even worse social lives than mine. It was all nonsense.

This coming from a boy who had painted the future, a small part of me thought.

Shut up, the rest of my brain told it. *Nobody asked you.* When it finally got too late, I decided to go to bed. But after half an hour of tossing and turning with no success, I decided that wasn't happening and went outside for a walk. Sure, it was late. But at that point, I needed fresh air. I disabled the downstairs alarm, put on a jacket over my pajamas, and walked out into the brisk October air.

It was cold, but not bone-biting cold. Just cool-you-down-while-you're-freaking-out cold. I walked down my lawn and into the streets, following the curb, seeing by the bright streetlights overhead. It was quiet. No teenagers out trying to amuse themselves...or at least not here. This was the quiet neighborhood. If I were in The Pit, there would be drunk kids with busted beer bottles on every street corner. If I were in Wind Eye Hills, I wouldn't be able to step on a single lawn without setting off an alarm. But here, in the one neighborhood without a stupid nickname, everything was calm. The air itself seemed to be drifting around, doing whatever. The cold was causing night dew to appear on the grass, and the stars were out like bright diamonds etched into the midnight canvas, with a huge, white slit that was the crescent moon. Everything is beautiful at night, so what I saw next was only fitting. As I turned another corner in the residential labyrinth, there she was. I could barely make out the curtain of jet-black hair that framed a perfectly bronzed face. Her slim, curvy figure slowly stood at the sight of me.

"Hello?" she called.

"Whoa!" I whisper gasped and stumbled back, mainly from the exquisite happenstance.

There was fear in her eyes, before she saw who I was. "Daniel?"

"Annabelle Martin," I said, taking a cautious step out of the shadows

Her face wore a look of concern. "What are you doing?" she asked.

"Uh..." I struggled momentarily for an answer to that question. "Meandering?"

"Are you feeling alright?" My heart actually pounded against my rib cage. "I mean, because of the fire. And now...whatever it is that you're doing…"

It all came rushing back to me. In the moment of seeing Annabelle, I had actually forgotten about what happened in the last week.

"Oh, right," I said. "I'm fine. It really wasn't that bad, I kinda got off easy."

"Oh, well that's good," she said.

"Yeah," I said. There was pause as I struggled to think of something else to say. "So, what are *you* doing here?"

"Oh. I live here," she said, gesturing at the modest Tudor-style, eggshell colored house behind her.

"Of course," I said. She looked embarrassed to be loitering in a driveway late at night, so I added, "almost everybody lives in this neighborhood."

"Ah," she said. "So can I ask, why you're out so late?"

"Or I could point out that you are too," I said with a smirk. *Is that okay to say?* She grinned, so I suppose it was.

"Good point," she said. "You tell me, I'll tell you?"

"Fair enough," I said. "I just…" how did I actually tell her why? "needed some fresh air."

"Oh, come on," she said. "Give more details than that." I smiled.

"Okay," I said. "I'm…kinda confused about some stuff, and I'm having trouble figuring it out."

"What kind of stuff?" she asked as she started walking down the sidewalk in the direction I was headed. I continued next to her.

"Some stuff…about me…that some other people know more about. But they aren't willing to share."

"Why not?"

"No idea," I said sadly. "That's part of what I'm trying to figure out."

"Mysterious," she mused. I grinned.

"What about you?" I asked. She shrugged.

"Not as mysterious. I just moved to a new town—"

"Tiny, podunk town," I blurted out. She giggled.

"Right," she said. "I just moved to a *tiny, podunk* town where everybody's known everybody forever, and there just doesn't seem to be any room for a new girl."

"I, uh, know how you feel," I responded. She raised an eyebrow. She was so beautiful when she did that.

"How's that?" she asked. I shrugged, but didn't say anything. I didn't like where this was going. "You don't share much do you?" she asked. I chucked nervously.

"Not really much to share," I said.

"Try me," she said.

"It's pretty boring."

"Well then, bore me," she said, smirking. I grinned. For some reason, I really wanted to tell her.

"I don't know. Feeling lonely. I...understand that. I'm just...not the most...social person in the world."

"Is that all I'm getting tonight?" she asked. Again I shrugged nervously. She nodded. "Meaning, yes."

"Sorry," I said.

"It's cool," she answered. "I get it." But I could tell she was disappointed. At the sight, I felt terrible. I felt the urge to tell her every little thing about me. Anything she wanted to know. Anything. "It's really okay," she said, looking concerned. She looked like she could see how bad I felt. Which was weird, because normally, I was really good at plastering on a fake smile and pretending to be fine.

"I'm trying to figure something out," I said anyways. "Someone really close to me knows the answer, but for some reason, he won't tell me. And I'm having trouble figuring out why." She nodded.

"Can I ask *who* this close someone is?" she asked. "Or am I overstepping my bounds?"

"Nico," I said after a moment's hesitation. "Which I don't get, because he's never lied to me before."

"How do you know he's lying?" I paused, considering that for a moment.

"His hand," I said.

"Huh?" she asked, confused.

"His hand," I said. "Whenever he lies to someone, the ring finger on his left hand gives this tiny little twitch. It's his tell." She raised her eyebrows again, but this time it wasn't sarcastic or questioning. She was impressed.

"You can actually notice that?" she asked.

"Yeah," I said.

"You guys are that close?" Again, I shrugged.

"I guess so. I mean, we've been friends since we were nine."

"Well then, do you mind if I say something invasive?"

"Um...I guess not," I said uncertainly.

"If you guys are really that close, then whatever this big secret is, you shouldn't let it bust you up." I looked over at her, and in her deep, Hershey eyes, I saw sincerity.

"Maybe you're right," I said. She smiled. "Thanks," I said.

"You're welcome?" she said uncertainly. We were silent for a very long moment.

"Well, how about we talk about something else?" She laughed and let out a relieved breath.

"Sounds good."

"So," I began. I racked my mind trying to think of something to say that could strike up a conversation, but my mind blanked. "What...what's your favorite color?"

She broke out in laughter and looked at me in bewilderment.

"Okay," she said. "Why not? Um...I think I would have to go with...cerulean blue. It's so peaceful and serene. It's like the color of the ocean before the sun comes up, when the surface of the water is still."

"Wow," I said in wonder. "That's beautiful."

"Well, I try," she said, feigning modesty. I had to laugh at that. "Back home whenever I was feeling sad or angry, or just generally had a crappy day, I would go out onto the beach and stare out at the ocean. Close my eyes and hear the sound of the waves."

"I know what you mean. Sometimes I just have to get away. Find something beautiful." I couldn't take my eyes off of her as I spoke. "Life's all about finding beautiful things, I guess." She stared at me after I said it, and I shook my head and let out a breath. "Holy crap, did I really say that? My god, I sound like a Hallmark card."

"No," she said, smiling brightly. "You're right. Nothing makes me feel better faster than finding something beautiful and getting it on canvas. It's like... it's like taking a moment in time and capturing it. Taking something beautiful and making it last forever."

"Yeah," I said dreamily. "I never thought of it like that, but...wow." At that moment, my hand itched for a pen, or some colored pencils, maybe some pastels. I wanted to draw her. To preserve her beauty and grace for all of time. "Like this."

"What?" With a shock I realized I had spoken aloud. Panicked, I grasped for a lifeline.

"Um...like...like the sky," I pointed up at the great expanse of inky night. "One of the perks of living on a little blip on the map. No smog, no smoke, all stars."

"Wow," she breathed softly as she stared up at the stars.

"Bet you haven't got that in Destin," I said quietly.

She laughed, though didn't take her eyes of the cluster of twinkling stars above. "No, can't say we do." She continued to stare at the sky in wonder, the shining pinpricks of light reflecting in her eyes. "Now *that's* beautiful."

I looked over at her rich, tanned skin in the dark, the gentle curves of her slim figure, the way her jet-black hair came down over one shoulder like it always did, the way her eyes looked up at the stars, as if anything up there could come close to the beauty I was seeing.

"Yes, it is," I said softly.

Something about that must've gotten her attention, because she turned her gaze away from the stars and back to me. Our eyes locked for a moment, and the entire world seemed surreal.

"Well what about you?" she asked.

"What–what about me?"

"What's *your* favorite color?"

She looked up at me with those dark chocolate eyes. It's impossible to believe that any shade could be so warm, so welcoming and so magically comforting, like being wrapped in a soft fleece blanket.

"Brown," I said without thinking. "Deep, chocolate brown."

She looked back at me with a surprised, but not altogether displeased expression. Slowly, her face broke into a smile that I mirrored.

"Thank you," she said quietly.

"No. Thank you," I said. "It feels good to talk to someone."

"You never seem to do that," she said.

"Yeah well," I said. "For good reason."

"Well, hey, I'm not gonna push," she said.

"Thank you," I said. I looked at her then. I noticed that her hair had gotten a little messed up when we had collided, and a single strand had fallen into her face. Without thinking, I reached out and brushed it back to tuck it behind her ear. We both froze when my fingers touched her face.

Suddenly, the entire world around us stopped. I could feel my heartbeat racing, something I couldn't really identify swelling to the surface. It felt like a fire was raging in my chest, but nothing like the fire in the gym. That fire had been harsh and cruel. This one felt powerful as well, but it made me think of a warm summer's day, running around under the sun, of blood rushing through your veins, of feeling like the only person in the world. The bright, kind flame seemed to have enveloped both of us, wrapping us in its warm glow, shielding us from the cold night around us. Safe and warm, but also excited, blood pumping. I'm not sure how, but I knew Annabelle could feel the flame, same as I could, and it was closing in on us, pushing us closer together. My hand somehow moved to cradle her face, brushing her soft, beautiful skin, and she leaned her cheek into it. I was closer to her, and I could feel her body close to mine. My heart pounded so hard, it might have burst right out of my chest. I had no idea what was about to happen, but I knew that I wanted it to happen. I so badly wanted it to happen. But something burst through the fiery walls surrounding us.

A cold, terrible memory that I had almost died, and I had predicted the deaths of two people. I wouldn't let anything bad happen to Annabelle. As long as I was alive, nothing bad would ever happen to her. So, fighting every instinct in my body, I pulled my hand away from her face.

"I should, uh...I should probably get back to bed," I forced myself to say. Immediately, the fire vanished, the October night rushing back to us. She looked at me, as if waking up from a dream.

"What?" she asked, confused.

"I said I should probably head back to bed. And so should you." It was killing me. Each word tasted like acid in my mouth.

"Oh," she said, as if barely comprehending my words. "Yeah, um, okay. You're probably right."

"Okay," I said, and, realizing one of us had to do it first, I slowly turned away and started back to my house. I didn't look back, because I knew if I did, I wouldn't be able to keep going.

Chapter XI
Whitmore House

If I was ever going to get answers, I couldn't keep waiting for people to give them to me. I had to make them tell me. I wasn't exactly the confrontational type, and no matter how much more comfortable I was with Nico than other people, I still didn't feel good demanding answers from him. Plus, after my encounter with Annabelle the previous night, I was pretty much feeling like absolute crap. But, nevertheless, when morning came, I dragged myself out of my bed, showered, got dressed, brushed my teeth, and head out to Nico's.

As I approached the door, I looked inside my parent's bedroom. They slept on opposite ends of the bed, of course, as far away from each other as they could. They didn't actually sleep in separate beds, only because they knew it would upset me. I knew I had been shutting my parents out, but I had good reason. My dad was being just as, if not more than, secretive as Nico, and my mom...I don't know. I guess I'm used to keeping it all to myself.

I wanted to slip out early to avoid talking to my parents. I had avoided them the previous day when I got back from Nico's, and when they came up to my room I had been asleep. But it occurred to me that my mom really was trying to help me. Just like always. Even if she got a little too clingy. I felt a stab of guilt at how I had been acting toward her. I made a silent promise to myself that when I got back, I would talk to her, and try to put her mind at ease. Or, as at ease as she could get. I then slid out the door into the fresh morning air.

The walk wasn't long to get to Nico's house. At dawn, the grass glistened, my vision slightly obscured by the morning fog. I tried my best to build up the nerve to do what I was about to. Thing was, I wasn't exactly the "nerves of steel" kind of guy. I was more the "knees of jelly" kind of guy. I found myself wishing Nico's house was further away so I'd have more time to talk myself up (or shorter, so I'd have less time to talk myself out of it). At least twice I stopped and contemplated walking back home. But I knew I couldn't. Deep down, no matter how much I didn't want to do this, I knew I had to. If all of this was to make any sense at all, I was going to have to face up to all of them. As the top of Nico's house came into view, my heart started hammering. On one hand, I'd have to defy everything about my nature. On the other hand, I might find what I've been looking for. And that thought quickened my pace. I could feel that missing part of me, a hole that needed to be filled, and I was aching to have it all click into place.

Before I knew it, I was on the lawn, rapidly walking toward the porch. I was going up the steps. I was at the door. I don't remember ringing the doorbell, but there was the ding. I waited anxiously as I heard footsteps coming toward the doorway, my heart rising to its pique...

"Daniel, what are you doing here so early?" My heart fell.

"Mr. Marshall?" Nico's father stood in the door, as big as his son "Um, hi. Is Nico here?"

"No, he took off about an hour ago." I was very confused by that. I had a reason for being up so early, but where could Nico possible be going?

"Well," I said. "Can you tell him I stopped by and tell him to call me?"

"I'll be sure to do that," he said.

"Thanks," I replied.

"Daniel," he said as I turned to walk away.

"Yes, sir?"

"Are you and Nico fighting about something?" I hesitated for a moment. *Had Nico said something to his father?*

"W-why do you ask?"

"He seems upset. I thought you might know something."

"Trust me, Mr. Marshall..." I sighed. "I wish I knew." He nodded and went back inside.

I tried calling Hayley but got voicemail. I left a message saying to call me back, or tell Nico to call me if she saw him. I needed to find him. I could slowly feel my edge ebbing away. If I didn't do this soon, I didn't think I would ever be able to. I kept my eyes open, hoping to see him taking a walk or something. But no such luck. I ended up walking by Whitmore House. I looked up at the macabre mansion, letting my eyes wander all over the rotten outside until they came upon a window. A window with dust-covered glass, ripped curtains, and a splattered red stain that looked suspiciously like blood. Something stirred at the back of my brain. The teasing of a memory, tickling my consciousness, barely out of reach. There was a shift in the window. Nothing more than a shadow, but it was enough to tell me that something, or someone, had definitely moved in there. I found myself recalling a dream. Three familiar people arguing in a very old bedroom.

"Oh my God," I whispered, before jumping over the sidewalk, bolting across the overgrown grass, and running onto the porch. I stopped myself from wrenching the door open, as they would surely hear me, and eased it open instead. The inside was even more decrepit than the out, but I didn't stay to observe it before easing my way up the stairs, fighting the urge to run up three at a time. I could hear voices drifting down the steps and hurriedly walked toward them.

"...problematic!" I crept up the last stair to decipher the first recognizable word coming from the furious group.

"Well it would line up with what happened in the church, and why Daniel was at the front of the crowd, or the sole witness to both murders." I couldn't believe what was happening. My dream was unfurling right before me. I looked over to the next room. If this was truly my dream, then that was the room from where the scream had emanated. I hesitated for a moment, before slowly creeping further across the hall and putting my ear to the door. I didn't hear any voices, just some kind of labored breathing. I took a careful step back, wondering what could possibly be in there. I looked back to the room where the others were. I should go in there, confront them, like I'd planned. Get my answers right then. But I wouldn't find answers in there. Nothing but hastily imagined excuses and lies. In here was where I would find my answers. It was like an internal compass leading me where I needed to go. And it was wrenching me in the direction of the door.

I cautiously put my hand to the knob, keeping my eye on the other door to make sure they didn't hear me, and turned it slowly. Holding my breath, I pushed it open, looking through the cracked door. There wasn't much difference between this room and the others. Same layout, same dusty, mildewed sheets, same moth-devoured curtains. But on the bed, wrapped up in the sheets, was a person. I couldn't see the face, but the sheet seemed to be shaking. Small, weak moans were coming from the musty bundle, and whoever it was seemed to be in pain. I took a tentative step toward it, and the bundle exploded, tearing out of the covers, head flying out, wild eyes fixing on me. I froze. The person was a boy. He looked about nineteen or twenty, with disheveled, unkempt, hair of a raw umber brown, and chestnut eyes, wide open in terror. He was drenched in sweat, pale and sickly. His look of fear, combined with his fragile, malnourished physique gave me the impression of cracked glass. Not quite broken, but if tested, it would surely fall apart. But the most surprising thing was, I recognized him. Barely.

"Cam?" I said. "Cam Wilson?" It was him. I hadn't seen him in years, and he hadn't looked nearly so damaged, but the hair, the eyes. Underneath it was the same person. Cam had lived here about eight or nine years ago. He lived with his parents, and there were rumors that they were neglectful. Sometimes he would come to school and pig out at snack time because he hadn't gotten dinner the night before. But he had disappeared. The entire town had launched a manhunt to find him, but he was nowhere to be found. And yet here he was. Right in front of me. In a haunted house where Nico, Hayley, and Natalie were mysteriously fighting over *me*.

My blood ran cold as a terrifying thought formed. Could they have started that fire somehow? Kidnapped Cam, killed Ms. Fairchild and Angie? No way. Nico was my friend, Hayley too (sort of). Natalie...well Natalie may have been a bitch, but that didn't make her a murderer. But I didn't know how else to explain the situation. Why else would they lie about each death? Why else would Cam be here? My knees shook as I gawked at him. At the broken shell of the boy who used to always share his toys at recess and give other kids his leftover snacks.

"What did they do to you?" I asked. He didn't say anything, but seemed to be studying me. There was a glint in his eyes, like he was looking into a bright light, trying to read it. He put his hand out, as if feeling the air. Stroking it. "Cam—" But I cut off when I saw the look in his eyes shift. It was like he had seen something incredible and terrible at the same time. His breathing became labored and rapid, as if having an asthma attack. His body seized and he let out a scream. A terrible wail of agony that echoed through the huge house. I fell back a step out of surprise as he collapsed back onto the bed, cutting off the scream. I kept retreating until I felt my back hit the wall behind me. There was the sound of a door opening to my left. My head whipped around to see Natalie running out the door, golden blonde hair flying behind her. Nico and Hayley came right behind her, their faces morphing into shock.

"DANIEL?!" Hayley cried out.

"What did you do?!" Natalie yelled, coming at me. I dodged her, and she ran into the room with Cam. She tried to pull him up, but he didn't budge. She yelled his name, and screamed for him to wake up.

Swiftly, Hayley was by her side, checking his pulse. "He's alive, but he's out cold," she said.

Natalie turned to me, rage plain on her face. "What the hell did you do to him?" she shrieked. The lamp on the table next to the bed flew up and shattered against the ceiling. Then the table itself flew at the wall, completely unsupported, and put a hole in the rotted drywall. My blood pumped through my veins, filling me with terror.

"Nat, you wanna stop it?!" Hayley screamed. I looked over to Nico, terrified.

"Daniel, it's okay," he said. But whatever was happening, it certainly was not okay. I had no clue what was going on, just things were flying because Natalie was clearly furious at me.

"No, it's not okay," she said, storming toward me. "You tell me what you did right NOW!" She slammed her arms down at the last word, and I felt some invisible force rush at me, and I was pushed onto my back. I looked back up at Natalie, and saw a look of horror replace the fury. "Oh, God."

"Daniel—" Nico began, but I didn't hear the rest. I jumped to my feet and ran.

Chapter XII
The Will-o'-the-Wisp

I heard Nico shout after me, but I kept running. I managed to jump down the stairs, four at a time, to escape from whatever I had gotten myself into. I made a beeline for the front door, but I felt my feet pulled out from under me, as if by a rope. I fell to the ground, splinters stabbing into my face from the rough wooden floor. I pulled myself up, ignoring the blunt pain in my chest and knees, and the stabbing pain in my cheeks. I looked back up the stairs and saw Natalie, hand outstretched as if she had just pulled the rope that had brought me down. I turned back to the door, but out of nowhere, a couch moved to block my path. Adrenaline pumping, I ran through the living room, and went into the kitchen, desperately searching for an exit.

The back door was ten yards away, in the dining room hallway. I rushed through the kitchen, past the dining table and cobwebbed chandelier, into the hallway, and wrenched open the door. I jumped onto a large patio then bolted across the backyard, legs aching, face bleeding, but I ignored the pain. Somehow, it was dark. I had no idea how that had happened. It shouldn't even be noon yet, but somehow, night had fallen in the few minutes I had been in the house. I hit the tree line of the backyard, and went into the forest.

"Daniel!" I heard Nico call from the house, but I didn't turn around. I kept running past the trees, leaves crunching under foot, and I could barely make anything out in the cold night air. Nothing seemed to have any shape. It was all black shadows. I kept running, but I stopped when I almost slammed face-first into a tree. I collected myself, took a deep breath, and tried to process the recent turn of events.

Natalie had attacked me, but what she did wasn't natural. She had made lamps and tables and couches fly. She had thrown me and yanked me without even touching me. And she thought I had attacked Cam. But I had no idea what had happened to Cam. He had looked so broken down, so fractured, so...*scared*. As if something about me had terrified him, but I had no idea what that could be? Maybe he thought I would rescue him and he had Stockholm syndrome or something. He didn't want to leave. But that doesn't answer any of the questions I had gone there to get answered. All I knew was that the three of them had been keeping Cam in Whitmore House, possibly as a captive, and possibly committed murder. And tried to kill me in that fire. I was so scared, so confused, I didn't even know where I was.

How had it become dark so fast? I knew I was in the woods, but I had no clue where. I had never been in this part of the forest around my neighborhood, but I knew that they would be coming after me. *To kill me?* I had no idea. Or keep me hostage like Cam. I was so terrified it was hard to think straight. Without warning, light flashed through the darkness in the corner of my eye. My head whipped in the direction of the brief flash. It was gone as quickly as it had come. Scanning the oily black, I saw it again. A small flicker of arctic blue light. Wispy, intangible. Like a ghost. It seemed to call me to it. In the blink of an eye, it disappeared again. I looked back in the direction of the house. They could be coming for me at any moment. The eerie light flickered again, farther away this time.

"Hello?" I called. The light vanished only to reappear even farther away. Hesitantly, I took a step forward. The light moved again, beckoning me to follow it. I took another step, keeping an eye over my shoulder, wondering why I was doing this instead of going to the police. The light kept up the pattern of appearing, only to disappear, and then reappear a little further. I followed it, barely noticing how much time had passed. My head felt fuzzy. I didn't even feel myself walking. I felt like I was dreaming, slipping deeper and deeper into a sleep.

I stopped dead in my tracks as an icy premonition slammed into me.

Stop. Don't follow that thing. Turn back. I looked ahead, where the ghastly light was stopped, waiting for me to follow. But I didn't. I didn't want to follow it anymore. Wherever it was leading me to, I did not want to go there. This thing, whatever it was, wanted to trick me.

"Go away," I called to it. "I'm not going to follow you. Just leave me alone." And just like that, the wisp of light was gone, and it did not reappear. I stood in the same spot, half-waiting for it to reappear further down the trail, but it remained dark.

"Daniel!" a voice came through the darkness. Nico. A more powerful light filled my eyes, blinding me. My hands went up to shield my eyes as the thick darkness dissolved, and then it was afternoon. I slowly brought my hands away from my face and saw the light streaming through the canopy of leaves overhead. It had never been nighttime. Somehow, I had seen darkness, and only darkness. "Daniel?" I brought my astounded gaze down to Nico, eyes filled with concern. "Are you okay?" He examined the scrapes and wounds on the side of my face and on my hands.

I pulled away from him, ready to bolt again if my legs would allow. But looking into the cool eyes that had so many times instilled me with calm, I thought, *No. No way.* This was Nico. And whatever secrets he had kept from me, he was no killer, and he would never hurt me. He could never hurt anyone. He was Nico. The guy who worked his fingers to the bone every day for his family. The guy who would sit and listen to me talk about my problems, and never once complain about his. The guy who brought me horror movies, and backed me up when I needed him, and gave me my first real friend. My only real friend. No matter what, Nico was my best friend. For what felt like the thousandth time in my life, I felt Nico's calm wash over me, making me feel safe and secure.

"No more lies," I asserted. "I want the truth." He didn't dare say a thing. I calmly waited for my answers to come. Finally, he opened his mouth.

"I think you know."

"No, I—" I started, but the words caught in my throat. I wanted to say that I didn't know. But I did. I had been hiding it from myself. It had been buried beneath the part of my brain that said it couldn't be real. But something deeper was more powerful. It was a primal force that raged against the rest of my mind, but it finally won out.

Another term came into my head, like a flower blossoming into full bloom. A single word that connected all the other terms, like the roots of a tree that grew into the branches that formed the other words. A magnificent tree that connected everything in the world. I could practically hear the *click* resounding through the universe as it all fell into place. All the terms on that page that had revealed the world to me. They were all just the branches and leaves that grew from this one word. This one force. *Mana.*

Part Two
The Rising

Chapter XIII
Silence

Do you ever think that silence is worse than pandemonium? That it would be better for everything to be falling down around you, a thousand noises tearing through your skull, than to sit in the strangling tightness of quiet? Maybe it's not a fair comparison. Maybe it's like comparing a death by clumsy bludgeoning to a death by euthanasia. Like comparing Jack the Ripper to carbon monoxide. On the one hand, chaos confuses you, leaves you vulnerable. But with silence, it's like you already know you're going to die. You know how, and when. Where and maybe why. But there's nothing you can do. Just sit and wait for your life to end. Oh, yes. Silence is much crueler than noise.

I would have given anything for a cacophony of noises as I sat on the dust-encrusted couch of the Whitmore House's living room, with Nico, Hayley, and Natalie staring me down. Nico was sitting in the chair opposite me, silver eyes filled with sympathy. Hayley was leaning against the wall behind him, emerald eyes looking me over curiously. Natalie was sitting on the staircase, hazel eyes drilling into me, as if she could force me to spill my guts by nothing more than the force of her stare. Now that I wasn't rushing to see my dream literally come true, I had the chance to really see the place. The rickety staircase I had bolted up was straight across from the front door. To the left was the living room, where a dirty couch rested in front of the window, whose shades were closed. Across from the couch was a high-backed chair, with a small glass table in between, a mid-sized love seat on the other side, and on the far side of the room was the fireplace. On the right side of the staircase, I saw the dining room, with a mighty mahogany dining table, worn down and aged.

I looked back to the others. I didn't exactly know what to say. What do you say to people who told you about your mystical powers? "Thank you?" Or maybe, "oh, okay. Now you wait right here while I call some nice men who'll take you to this really neat room with really soft walls." But the men would have to take me too. Because I bought it. As crazy as it was, I didn't doubt them. I believed I had supernatural powers. That we all did. Consciously, I knew it was insane, but every other part of me knew what they were telling me was true.

"So… of all the things to meet over, huh?" Mother of God. That was the best I had?

"Yep," Hayley said, nodding. "This one sure is a doozy."

I nodded. "And…you all…" I struggled for a word.

"Yep," Nico said.

"And…I…"

"It would appear so," Hayley replied.

"Hang on," Natalie said. "Why are we telling him all this?"

"Because he's one of us," Nico said.

"How do we know that? I mean, he shows up claiming to be able to see the future, and we just believe him? And what about that thing you said, *mana?* What the hell does that mean?" I shrugged. The word had popped out of my mouth. I had no clue what it meant. Honestly, I thought they would. Despite the confusion, the word swirled in my mind, touching it with light and energy.

"Oh, come on Nat," Hayley droned. "You know as well as we do what Cam saw in him. He has a supernatural aura, and a strong one by the looks of it." I tried to butt in, but Natalie jumped on Hayley.

"We don't know what Cam could've been reacting to. He could've been freaked out to see a stranger." Hayley turned to me. "What did he look like before he passed out?"

I tried to remember. "Like...like he saw something...bright." Hayley turned back to Natalie with a triumphant look. "Why? What does that mean?" Natalie turned her daggers back to me.

"It means you overloaded him, you dumb mother—"

"CAM," Nico cut her off, doing his yelling-but-not-yelling thing, "is an empath."

"Empath," I repeated. "So, he can feel what other people feel."

"Well..." he said, "it isn't that simple. He can see into a person's soul. Feel its energy, know their deepest fears, their most powerful desires. And he can see when something is special about them."

"Meaning he can tell when someone is a little more than human," Hayley finished. I nodded.

"But...what..."

"Happened to him?" Natalie said. "Do you know how much pain, resentment, anger, and regrets are in this town? You try having every bit of that running through you every second of the day, and see how you deal." With that, she stormed back up the stairs, leaving each step to groan in protest behind her. I looked over at Nico and Hayley.

"Sorry about that," Nico said. "She's kinda..."

"She's an emotional mess," Hayley said.

"Yeah," I said. "So," giving my head a shake, "let me get this straight. Cam is an empath. And you guys, are..." They were both silent.

"We don't really know what it's called," Hayley said.

"We haven't really found a word that matches what we can do."

"Which is?" I asked.

"All sorts of things," Hayley said.

"Like reading minds?" I asked, addressing Nico.

"And broadcasting them," Nico said.

"Broadcast." Something formed in my head. "So, send people thoughts?"

"Yeah," he answered.

"My friend voice," I muttered.

"What now?" Hayley asked.

"Nico...that was you. Sending me calm thoughts when I panicked." Nico shrugged, but his eyes seemed to be trying to say *it's no big deal*. But it was. My friend voice, so many times, had been my savior. I knew it had sounded like Nico, but I assumed that was because he was my best friend. But it actually *was* him. I didn't even know what to say. "Thank you," was all I managed. We were all quiet for a second, before Hayley cleared her throat to cut through the silence.

"So, yeah. Nico is your telepathic rock, and you're the pen-happy precog."

"And you can..." I waited for her to finish that thought. I thought I knew, but I didn't want to say anything in case I was wrong.

"Astral project," she confirmed.

"So, your migraines?"

"Are really a devilishly clever excuse to stay still for a little while, while I wander around." She gave me what she probably thought was a wicked grin.

"Okay," trying to soak it all in. "So, Cam's an empath, Nico can read minds, you can just hop out of your body, and Natalie is telekinetic?" I paused.

"Well that's really just a taste. It's hard to describe exactly the extent of our powers," Nico said. I nodded, confused.

"And what about Leo?" They both looked surprised at that.

"Leo?" Nico asked.

"Yeah," I said, feeling even *more* self-conscious. "I–I heard you talking to Natalie about his gift. So...what is it?" They both fell quiet. The still, tight air seemed to turn heavy and grim.

"Leo's kind of..." Nico began, "dangerous," he decided.

"I've gathered. But what does he do?" "He can—"

"He's the Human Torch," Hayley said. Nico winced at his girlfriend's bluntness.

"He's a pyro. He can start fires with his mind," he said softly. I took that in for a moment. Images of smoldering papers, burning bodies, and smoke-infused air filled my mind. The fire came rushing back to me. The stinging hand and eyes, the blistering heat. Throat searing from smoke, the air far too thick to breathe. The fear, the helplessness. I gagged as I could almost feel the terrible choking sensation. Nico was immediately at my side, hand on my back, ready to pound if I needed resuscitation.

"I'm okay," I said through my panting.

"Take deep breaths," he said, demonstrating some slow, deliberate breaths. I did as he showed me, and in a couple of minutes I was breathing normally, but I was far from calm.

"Leo did it," I said. "He started that fire. He killed Angie, and Fairchild. Didn't he?" Even Hayley didn't seem to want to answer me.

"We think so," she said slowly. I tried to process that. I had always known that Leo was messed up. That was pretty much common knowledge. But a *murderer*?

"W–why?" I forced out.

"We don't know," Nico said. My thoughts were all swirling around in my head, making it impossible to think straight. Nico grimaced, as if tuning out a loud racquet. It occurred to me that he could hear the pandemonium of thoughts going on in my brain right now. My thoughts, my panic, was hurting him. I tried to focus on something calmer that wouldn't bother him as much. "No, it's okay," he said. "I'm alright." He straightened his face and did his best to smile, but his eyes gave him away. They still kept twitching, like he was trying to not hear it all.

"I'm sorry," I said.

"Why are you apologizing? We're the ones who just told you that you're going to school with a killer," Hayley said. Nico shot her a *be quiet* look. She put up her hands in defense and didn't say another word.

"I was just saying sorry for...I don't know...thinking

too…loud?" I said uncertainly.

"It's not that," he said. "You're thoughts are kind of…abnormal." My brow furrowed at that.

"What do you mean, 'abnormal'?" I asked.

"They kind of…echo in your head. They don't form completely. They seem more like…" He seemed to be struggling with the description. "pictures than words." I didn't quite get what he meant. I always understood my thoughts perfectly. Occasionally, I had to talk to myself to articulate a thought, but only when it was something that I couldn't get quite right in my head.

"So, I think weird?" I was silent for a moment as I tried to process that, but for some reason, it wasn't sinking in. That actually hit me harder than the whole plethora of preternatural abilities. "Okay, I need to go," I said, standing up and heading toward the door.

"Daniel, wait," Nico said, getting up to follow me.

"Lying by omission is still lying, you know," I scolded him.

"I'm sorry."

"No, it's fine, it's…. Look, I believe you, Nico. I do. As insane as it is, I believe you. But, I think I'm at my limit for today." Nico nodded understandingly. He took a step back, resigning to the couch as I turned and walked out, leaving my concerned friends to stare after me.

Chapter XIV
Guide Me to Salvation

I walked home in a stupor. I didn't even tell my legs to move, they just kind of did it of their own volition. As I walked home, I tried to sort through the swirling hurricane of thoughts and emotions coursing through me. Is someone supposed to feel different when they realize that they have paranormal powers? I sure didn't. I would've expected to walk a little taller, like "He, he, I'm better than you. What's gonna happen in the next two minutes? You don't know? I do!" I certainly wouldn't have to worry about muggers at night, so I should feel safer. But I didn't feel anything of the sort.

I tried to ponder why Leo would possibly want to kill those people. Could he really have killed Fairchild just for bugging him during their counseling session? I knew the woman could be annoying, but was she annoying enough for Leo to want her dead? And what about Angie? She always kept to herself. What could Leo have had against her? Maybe it was that I was having trouble believing that Leo killed anybody. I mean, only he could've started that fire, and he had always seemed scary, and sure, violent. But did he really have it in him to become a killer? I was having a tough time believing it. Still, I looked over my shoulder the whole way home. To add to it all, there were other things that didn't add up. Like that light I had seen behind the house that I knew had been trying to lead me somewhere bad. Or how I had mysteriously seen nothing but darkness. And not one of them had fessed up to pulling me out of the fire and healing me.

As I approached Annabelle's Tudor home, I glimpsed a speck of black against the creamy eggshell exterior. My heart leapt to see her standing in her driveway, bent over an easel, hard at work on a painting. She was wearing dark denim jeans and a white, paint-splattered button up over a thick turtleneck. The cuffs were rolled up to her elbow, her hair pulled up in a messy bun. I was seized by a sudden desire to call out to her, talk to her, hear her voice, her laugh. I knew I would feel okay if I could hear her laugh. But I didn't. I couldn't. After learning of Spirit Ridge's supernatural teens, I had confirmation that my life was in danger. And as much as that terrified me, I would *not* drag Annabelle into it. I cowardly took a detour before she noticed me.

When I entered my house, my mom was at the stove, cooking eggs in a cast iron frying pan. She tried to ask where I had been, but I barely registered, kept going until I reached my room, locked the door to keep myself from bolting back to Annabelle's house, and flopped onto my bed. I tried to get the picture of her out of my head. That proved easier said than done, so I distracted myself by trying to digest the day's insanity. In the past four hours, I had discovered someone was out to kill me; I could possibly never talk to my crush again; and, oh yeah, I'm not human. I kept repeating that in my head. *Not human. Not human. Not human.* But not because I couldn't believe it. Because I did believe it. It was completely insane, but I couldn't make myself doubt it even for a minute. I wasn't human. I knew they hadn't actually said that, but come on. Humans couldn't do stuff like this. And I thought I was a freak before. Look at me now. I drew people who were going to die, and God knows what else I could do. I was not even close to normal. I didn't feel special, or better than anyone. I felt like a freak. Because I was a freak. Nothing but a big freak.

"*Freak,*" I muttered to myself, frustrated. I didn't know what to do. Normally, when I felt like this, I would draw. But what would I draw? The sunset? Or some poor victim who would end up dead in twenty-four hours. I felt trapped. Drawing was usually my only escape. This power had stripped it away from me. It had taken any chances with Annabelle away from me. Any feelings of happiness, or connection, or contentedness were gone, and all I felt was resentment. Bitter, terrible resentment at this *thing*. I had never asked for this. Ever since I was seven, I wanted to be like normal kids. And what did I get? The psychic ability to draw the soon-to-die. Was this some kind of sick cosmic joke? The universe's idea of a prank? I couldn't see how Nico and Hayley were so calm about it. How they could talk about their powers like they were some kind of gift. *Because they were normal before,* I thought. *And now they're special. And you're just even weirder than you've always been. They're not like you. Even with this, nobody is like you. You're even a freak among freaks.*

***

I wish I could say that while I sat in my room, I had some kind of startling revelation, or this moment of blissful acceptance. That I came to terms with what had happened, and what I was, and what it meant. But then I'd be lying through my teeth. Truth is, I sat there on my ass all day thinking about how much my life sucked, and then berating myself for sitting there on my ass thinking about how much my life sucked. But I really had no clue what to do. I mean, what do you do when you find out all of these things? When you find out the school thug is a murderer who can set fires with his mind, and that you can predict each and every death by drawing it. I decided no good could come from starving myself, so I dragged myself downstairs for breakfast.

My mom was at the refrigerator when I walked in. "Hey," she said.

"Morning," I said.

"So what happened this morning?" Sometimes my mom was as blunt as Hayley. That's why she liked her. I contemplated my options for a moment, and decided to try playing dumb.

"What do you mean?"

"Well, you took off at the crack of dawn, then came in a minute ago without saying a word." Okay, so playing dumb probably wasn't going to fly here. I grappled for something to say, but, as always, my mother beat me to the punch. "You're still having trouble with the fire, aren't you?" Figuring my mom was supplying my excuse, I decided to roll with it.

"I don't want to talk about it," I said in my most unconvincing voice. The look she gave me told me it didn't work.

"Daniel, you need to talk to someone about this."

"No, I don't, okay? I'm fine." I was not fine, but hell if she was going to find that out.

"Look," she said in her gentlest tone that told me she was about to suggest something I wouldn't like. "It's Wednesday, and they're having a church service tonight. Maybe you could go and talk to someone." I groaned. Complaining to some priest about my supernatural powers did not sound like something that would go over well. I had once heard that, supposedly, God was the only one who was supposed to know what was going to happen. I wondered if that made me unholy. Wouldn't be a surprise. God never seemed to be rooting for me in the past.

"Mom, I really don't think that a confession is going to help." I was being sarcastic. Ours was a Methodist church. We didn't have confessions. But we did have pastors who were happy to talk to people, should they feel the need.

"Well, I wasn't thinking confession," she clarified. "There's a group counseling session tonight for kids who are having a rough time dealing with what happened at school."

"You want me to go to a talk group?" I asked, immediately cringing at the idea of exposing my feelings to a bunch of crying strangers.

"I know it's not something you feel comfortable with, but it could really help."

"Yeah, I really don't want to do that."

"Well, that's too bad. You're gonna," she said with conviction.

"Mom—"

"No buts," she said, holding up a hand to silence me. "You're going to church tonight. End of story." With that, she walked out of the room.

***

In retrospect, I should've known the delicacy she'd been treating me with would be going any day now. Now she was back to forcing me into things I hated, hoping to further my social skills. True, the idea of going to church and weeping about my feelings didn't sound too awesome, but part of me did like the idea of going to a place so familiar and comforting. I thought maybe even if I went to the group talk, maybe I could sit quietly and make sarcastic comments in my head like always. When my mom and I got into the car, I had some hope that tonight wouldn't be a total disaster. As we drove, she went on and on about some grief counselor who was supposed to be heading up the talk. Apparently she had references and degrees and stuff like that. Although considering she ended up in a church counseling kids in some off-the-map town, I think we can speculate on how much good those did her.

The talk was being held in the fellowship hall, and the door was wide open. Inside, I could see a lady with dirty blonde hair and glasses speaking to a girl I vaguely recognized from school. Don't ask me what her name was, though. She had black hair, pale skin, and was wearing a dark cobalt lipstick. She was wiping her eyes with a tissue while the counselor lady was rubbing her shoulder in a consoling way. I noticed that she had a bandage on her shoulder, with stray red spots sneaking out of it. My breath hitched in my throat. I stopped, causing my mom to look back at me.

"Daniel?"

"What happened to that girl?" I asked, pointing at the crying Goth girl. My mom looked back at me, sympathy in her sea foam green eyes.

"She was a friend of Angie's. When she heard that it was Angie in the fire, she tried to run in and see for herself, and she got burned." I looked up at the tears streaming down her face and I wondered how much of her tears were for her friend, and how much were for the physical pain from the hidden burns. Nausea rose in my stomach as my mind went back to the fire. To the searing pain, the lack of oxygen, the blistering heat. The floor seemed to spin underneath my feet.

"I can't," I whispered. "I can't go in there."

"Daniel," my mom spoke with loving care and concern. I looked up into her green eyes. I always wished I would've inherited her eyes instead of my dad's. Her eyes are soft and warm, whereas mine are nearly phosphorescent.

"Mom, I don't want to go in there," I said, my voice sounding fragile and scared in my ears. There was a pained look to her at the sound of that tone in my voice.

"Are you sure?" I started to nod, then a thought occurred to me. Something I thought might help calm my stomach.

"Can I go into the sanctuary? Sit in on the sermon?" They had services every Wednesday night.

"Yeah, sure," she nodded, before giving me a hug.

I pulled away and went straight to the double doors leading into the sanctuary. There were a few people there. Wednesday services were never as packed as Sunday afternoon, but there was a fair turnout most of the time. Today, most of the pews had someone there, but a few were empty. I took a seat next to the door so I could admire the windowed walls. Such intricate work, making something as fragile as glass intricately fit to make something so elegant. It was the best part of being at church. The work that must've gone into making those...I imagined people forming the glass to just the right shape and thickness, coloring them so many different colors, arranging them all together like a jigsaw puzzle. Drawing may have scared me at the moment because of what could've happened, but if I couldn't make art, I could at least admire it. One of the scenes it showed was the return of the prophet Elijah. His return is supposed to signal the second coming, but it sounds to me more like a death omen. I remembered the Bible mentioning earthquakes and thunderstorms, and to me, that meant death. It seemed more to me that Elijah was the bringer of the apocalypse. If I tilted my head just right, it looked like the stained glass Elijah was grimacing at me, the rays of sunlight behind him, lightning that he carried in his wake.

"Beautiful, aren't they?" I turned to see Craig sitting beside me, looking as meticulously groomed as the last time I saw him. "Hello, Daniel," he said with a smile.

"Hi," I said, turning my attention away from the window.

"Say, I heard about the fire at your school. I hope you're alright." Oh great. I shouldn't have been surprised people already knew that I was the one in the fire.

"Yeah, I'd really rather not talk about that."

"Oh, of course," he said, and dropped the subject. "Good sermon tonight, huh?"

"What? Oh yeah." I hadn't been paying the slightest bit of attention.

"But I would've guessed you were here for the grief talk. I mean, since you were so involved in what happened."

"No, I'm alright," I said automatically.

"Are you sure?" I clenched my teeth. Why did everyone have to freaking ask me that? If I said I was alright, why couldn't they let it go? Sure I was lying, but that's beside the point.

"Yeah, I'm fine," I answered. He was silent for a moment.

"You know, in times of grief, people usually turn to their faith to guide them through it."

I grimaced at that. "Right," I said. "Faith."

"What does that mean?" Craig asked, cocking his head at me.

"Nothing," I said automatically. "Sorry."

"Daniel," he said. "You sound like something is troubling you. Why did you say 'faith' like that?

I didn't really want to talk about my faith (or lack thereof) with anyone, let alone a youth pastor, but his look told me he wouldn't let up.

"It's just…with recent events I'm finding it hard to have much faith."

"Recent events," he said. "You're talking about the fire?"

"Yeah," I said quickly. "And the murders."

"Daniel," he said gently. "I know when something like that happens it's hard to have faith that the Lord has our best interest at heart, but we have to have faith that he has a plan for us."

I didn't say anything, because nothing I could say wouldn't sound offensive. It wasn't just the murders, it was everything. I mean, where in the Bible does it say, "And man shall be able to predict ugly, bloody death scenes and read minds and throw coffee tables with their minds. So sayeth the Lord." I mean, aren't people like us who the Protestants used to call witches and burn at the stake? Were some of the people burned back then like us? How could any god curse someone like that and then let them die for something they couldn't control? What could I have done to deserve it?

"Daniel?"

"Hm?" I turned back to Craig. "Oh, sorry."

"I was just saying that we have to have faith. Our Lord is always watching over us. Don't try to understand his plans for us. He's a lot smarter than either of us."

"I don't know…" was all I said, which was Daniel-speak for, *I don't want to tell you to leave me alone, but leave me alone.*

"I know it's hard," he said, causing me to inwardly groan. "I wasn't exactly the picture of a perfect Christian when I was younger. I could've used a little Jesus back then."

I looked Craig over, with his meticulously assembled appearance, bright smile, and perfectly pressed clothes, and I couldn't quite get the image of him as any kind of troublemaker or street kid. I tried to picture him living in the Pit with Hayley and Leo and decided he probably would've been stabbed and robbed within ten minutes.

"But the point is, everything is easier when you have faith in the spirit. Faith, Daniel," he said, leaning in closer. "Faith. Why else would you have come here tonight?"

"My mother made me," I told him.

"But why come in here instead of the group session?"

I shrugged, uncomfortable in the whole conversation. "I don't know. Because it's familiar, I guess."

He nodded for a moment. "People tend to find the most solace in what's familiar to them. What has always given them comfort. Maybe that's a good place to start."

He didn't say another word after that, but his words did make me think about something. That girl in the discussion group, the one who had run in after Angie. Her actions seemed like something Nico would've done for me if I hadn't gotten out. He had always been there for me. He and Hayley, even if it was fake with her. But the problem was, *they* were the problem now. How could they offer me comfort when they were walking reminders of my problem? It doesn't matter, I decided. I couldn't just stay away from my best (and only) friend. I needed Nico in my life, regardless of what it was becoming. And there was only one way I could do that; *shut up and deal.* Just like I had for so long. What I'd done for almost ten years since that fateful day when the doctor called our house. *Shut up and deal. And hope you survive.*

Chapter XV
Playing with Fire

On my way out of the church, I ran into someone I had been hoping to avoid. Though my body betrayed me with the kick of adrenaline that the sight of her produced.

"Annabelle," I said when she saw me.

"Hey," she said, walking through the atrium. She was in a plain white tank top, holding a blue jean button-up jacket, with her hair pulled in a ponytail. I'd be lying if I said my eyes didn't linger a bit on her exposed shoulders and neck.

"Hey," I said stupidly. "Hey," she replied, pulling her jacket over her goose pimpled arms. I got the feeling she didn't own much warm clothing. The air was thick with awkward silence. "So, how are you?" *Probably the most inopportune time to ask me that question,* I thought.

"Okay," I lied. I wondered vaguely if it was possible to die of awkward silences. Probably not, or I would've been dead long ago. "You?"

"Alright," she answered. I didn't know whether or not I should be looking at her or my shoelaces. "Look, Daniel, whatever happened the other night—"

"Yeah, I'm sorry." She looked a little confused. "For what?" "Well...I don't know. It...seemed like...I don't know." She nodded uncomprehendingly.

"Okay, then," she said. "But, can we...talk about—" "Annabelle," I interrupted. "I have to go." She gave me a look like she didn't understand. "It-it's that my mom is waiting, and I don't want to keep her waiting," I stammered. "So, you know, I...should go."

"Oh," she said, with a look of understanding, like something just clicked into place.

"You understand, right?" "Yeah," she said. "I totally get it." She sounded like she did understand, but not what I was saying. Her arms were crossed and her jaw set, and for some reason, she wasn't making eye contact anymore.

"So, I'll talk to you later," I said.

"Yeah," she said a little coldly. "Later." She turned around and walked into the sanctuary, disappearing through the double doors. Quelling the churning feeling in my gut, I turned and left.

***

"So how exactly does one go about having supernatural powers?" I asked in a hushed tone.

Nico chuckled. "There isn't exactly a handbook, Daniel." We were at the café with Hayley. Nico was working, wiping down the already shiny surface of the counter, I was munching on a bagel, and Hayley was rapidly drumming her fingers on the countertop. I had, by no means, acclimated to anything but step one of shut up and deal; I needed to know everything I could.

"Well you two know more than me, and there has to be more than what you said last night." Hayley turned in her swiveling chair toward me.

"Ask away, young grasshopper," she said with an air of mock-wisdom.

"Well," I began. "What do you know about my power?"

"You're a seer," Hayley said. "You see."

"I know that much," I said, flicking a bagel crumb at her face. She swatted it down with a smile.

"You're precognitive," Nico said. "It means you can see the

future, or you can see things that have already happened; retrocognition. Or see things that are happening currently, somewhere else, which is remote viewing."

"Wow, those are some big words," I said with mock-impression. "Very good, Nico." I clapped derisively, with Hayley joining in.

"Very funny, asshole," Nico shot back.

"Okay, so what about when I'm not so much *seeing* as *feeling?*"

"What do you mean?" Nico asked.

"Well, sometimes I get these really strong..." I grappled for a word to describe my premonitions, "vibes. Like...intuition, I guess."

"Well that could be true too," Nico said. "Being a seer means you can see things that normal people can't." I nodded. Like touching a painting and knowing who painted it, or touching a safe and learning the combination.

"How do you guys even know all of this?"

"We've done our research," Hayley said, winking.

"Which means we mainly checked out every stupid library book about psychic powers and the supernatural that we could find," Nico clarified.

"Which by the way was boring as hell."

I grinned at Hayley's classic hatred towards studying. "And you can do other things."

"Totally," Hayley said.

"Like what?"

"Like..." Nico was now struggling for words.

"Here," Hayley offered. "Let me help you out." She snatched the bagel right out of my hands.

"Hey!" I protested. "I was eating that."

"Suck it up." She took the bagel and squeezed it in her fist, sending a cascade of crumbs falling onto the counter.

"Hey, that was clean!" Nico said.

"Seriously? Come on, ladies," Hayley said exasperatedly to us both, then turned her focus to Nico. "Help me out?" She stared meaningfully down at the crumbs. Nico, seeming to get the hint, grinned and looked around us. Once he seemed sure nobody was looking at us, he took her hand. I raised an eyebrow at them suspiciously, but then they both closed their eyes in concentration.

"Um, what are you—" I started, but Hayley cut me off with a sharp *sh!* I felt a surge of energy extending from them. Right before my eyes, the crumbs on the counter started to twitch, then moved. They rose into the air by some unseen force and hovered a few centimeters above the bright linoleum. "Are you guys doing that?"

"Yep," Hayley said, opening one eye to look smugly at me. "And the best part is, with just a touch of a hand," she indicated her and Nico's interlocked hands. "We can team up with others and borrow or consolidate power."

"It's called channeling," Nico said, opening his eyes to smile at the levitating crumbs. "Using someone else's power to strengthen your own."

"Wow," I breathed. "Kind of like what happened in the church." I turned to look at Hayley. "You were astral projecting through the hallway and I must've passed through your spirit. You must've accidentally channeled me, which is why I was able to see you."

"Sounds about right to me. Wanna try?" Hayley asked eagerly.

"Hayley," Nico said hesitantly. "I don't know about that."

"Oh come on," she said and offered her other hand to me. "He's gotta learn." I stared at Hayley's outstretched hand tentatively. Nico certainly seemed to think that wasn't a great idea. But I had to admit that floating things was pretty cool. Plus the way she said it, like I was joining some exclusive group, didn't sound exactly unappealing.

Slowly, I reached out and took her hand, closed my eyes and mustered the same energy I had felt radiating from them. Almost immediately, I could feel their energies interlocking with mine. The feeling was almost surreal, but good in a way. I focused my energy where theirs was directed, at the crumbs. I snuck one eye open to look at what would happen. Almost as soon as I focused on the crumbs, they went flying. They shot up into the air like mini-rockets, as if they had been electrocuted. But not just the crumbs. The rag Nico was holding shot into the air, as well as the crumbled remains of my bagel itself.

"Well then," Hayley said as crumbs rained down on us, to strange looks from the surrounding customers. "Somebody put a little extra juice into that."

Nico caught his washrag in midair, but failed to catch the bagel before it thudded down in front of us, spraying all three of us with crumbs. "Yeah," he said. "You could say that."

I was stunned at what I had just done. Wondering how I had done it.

"So," Nico said, trying to keep the conversation moving. "Anymore questions?"

"Uh," I tried to think of any other inquiries I had. "One more thing. Do you have any idea where these abilities come from?" They both shook their heads.

"You want to ask something," Nico said. "A theory?"

I was taken aback. I had always known Nico was good at telling when I had something on my mind, but this whole telepath thing was going to take some getting used to. I hesitated before asking, "Is it possible that they could be inherited?"

Nico considered that for a moment. "I'm not sure. We don't know if we were born with our gifts and grew into them, or if they happened somehow, so we don't know if they could be passed on. As far as I know, neither of my parents could read minds." "And my mom may space a little, but I'm pretty sure she's just drunk," Hayley said. "No astral projection involved. Why do you ask? Thinking of having some psychic babies with a certain raven-haired painter?"

"No, and before you ask, I don't want to talk about it. I was asking because... well my dad seems to know something about it." Nico's head snapped up from looking down at the counter, taking on an air of urgency, and something perhaps a little graver. "Are you sure?" he asked.

"Well," I said, feeling very self-conscious. "H-he was talking about how I had 'special gifts' and, he was never surprised when I acted weird, and I had one of those vibes, that he knows something."

"What about your mom?"

"I don't think so," I said nervously. "Are you okay?" There was a yell from behind him as Mr. McCall called him back to clean the cappuccino machine.

"I'll be right back," he said before disappearing in the back. I turned to look at Hayley, and she shrugged.

"He wants this kept a secret. We all do."

"Believe me, I get it," I said. I definitely didn't want anyone knowing about this either. I already couldn't stand people judging me. Imagine what would happen if they found out that I drew dead people.

"*Soooo,*" she mused. "What's up with you and your mundane lover?" I nearly choked on what was left of my bagel. "What?" I said through a throat full of bread. "You said you didn't want to talk about it, meaning there's something to talk about."

"No there isn't," I said sarcastically.

"Sure there is," Hayley said. "Otherwise you wouldn't be nervous."

"I'm not nervous."

"Sure you are. You're voice always gets derisive whenever you're nervous."

"No, it doesn't." "Yes, it does." "No, it doesn't."

"Yes, it does." "No, it doesn't." "Daniel, I have two little brothers. I can do this all day."

I sighed. I knew she was right. Hayley was by far the most stubborn person I knew. But I really, really didn't want to explain what happened between Annabelle and me the other night. Mostly because I didn't even understand it myself. But Hayley kept staring at me, eyes trying to pull the answers out. I took a deep breath and tried to gather some words, when something in the window caught my eye. I turned toward the black, dull jacket atop the dark, gray jeans in the lanky, pasty body with flat, charcoal hair. My stomach sunk. "Oh God," I said. Leo was standing there in the window, staring at me with those intense, frightening eyes.

"Oh, no, that distraction tactic isn't gonna work on me. I have a one-track mind." Hayley said. "Hayley, turn around," I said. She opened her mouth to argue, but I turned her chair toward Leo with my foot and she froze. Leo held our gazes for a moment before jerking his head to the side. Hayley and I both followed his gesture to the public library across the street. We returned our looks to Leo, and he gave us one final glare and moved down the sidewalk. I don't think he realized it, but people subtly altered their routes, clearing a path for him. Hayley turned back around in her chair.

"He wants us to follow?" I said.

"Looks like," she said warily. "Wonder what he wants to talk about." "Don't assume he wants to talk," I said sarcastically. Hayley took on a sly, sneaky smile.

"Well there's only one way to find out," she said. She got up from her seat and started toward the exit.

"Hayley, what are you doing?" I asked.

"Well," she whispered. "Do you know another way of finding out why he's killing people?"

"It's because he's nuts, now sit down!" I said in a hushed tone. I cast a look toward the back, praying for Nico to come back and talk some sense into her.

"We need to know Leo's angle, if we're gonna put a stop to this without having to, you know," she dragged her finger across her throat in a cutting motion. "So I'm gonna see what the psycho wants, and if you want, you can come with."

"Hayley, you can't!" "Well I am, and if I'm alone, then there's a much bigger chance I might get hurt," she was taunting me. She grinned at my pained expression before walking out the door. I shot one last look back toward Nico before making a split-second decision, followed by a muttered string of profanity.

***

The library wasn't a big place. We passed the checkout counter. Books were out of order, tossed on the desk with absolutely no rhyme or reason, and then we saw the ancient, blue-haired librarian slumped over, asleep in her chair. Or at least, I hoped she was asleep.

"Where do you think he is?" I asked.

"He could be anywhere in this hellhole," Hayley replied. We searched the labyrinth of shelves, trying our best to navigate it.

"Hayley, what exactly do you expect we'll see here?"

"Oh, I don't know," she said. "Maybe, Leo setting that librarian on fire while he barfs up pea soup and his head rotates 360 degrees."

"You're not funny," I said.

"I agree," I heard Leo's voice drifting from behind one of the bookshelves. Hayley and I both whipped around and saw him walking slowly out from behind the shadow of a tall shelf. His gait reminded me of an animal sneaking out of a cave to attack its prey. "So I'm guessing he's in on our little secret," he said with a nod in my direction.

"He's one of us, Leo," Hayley said, taking a few confident steps toward him. Her face was completely unafraid, which I really don't understand, since even if I didn't want to admit it, Leo scared the living hell out of me.

"Oh, I know," he said. "I wondered how long it would take you and your little boy-toy to figure it out." Leo wasn't taking his eyes off of me. He was studying me. It was making me very uncomfortable. Of course, I was in the presence of a killer. I became very conscious of the fact that nobody else was here, aside from the snoozing elderly. We were alone with him. "What is it you want, psycho?" Hayley asked, cutting to the chase. Leo's expression remained unreadable. He was completely ignoring Hayley, his onyx eyes locked on mine, drilling into me, like they were trying to drag something out of me. He took a step toward me. I didn't dare move. He took another step, and then another, and another, until he was right in my face. I could see the whites of his eyes, what little there was, and at this proximity, I could see that his irises were actually slightly lighter than his pupils. My pulse sped up and my palms were getting sweaty. I couldn't help but remember the fire again. How helpless I had felt, and I realized he was making me feel this way again. Making me feel like I was at his mercy. Like there was nothing I could do to save myself. I wanted to look at Hayley, but I couldn't pull my eyes away from his. Slowly, he opened his mouth and spoke four words.

"What do you know?" I didn't understand. I had no clue what he was talking about. "Leo, back off," Hayley said angrily. Leo didn't take his eyes off of me for even a second.

"What do you *know?*" he asked me again. Somehow, I managed to find my voice.

"I don't know what you're talking about," I said weakly.

"It's a simple question," he said.

"I don't know anything," I said.

"You're lying."

"Leo, leave him alone!" Hayley said. "He's new to us, he doesn't know anything."

"He knows more than he's letting on," Leo said. His voice began to give away his frustration. "I'll ask one more time. What. Do. You. Know?"

"Nothing!" I blurted out. "I don't know anything you don't know."

"That's not what I asked," Leo growled. "I asked what you *do* know."

"Not much! Everybody is supernatural; I can see the future; Nico can read minds; we can do things nobody can explain! Cam's messed up because everyone around him is messed up; Natalie is really emotional for some reason; I draw people who are gonna die, and *you* killed them!" Good God. I hadn't ranted like that since I was twelve years old.

"You're a liar," he deduced. "You may have everyone else fooled with your little innocent act, but I know you know something."

"Hey!" Hayley exclaimed, pushing Leo away from me and putting herself in between us. "Back off! You don't know anything about him."

"I know he's a liar!"

"Oh, really?" Hayley snapped back. "He's not the liar here, *you* are!"

"If you even knew half of what you thought you knew—" Leo growled angrily.

"Don't even!" Hayley yelled. "We know you killed those people. You killed Fairchild because she bugged you, and you killed Angie for God knows what reason. Nobody else could've done it. Only someone with your powers could have done something like that."

"You think you've got every little piece of the puzzle. This is bigger than you think."

"Oh really? You're gonna go with the whole, 'higher purpose' excuse. You're a murderer, Leo. Plain and simple. You killed innocent people and you know you did. And we're gonna prove it."

"How're you gonna do that?" he asked viciously. "You gonna go all espionage? Dig up some dirt and prove me guilty? You're not detectives! The only thing you've got linking me to the second murder is the fire, and it's not like you can tell the cops that I set the building ablaze with my mind!"

"We'll prove it," Hayley snarled. "And we'll make sure you pay for what you did."

"Hayley," I said. "Let's go."

"Yeah, go running off. Do the smart thing for once."

"We're not going anywhere, Daniel."

"You really need to learn how to back down," Leo said, his eyes started to give away his fury.

"Hayley, it's starting to get hot in here," I said. I could feel sweat on the back of my neck as the temperature started to rise. Leo's fists were clenched so tightly I swore he was shaking, and his eyes were practically ablaze, but Hayley didn't even seem to hear me.

"Why don't you admit it and save yourself the trouble. You killed those people!"

"Why don't you take your accusations and shove them up your—" "Hayley, we need to go!" I shouted. The temperature in the room had gone up to the point where my hair was damp with sweat and it was starting to sting my eyes, plus I could feel energy radiating off of Leo in waves. I couldn't describe the feeling; it was like feeling someone's breath on your neck, or sensing the warmth from their body when they were standing right in front of you. "Are you gonna try and set us on fire now too? Kill us like you killed them?"

"Well maybe you have it coming," Leo snarled through a curled lip. I could feel the heat starting to condense, and I could smell the acrid stench of smoke. "Hayley!" I yelled, grabbing her arm and tearing her out of her death staring match. "We need to get out of here." I looked her in the eyes, and there I saw a manic anger that scared the hell out of me.

"He needs to be stopped," she said. "Well we can't stop him if we're dead! Let's go!" I pulled her toward the door. "DON'T YOU WALK AWAY FROM ME!" Leo shouted so loud that it echoed throughout the entire building. I looked back at him. His whole body was trembling with rage, and his eyes blazing with intense fury. "Come on," I said to Hayley, eager to get out of there. "NO!" Leo shouted. A harsh light tore through my line of sight, followed by a frightened scream. I looked to my left and saw that the librarian had woken up, and was screaming in terror at the stack of books next to her that had caught fire. "Damn it, Leo!" Hayley said. She ran to the checkout counter, grabbing a vase of flowers and dumping the content all over the blaze. The flames went out with a *hiss* and a cloud of steam. The librarian took a second to stop screaming. I looked back at Leo, expecting to see the same fury and contempt that had been so evident seconds ago, but instead I saw a look of horror, and something close to guilt. Hayley spouted out some excuse to the old woman about Leo sparking up a cigarette and dropping it on the books before walking quickly to me. "Let's get out of here," she said before pushing the door open and leaving.

What a wonderful idea. Wish I'd thought of it. I started to follow her, before taking another look back at Leo. I didn't know if I should say something spiteful or…comforting.

"What are you looking at?" he growled before we got out of there.

Chapter XVI
The Sun Always Sets

"Are you two both complete idiots?" Nico asked. I was alone in the parking lot of my art studio, talking to him on my cell phone.

"Hey, I was following your psycho girlfriend," I scoffed. "Lay off," Hayley said from the other end of the three-way conference call. "I just wanted to rattle his cage a little." "Because he needs more incentive to want us dead?" I said sarcastically. "To throw him off," Hayley argued. "If we can throw him off his game, he'll slip up and we can catch him." "You know that 'rattling his cage' almost got you and Daniel dead," Nico asserted. "It was a small fire," Hayley parried. "And if you had pushed it anymore, it could've just as easily been a building fire." "Well it wasn't!" "Look, all we really accomplished yesterday was pissing Leo off," I pointed out. "Can we please meet?"

"Can't," Nico said. "Me and my dad are visiting my mom. What about tomorrow?"

"Yeah sure," I said, with Hayley echoing me. Neither of us were going to argue Nico's right to that.

We said our goodbyes and I threw my phone into the passenger's seat. I thought about the look I had seen on Leo's face when he started that fire. I could have sworn I had seen something close to remorse. Like he hadn't meant to start the fire, or almost hurt the librarian. What kind of person (who already killed two people) felt bad about almost hurting an old woman probably a few years from death anyways? When I looked back, it was like he covered it all up. Put up the anger and hatred. Almost like he was trying to hide a different Leo. One who didn't want to hurt people. The Leo I had seen before, the angry, unstable one who had threatened Hayley and me and tried to scare answers out of me. That guy, I had no trouble believing could kill someone. But the Leo I saw for that one second...I wondered if *he* was even capable of such a thing.

I must've sat in the Honda for at least twenty minutes after hanging up with Nico and Hayley, staring at the building before me. The art studio hadn't changed since the last time I was there, but I was scared to go in. What if my earlier admonitions were right and going in there would just pull up the memories of that first drawing? I didn't know if I was ready to find out. To officially lose my safe place.

It was a true testament to the state of my social life that I had the entire day to myself, and this is what I was choosing to do. Shaking my head, I cranked the car and pulled away from the studio. I drove back through town square, not really going anywhere. I didn't know what to do to occupy the day. Nico was at the hospital, and I suppose I could've gone with him, but sitting with him, his father, and his comatose mother would exactly brighten my mood. The art studio was out of the question, I was terrified to paint, and I even tried calling Hayley back, but she didn't answer.

I groaned. *I need caffeine,* I thought, and drove over to the café. The barista was some girl with dyed-black hair and nose piercings. When I placed my order, she glared at me as if asking her to do her job was some kind of personal offense. I mouthed a silent *wow* behind her back. Once she produced an Americano in a to-go cup she curled her lip at me. Feeling I needed to get out of there before she decided to open her mouth and bite me, I gave her a weak "thanks."

"Yes mom, I promise I'll—oh!" I internally swore as I ran smack into the person walking into the café.

"Oh I'm so sorry—" I started before I caught sight of who it was. *Damn you heart,* I thought. *Calm down.* "Annabelle."

"Daniel," she said, freezing where she was. "Hey."

"Hi," was all I could respond with. We remained silent for a few seconds, though it might has well have ten years for how long it felt. "Um, weren't you talking to someone?" I pointed at the cell phone she had dropped to her side.

"Oh, right!" she pulled the phone back to her ear. "Mom? No, no, I'm here. Yeah. Yeah sure, I got it. Okay. Love you too. Bye." She hung up the phone.

"That your mom?" I realized a split second after it came out my mouth that that was a very stupid question. "Of course that's your mom. Otherwise you wouldn't have called her mom. Right, nice deductive reasoning there, Daniel."

She smiled hesitantly. "Well it's valid. That was, in fact, my mom."

"Good," I said. "Wouldn't want to look stupid or anything."

She giggled, but then seemed to remember she shouldn't and put on a straight face.

I furrowed my brow in confusion. "What?"

"You blew me off the other day and now you're making me laugh, and giving me that look, and being shy. Not sure I get it."

"I didn't—"

"Never mind..." She ran a hand through her hair in frustration. "I can't deal with this right now. I just need to grab some coffee and be on my way." She walked around me towards the counter, but I turned around and touched her shoulder.

"Hey look. I'm sorry for being so...*that* at the church the other day, I was just..."

"Daniel," she stopped me. "I really don't have time for this, okay?" She turned around and shrugged off my arm and started to walk away. I knew I had promised myself to keep her at a distance to keep her safe, but sensing her obvious disappointment, for some reason my mouth decided to do that thing where it rebels against my brain.

"Have lunch with me!" I blurted out.

Immediately, she whirred around, her face as shocked as I was.

"What?"

"Um…" *Damn it mouth, what the hell did you do?*

"Did you just ask me out on a date?" she asked hesitantly. Had I? Had I just asked a girl out on a date? I wasn't sure I had meant to.

"Yes," I conceded. "I think I may have just done that." Fear coursed through my veins and set my heart pounding against my ribs with the speed and force of a jackhammer. "Well? Will you?" For a moment, a terrible, agonizing, petrifying moment, I was scared she was going to say no.

"Okay." A smile snuck onto her face. "Sure."

I thought I must've misheard her. But unless that was a twisted smile at having turned me down, she had said *yes*.

"Y–yes?"

"Yes," she repeated. I could barely speak. I had to be dreaming. "I've still got to run a couple of errands for my mom, but we can meet back here in about half an hour?"

"Okay," I said simply, still stunned.

"Okay," she said, smiling, and headed into the café to get her coffee.

What in the name of God just happened? Simple. I had run into the most beautiful and amazing girl on the face of the planet who I for some reason had blown off, then asked her out on a lunch date, and she said *yes*. I walked to my car almost in a daze.

I had about half an hour to kill before my…date. I decided to head back home for a little bit. Cranking up the car, I pulled out of the parking space. Once I got there, I immediately shut myself in my room.

I have a date, I kept thinking to myself. *A real, bona fide date with an actual girl. And not just any girl. Annabelle* freaking *Martin.* What was I going to say? Would she be expecting me to be talkative, suave? Suave is definitely not my forte. What should I wear?

I took a good look at what I had on. It was a dark sweatshirt and some blue jeans. Surely I would need to be dressed nicer than this. I mean, it was just an impromptu lunch date, but I couldn't just show up wearing whatever.

I went over to my closet and took a cursory look at my wardrobe. It consisted mainly of sweatshirts, plain T-shirts, and standard blue jeans. What can I say? I'm not a fancy dresser. When I get dressed in the morning I'm not trying to impress anybody. If anything, I'm trying to *not* be noticed.

I sifted through the hanging clothes trying to find *something* I could wear on this–oh God–date. The jeans would work, I supposed, but I needed something else.

All of a sudden, I was no longer in my bedroom. I was somewhere else. I was *someone* else. I was still rifling through clothes but they weren't my clothes. They looked like girl's clothes. I saw skirts and dresses and several women's shoeboxes.

I was nervous, excited, apprehensive, all of the emotions I had been feeling before, only again, they weren't *mine*.

They were hers.

But who was her? I couldn't see any details. It was as if I was seeing through her eyes. I could see, hear, and feel everything she saw, heard, and felt.

She cast a glance at the clock on her bedside table and I saw that it was…one twenty seven in the afternoon, just like it was right then. Wait, Nico had mentioned something about this–remote viewing, he had called it. Seeing something that was happening in the present, but somewhere else.

I–she, whatever—grabbed a soft lavender sundress and held it up, turning towards the mirror to see it. It was Annabelle.

I thought she had said she had errands to run for her mom. As soon as that thought formed, a memory floated towards me. Her memory. She had lied about the errands. She had only been out on a coffee run, but when I asked her out she wanted to have time to get ready, so she said she had errands.

She examined herself with the dress in the mirror, standing in every possible position. It looked perfect to me. The violet went well with her hair and skin tone, but I could sense that she disagreed. It was too shapeless and childish. And it was a *summer* dress. She tossed it into a pile on the floor and turned back to her closet.

This is stupid, she thought. *Why are you stressing? You just met this guy a couple days ago and you're running yourself mad picking out an* outfit? *It is* just *a lunch date.*

But then she thought about me and the way *he makes me laugh, his adorable shyness, those mesmerizingly blue eyes.*

Mesmerizing? Adorable? For a moment I had to wonder if she was thinking about a different Daniel.

Before I knew it, the experience ended and I was back inside of my own head. I marveled at what I had just seen. How could it be remotely possible that Annabelle was standing before her closet, compulsively trying to pick out the perfect outfit to go eat lunch with me, just like I was? That she was so nervous to go out with me that she would go through that? That she really thinks my shyness is adorable, thinks I'm funny, thinks my eyes are *mesmerizingly* blue instead of frighteningly blue? Part of me felt ashamed for what I had just done. Those are her private thoughts and emotions and what right did I have to use my powers to invade them, even if by accident? Though another part of me couldn't help the smile that crept onto my face.

I decided on a simple T-shirt with a jacket over it. Not too casual but not too dressy for a lunch date. I gave myself a once-over in the bathroom mirror. *Mesmerizingly blue?* I thought. *Really?* Whatever she saw, I couldn't see. But who am I to argue?

Steeling my nerves, and clenching my suddenly *very* sweaty hands, I grabbed my car keys and headed out the door. My hands were tight on the wheel, even when I was nervously rapping my fingers on it. Annabelle had said to meet her back at the café. Sure enough, when I pulled into the town square and approached the coffee house, there she was, waiting. I took another second before getting out of the car to breathe, calm my rapid heartbeat, and wipe my sweaty palms on my jeans. Her head rose when I approached. She smiled that dazzling smile of hers. Good god my knees felt weak.

I entered and sat.

"Hey," I said simply.

"Hey," she replied, smiling. She thankfully decided on a cerulean blue sundress with her hair falling easily down her back. A bulky white sweater and jacket compensated for the thin material, but she looked amazing, as always.

"Uh, you look nice," I stammered.

"Oh," she said, looking down at the dress. "Thanks." We stood in awkward silence for several more, extremely long moments. Things were off to a great start. "So, where are we going?"

I froze. I hadn't even thought about that. On a date, you typically *go* somewhere. Or at least, that's what I'd learned from TV and stories from Nico. I hadn't really taken the time to plan this out. We had to go somewhere.

"Well..." I racked my brain, but suddenly every restaurant in town completely vanished from my memory. There had to be somewhere. Anywhere. "I do know this one place I like going."

She smiled a smile that nearly made me implode. "Great. Let's go."

***

Really, Daniel? Really? Moore's ice cream parlor, really???

"Wow. Okay, that's...interesting. I mean...I love ice cream," Annabelle said as she looked up at the sign above us that read *Mr. Moooooore's Creamatorium.* The moo was emphasized by the giant image of a smiling cow right above it, with a motorized snout that spun like a wheel every five minutes.

"Yeah," I said awkwardly, mentally face-palming myself for this brilliant idea. Or, I wouldn't call it so much an idea as the only "restaurant" that popped into my head. "I...I used to come here with my dad when I was a kid. It's not so bad. Once you, you know...get past the stupid cow and...you know...the fact that they call it a crematorium."

"Yeah," she said, trying her best to feign enthusiasm. "It looks...really cool."

I heaved a sigh. "It sucks."

"No," she said quickly. "No, it doesn't. It's...it's very...I love ice cream," she repeated weakly.

"That cow is looking at me, I swear to God." She giggled at the comment, but it wasn't enough to wipe away my shame. I couldn't believe I brought her to Moore's. What kind of idiot am I that *this* was the only place I could think of? "I'm really sorry, this was a stupid idea. I'll just take you home." I moved to get back into the car, but Annabelle grabbed my arm and held me back.

"No," she said. "Really it's not that bad. Sure it's..."

"Horrible?" I suggested. "Inane? Idiocy the likes of which the world has never seen?"

"Not what I was expecting," she corrected, smiling. "But it's actually kind of...I don't know, kind of cute."

"Cute?" I repeated incredulously. "It's called a *creamatorium*. That doesn't say 'cute', that says 'come one, come all little children, this isn't a front for human trafficking at all.'"

Again she laughed heartily, and this time I smiled a little.

"Come on," she said, taking my hand and pulling me towards the door.

"You actually want to go in there?"

"Hey," she said, turning back to me, looking me in the eyes with her bottomless brown ones. I became very, very aware of the fact that I still had her hand in mine, her fingers interlocked with mine. "I love ice cream." She turned and kept pulling me towards the door, and this time I didn't argue.

The second we walked through the door, the overpowering smell of sugar hit me. In my artistic opinion, the interior of the building seemed to be modeled after some of the early work of Candy Land. The walls were white and pink and creamy yellow, with giant plastic gumdrops the size of my head set into the walls and a swirly lollypop design dominating the tiled floor. The ceiling was all brown, the color of hot fudge, with a red cherry painted in the very center, and sprinkles scattered all throughout, giving the entire room the feel of being inside a giant hot fudge sundae.

There was a very perky-looking woman standing behind the counter wearing a black-and-white striped apron and a bright pink hat. "Hey there!" she squealed. "Welcome to Moore's. Or should I say, Moooooore's!"

You really shouldn't, I thought.

"Come on up here, don't be shy!" she squeaked, excitedly beckoning for us to come up to the counter. Trading apprehensive looks, Annabelle and I made our way up to the glass case containing all the different flavors of ice cream. "Would you like to sample our Chocolate Lover's Swirl? It's super-duperly scrumptious!"

"I'm good," I answered.

"Are you sure? How about our Super Berry Blast?! It's *berry, berry* great!" She giggled violently as if her little joke was the funniest thing ever uttered by any human being.

"Well Daniel?" Annabelle asked. "How about it? I mean, after all, it is berry, berry great!"

The lady burst out in hysterical giggles again, causing both of us to take a slightly frightened step backwards. When we gave her our orders, she seemed genuinely ecstatic. As if filling our ice cream orders was all she had ever wanted out of life.

Once we had our ice cream, we went to sit down at one of the tables, but since the lady kept staring at us with that borderline-sociopathic smile, we decided to take our ice cream outside. The round umbrella tables weren't much better than back inside. They were bright neon yellow plastic, and the umbrellas attached to them were in the shapes of giant cupcakes. There were even saltshakers filled with sprinkles and syrup containers with chocolate syrup.

We sat down at the closest one and immediately entered another period of suffocating silence. We sat at opposite ends of the table, not touching each other, and barely even looking at each other. I prayed to God for *something* to talk about, anything at all, but nothing came to mind, so instead I tried to occupy myself by digging into my ice cream. At least in the years since I had last been to Moore's the ice cream hadn't changed. It still tasted like diabetes in a cup. Translation; it was delicious.

"So..." Annabelle said, clearly figuring out that she would have to be the one to drive the conversation. "You said you used to come here with your dad?"

"Uh, yeah," I answered, choking an uber-sugary chunk of chocolate. "When I was really little, like...five years old I think."

"That's nice," she said.

"Yeah," I said, struggling to hold on to the conversation. "My uh... my mom really hated it. This place really creeped her out. An ice cream parlor that called itself a creamatorium kind of sets off some red flags in a parent's head." She smiled at the comment, so I tried to keep going. "In fact, she used to joke for a little while that they were probably putting drugs in their hot fudge."

Her incessant laughter filled me with warmth. "That's hilarious. Is that why you guys stopped coming?"

"Uh..." I trailed off, not wanting to get into the topic of why my dad and I had stopped coming to Moore's. We had stopped when I was seven, after things at home got bad. "Not exactly."

"Then why?" she asked, absentmindedly poking her ice cream with her spoon.

In way of answer, I shrugged. "I'm not sure. Guess I just outgrew the place or something."

We drifted back into awkward silence. As she dug at her ice cream, I wondered if maybe I wasn't doing something I was supposed to be doing. Was I supposed to be carrying the conversation? Probably, but there was little to no chance of that happening. Was I supposed to be sitting closer to her maybe? Perhaps holding her hand or something like that? I became very aware of the fact that I had my hands tucked in close, one hand holding my cup close to my chest and the other holding the spoon. I tried to loosen myself up by leaning a little forward.

"So," I said, hoping that if I said something, more would just follow along. I was disappointed. "Is, uh... is that good?" I gestured towards the ice cream she was eating.

"Yeah," she said. "Sure."

"Coconut?"

She nodded. *What the hell kind of question was that? You were there when she ordered it; you know it's freaking coconut!*

"I kinda hate coconut," I said. Immediately, her eyes widened to the size of dinner plates and I regretted having said anything.

"How can you possibly hate coconut?"

"I don't know, I just never really liked anything coconut."

"What?! That's crazy!"

"I just don't like it," I repeated. "I'll stick with the classics, thank you," I said, gesturing to my two scoops of chocolate.

"Wha–have you ever even tried it?"

"Well...no, but I hate coconut candy."

"Oh my god!" she exclaimed. "It is not even in the same universe! No, this is unacceptable. You have to try it." She scooped a spoonful of ice cream out of her bowl and held it out to me.

"But—"

"No buts," she said, nudging the ice cream closer. "Come on," she coaxed. "Eat."

"Seriously?" I asked.

"Seriously," she responded. "Just close your eyes, and imagine you're on a beach in Hawaii, sipping a drink out of a coconut with a little umbrella in it. The breeze in your hair, sun on your face, the sound of the waves crashing against the white sand shore."

"You do realize that only one of us has ever actually been to a beach, right?"

"Just do it!" she said, giggling. Shaking my head, I consented, closing my eyes and opening my mouth. She slipped the spoon into my mouth and fed it to me. I tried to imagine what she was saying, or at least the best I could. When I opened my eyes, she was looking at me expectantly.

"It's...not terrible," I conceded reluctantly.

"Not terrible?"

"That's all you're getting."

She laughed, and pulled her spoon back. "All right, fine. I guess I'll take what I can get."

We smiled at each other for a long moment, though this time the silence didn't feel so awkward. It felt more comfortable.

"So, in fear of sounding cliché, tell me about yourself," she said. "I mean, we've talked about me before, now I want to hear about you." I immediately froze. Talking about myself was not really something I wanted to do. Especially since at least fifty percent of myself...I really didn't want her to know.

"Well," I started hesitantly. "There's not much to tell. Small town boy. Haven't exactly led the most exciting life." Not until recently, at least.

"I'm not asking for some epic tale of trials and tribulations and overcoming the forces of evil. Just some details."

"Like what?" I asked nervously.

"Like...aside from painting, what do you like to do with your time?"

"That's about it," I said. Then I added, "And hang out with Nico."

"Yeah, you guys seem really close."

"We are," I said, nodding. "He's always been there for me."

"How long have you guys known each other?"

"Uh..." I tried to think about that. It felt like Nico had been in my life forever, but then I reminded myself that we hadn't actually become friends until we were about nine years old. By that point I had been diagnosed for two years. "We've known each other all our lives," I answered. "But we didn't become friends until about seven years ago. He...he reached out to me."

"What do you mean?" she sounded curious now and I didn't want to get into that part of the story.

"I uh...I was shy. Or, shy*er*, I guess. But it was worse back then. I was that kid who stayed inside during recess with my crayons and refused to go and play with the others. Then one day, Nico saw me inside and offered to play with me. I said I was fine and that I wanted to color." She was paying close attention now, which made me feel slightly uncomfortable, but something about those brown eyes kept me going. "Instead of giving up and going back to the playground, he came inside and he... he sat down with me and started coloring with me." I felt a small smile creep across my face at the memory. "He was terrible at it."

She laughed and cocked her head at me in interest. I continued, "Every day after that he came inside and colored with me, everyday being terrible at it. So one day, when I couldn't take seeing him butcher the pages...I decided to play his way. I went outside and played with him on the monkey bars. Then I fell and hit my head." She laughed again, and I thought I saw the hint of a twinkle in her eyes. "All the kids pointed and laughed at me, and I started crying, but Nico..." I paused for a moment, my mind going back to that day, seeing the events almost as if they were right in front of me. "He just let himself fall too. Did a very intentional face-plant, and started screaming bloody murder. Everyone started laughing at him and it totally took the heat off of me. And ever since then we were best friends."

"That," Annabelle said, smiling. "Is the most adorable thing I have ever heard in my life." She kept smiling at me, and after a second, I smiled at her too. I could feel a glowing warmth on my hand, and I realized that at some point in my story she had slid her hand over mine. I didn't move it.

"Yeah, Nico is always doing things like that for me. It's heartbreaking that he never admits anything is wrong with him."

"What do you mean?" she asked, furrowing her brow.

"Nico's mom is in the hospital," I told her, not entirely sure why I was. "She had this aneurism a couple of years back and she's been comatose ever since. Nico tries to pretend that he's made his peace with it, but I know how much it hurts him to see her like that."

"That's awful," she whispered. "And there's no hope she could get better?"

"Not likely," I said shaking my head. "Nico and his dad visit her a lot though. They're actually there today."

"That's terrible." I nodded and we sat in somber silence.

"Hey, what do you say we get out of here?" I said. "I know this really cool place."

"Oh boy," she said apprehensively. "I've heard you say that before," she indicated the giant cow.

I laughed, and it felt really good to laugh. It filled up my lungs and made me feel a thousand times lighter. "Trust me, I won't be that dumb again." I stood up and, in an act of sheer and pure bravery, offered her my hand. She stayed where she was for a moment before taking my hand and standing up. With her hand in mine, we headed back to my car.

***

When we drove past the sign that said *Grover Park*, I pulled into a space in the parking lot.

"Okay," Annabelle said, getting out of the car and putting her hand back in mine. I didn't object. "So did you bring me here to see the duck pond or something?"

"Not exactly," I said, laughing. "Follow me." I led her down one of the gravel pathways that snaked through the woods. October equals early nightfall. I assumed she didn't mind staying till dusk, because she followed me with pure trust. When we were about a mile or so along the path, I spotted what I was looking for.

"Here we go," I said, pulling her towards a wooden bench on the side of the trail. We rested snugly.

"What are we doing here?" she asked.

"Hang on a second," I said, casting a look at the horizon. The sun was almost in the right position. "Okay, I come here to paint sometimes. Keep your eyes on the horizon, okay? In just a few seconds…"

As I pointed at the sun, it kissed the treetops at three o'clock. The orange sunlight broke through the leaves and shattered into a million colors. It illuminated the bright leaves and seemed to make them glow. All the different colors, golds, greens, reds, pinks, all seemed to perforate the entire forest. The entire world took on a tint of pinkish orange.

"Oh my god," I heard Annabelle mutter.

"Right?" I whispered. "It's unbelievable."

She leaned forward, her mouth wide open in marvel. "I never knew how much beauty was in this town," she breathed. "The sunset, the stars…this town is magical."

"Well…I don't know about magic. But it definitely has some beauty to it, if you know where to look." She turned to look at me and I could see the wonder, the amazement in her eyes. I felt myself shift, and suddenly I was her again. I was in her head, seeing through her eyes. Seeing all of this incredible beauty, and I could feel her heart swell at the majesty of it all.

And I saw myself standing before her. For the first time I saw myself through her eyes; tall and dark and handsome. The orange light shining through my dark brown hair, glowing off of my skin, making the blue of my eyes shine like bright beacons. She saw so much behind those eyes, so much held back, and yet so much glowing at the surface. Just like his eyes….

At that thought, I snapped back into myself. She looked different now.

"Is something wrong?" I asked her.

"No, no," she responded hastily. "I was just…I was just remembering something–er…someone." Whatever it was seemed to have bothered her. She was looking down at the ground now, her eyes somewhere far away from here.

"Do you...do you want to talk about it?"

"No," she answered sharply. "No I shouldn't, I...it's too..."

I could see how uncomfortable this was making her. She didn't want to talk about whatever it was. I felt an overwhelming sense of empathy, having many times been in her shoes. I could've asked her 'Are you okay?' Then she would say she was fine and I could ask 'Are you sure?' But how many times had I been infuriated by someone asking me that same question?

"It's okay," I said quickly. "You don't have to talk about it." She looked up at me and there was so much behind her eyes, but hell if I could make sense of all that emotion.

"Really?"

"Really," I told her. "I'm not gonna force you to talk about something you don't want to talk about. You want me to take you home?" I started back on the path towards the car.

"Wait," she said. I stopped in my tracks and looked back at her. She held my gaze, trying to make a decision. In the end, she sat back down on the wooden bench on the side of the trail. She motioned for me to sit back down, so I sat down next to her. She seemed to be gathering courage.

"Remember when... when you found that painting I did of my house and...and I thought you were stalking me?"

"I vaguely recall," I said, not wanting to relive that particular memory.

"Well...my jumping to conclusions wasn't entirely...without ground."

"What do you mean?"

"Back home..." she stopped for a moment, seeming to be having a very hard time getting this out. "There was this guy. And he..."

Oh my God. What she was saying began to sink in. Oh my *God*. "Annabelle...were you stalked?" I probably should've stayed silent, but it just slipped out. Curse my damned tongue.

She took a deep breath to steady herself. "His name was Jesse," she said quietly. "He was a couple of years older than me. We met in this community art class and we got partnered up on this one painting, and...I don't know, he was tall, dark, brooding. Sounds cliché, I know, but I fell for him. He was so intense, so deep and soulful. I felt like I was staring into this bottomless well of beauty every time I looked into his eyes." *I know the feeling.* "I never thought for a second he could be interested in me. And then he was." The pain I heard in her voice tore at me. I wanted to make her feel better, to take all of that pain away from her. "And I thought I'd won the lottery. The second he asked me out, I thought for sure I had to be dreaming.

"Of course as soon as my parents found out I was seeing him, they freaked. Told me I shouldn't get involved with that kind of guy, that he was nothing but trouble. And I just yelled at them that they didn't understand him and that I loved him. And I meant it, you know. I *loved* him. I guess I just have a thing for the broken ones or something." I wasn't sure how to interpret that comment, but I decided to shove it aside and address it later. "He may have loved me too, in a way. I thought we would be together forever. The perfect soulmates." She stopped then, seeming to get caught up in the memories. That was a feeling I knew very well; losing yourself in the past.

"And then?" I asked cautiously. "And then," she continued bitterly. "Things got heavy. We started talking about eternity and how all we needed was each other. I thought he was just being romantic. But over time, I started to notice things. How he glared at any other boy who looked at me. How he always held me too close to him when we walked down the street. I mean, if a cashier so much as winked at me, he would leer at him. And at first I thought he was just being protective but," she paused and I noticed that her hands were shaking. I wanted to take them in mine to steady them, but something held me back. She took a deep breath before continuing.

"But then I told him one day that I couldn't hang out with him

166

because my friend needed help picking out an outfit for some date she had that night. He started getting so angry, saying that I was choosing some dumb outfit over him and that my friend was a stupid bitch anyway. And I told him, I *told him*, that he was overreacting and that I loved him, but he just kept screaming." Her voice was trembling now, and she seemed to be struggling to keep it from breaking. "The next day of course, he apologized, but...it was never the same between us. He would always tell me how much he loved me and how much our relationship meant to him. How if I ever left him he would just... he would just die. Then one day my friends started avoiding me. I'd call to hang out with them, or try to talk to them during school, and they'd just come up with some excuse why they couldn't talk. Come to find out Jesse threatened them all to stay away from me. He told me that they were all just jealous of what we had and they were trying to come between us. Eventually I just couldn't take it anymore, I couldn't! It broke my heart, but I ended it. I knew I couldn't be with someone like that, no matter how much I loved him." She stopped and seemed to stare straight down at the ground for a moment, as if not actually seeing the ground, but rather reliving the events of the past. "I left him...but he didn't leave me. He started following me home from school, sending me texts and e-mails saying how sorry he was and that if I would just give him another chance, he wouldn't mess it up again. I tried so hard to tell him that it was *over*, but he just wouldn't let go! The next thing I know he's breaking into my locker and leaving presents, sending me messages saying if I wouldn't take him back he was gonna kill himself."

I heard the way her voice was shaking and said, "You don't have to keep going. You can stop."

"He wouldn't stop," she said, as if she hadn't even heard me. "He showed up everywhere I went; school, home, friends' houses, my brother's soccer games. I transferred out of that art class, and he transferred too just to follow me! The more I told him to leave me alone, the harder he came after me. I didn't feel safe leaving my own bedroom, and even when I was in my bedroom, I was being bombarded by texts, e-mails, IM's, posts on my Facebook wall. I couldn't escape him. He was everywhere! Then one day, I came home and—" At last, her voice broke and she took a moment to try and gather herself together. When she finally spoke, her voice sounded thick. "I came home after school and...and I saw...I saw my dog Oscar. He was outside...hanging from a tree. *His throat was cut.*" I remained in a disgusted trance until she broke again, and I heard a sob escape. I was seized by a sudden urge to wrap my arms around her, whisper in her ear that everything would be fine and that there was nothing to cry about anymore. I didn't want her to cry. "There was a note left tacked to the tree. All it said was; *I love you.*

"After that," Annabelle continued. "I had to tell my parents what was going on. We called the cops and they went to Jesse's house but they.... He was gone. They looked everywhere for him but he had gone from everywhere to nowhere. I still have no idea where he is. I was terrified he was just biding his time until he came after me again, so we packed our bags, I got a new cellphone, a new e-mail address, and we moved to the most out-of-the-way town we could possibly find. Somewhere Jesse could never find me."

"I don't even know what to say to all of that."

She turned back to me with surprise, as if just now remembering that I was there. "You don't have to say anything. I shouldn't have told you all of that, I shouldn't have just unloaded all of that on you."

"No, no, it's...it's okay," I assured her. "I just can't imagine what you must've gone through. *And* your parents."

"Yeah. My dad loved Oscar." She just nodded for a moment, but then she furrowed her brow and opened her mouth. "But I shouldn't even be telling you this," she thought for another moment. "I shouldn't even be here with you."

"What? W–why not?"

"I was *stalked*," she said. "A boy followed me and threatened my friends and family and overall made my life a living hell. I should be terrified to go on a date with another boy, and I should definitely be terrified to be alone in the woods with him for God's sake!"

"Well, I don't hang dogs from trees, so you don't have to be worried about me," I declared.

"But I'm not." She tried to giggle but couldn't. "Despite everything that happened to me, I'm not afraid of you Daniel. I don't think you'll hurt me. In fact...I feel...safe when I'm with you. I don't feel like if I look over my shoulder I'm gonna see Jesse standing there. For whatever reason, I...I trust you."

Our gazes interlocked and there again was that swirling behind her eyes. I couldn't identify what it was, but it looked different than before. Not as frightened, but in a way, even more intense. I became very aware of how close we were. We were no longer on opposite ends of the bench. Without conscious thought as to doing it, I had scooted closer to her, and her to me. We were barely touching now, and she was so close to me that I could feel the heat from her body. The smell made me feel a little bit dizzy, and yet everything seemed to suddenly be in sharpest focus. She seemed to be moving closer still. She was closing her eyes. She was much too close. I could feel her breath on my face. And everything in me wanted her even closer.

"Annabelle," I said, breaking the spell. Against every raging instinct in my body, I pulled myself away from her. "It will get dark soon. I should probably take you home."

She opened her eyes and stared at me in disbelief for a second. "Right. I guess that's just my luck."

"I'm sorry," I said. "It's just..."

"What?" she asked. "Cause I don't get it."

I opened my mouth, but no sound came out. I wanted to say the right thing to make her understand, but what could I say that wouldn't be wrong?

"Daniel? Tell me. Please just explain this to me. If I just poured my heart out to a guy who's not interested, then please tell me so I can avoid further embarrassing myself."

"Annabelle," I said. I didn't want her to think that. Even though it would probably be better if she did. Wouldn't it? "I don't...I just don't think I know how." I'm not even sure what I meant by that.

She nodded, not looking at me. "Yeah, it was...it was stupid anyway, you should...you should just take me home."

"Yeah," I said, nodding. "Yeah I guess I should."

We sat on that bench for what felt like forever. I couldn't tell if she was angry, disappointed, or embarrassed. Maybe a combination of all three. Emotions have a way of getting complicated like that. Sometimes it's impossible for me to keep up with normal people.

"Daniel please take me home," she said.

I turned my head and looked into those eyes. I couldn't say anything. So I just nodded. We stood up and started back down the trail. Annabelle kept her eyes glued ahead, the warmth that had been here a few minutes earlier completely gone. As silent as we both were, I might have been walking these trails by myself. The only sounds heard were the chirping of crickets, and the hoot of a night owl in the distance.

Chapter XVII
A View to a Kill

After I dropped Annabelle off, I drove home, feeling miserable, and gave some throwaway excuse to my mom when she asked where I had been all day. I went up to my bedroom and threw myself down on the bed. I knew that what I had done tonight was probably extremely stupid and the fact that I hurt Annabelle after she told me all of those things made me want to curl up into a ball and die. But I knew I had done the right thing, regardless of how much I didn't want to. Of course, telling myself that didn't help quell the churning guilt in my gut.

When I finally got to sleep, I should've known it wouldn't be a sound rest, because the second I fell asleep, I found myself in yet another nightmare. I was running. Running for my life. There was someone behind me, and they were trying to kill me. I couldn't see the face, but I knew I could never fight them off. My only hope was to escape. I heard the sound of high heels clicking on hard tile as I ran, and I realized where I was. I was running through the school hallway, and it was late at night. I got to the staircase and ascended angrily. The sound of high heels on marble changed to stone as I ran up the uncovered steps. When I hit the top landing, I dared to look behind me. There was nobody.

How could that be? I knew I saw someone. They had been just behind me. I had heard them chasing me. So where could they have gone? Is it possible I imagined it? It *was* late. Maybe I was so tired I had hallucinated, or misconstrued something else. Maybe I had seen the janitor and freaked out. Sure. I just needed to go home and get some sleep. Then I'd be fine. I was about to walk down the steps when I heard another footstep behind me. I whirred around, and suddenly, there was a hand clenched around my throat.

I tried to scream, but the hand had too tight a grip, and all that came out was a garbled, gagging sound. It was too dark to see who had grabbed me, but he didn't seem to be trying to choke me. Instead, he raised a hand to my forehead, and I felt all the heat leave my body. It felt like my insides were being pulled out of my body through a tiny hole in my forehead. Like he was draining away my soul. My limbs began to ache, kind of like when the blood pressure machine at the hospital squeezes too tightly. My whole body felt cold. Frigid. For a moment, I thought that the janitor had turned the air conditioner up too high. Then I couldn't think at all. I kicked and struggled, trying desperately to free myself. I felt my high heeled foot make contact with his leg, but all he did was grunt, his hand not for a second leaving my forehead. My vision began to go fuzzy, and I was conscious of a sharp, metallic taste in my mouth. Blood. The warm, thick liquid filled my mouth, and I felt it dribble down my lip. The sides of my vision began to go red, and I felt myself cry. I wasn't even conscious enough to realize I was crying until I felt the warm tears sliding down my cheek. Wait, those weren't tears. They were blood.

Blood was coming out of my eyes. My ears felt thick with it too. My arms beat against him pathetically, when I felt his grip loosen a little, but he was letting go of his own will. He was done with me. I fell to the floor, and as my vision went red, I tried to look up at my attacker. My killer. I couldn't say anything. My larynx was crushed and my mouth was full of blood. But I managed to get a glimpse of his eyes. They were like a cat's. Two luminous, venomous green bulbs floating in the faraway dark. I heard him say something, but it sounded like I was hearing it from underwater. What feeling was left in my arms showed that he seemed to be taking something from my wrist. But I couldn't even remember any more. The bright green bulbs began to fade to black. They were black. A minute ago those eyes had been venomous green, now they were a midnight shadow. But even that thought began to fade, along with the unbearable pain. Everything was fading. I shot up out of my bed, gasping for air, my heart racing at NASCAR speed. I struggled to breathe, but I felt like I was still being strangled. That dream had felt so real. More real than anything I had ever experienced. I knew with a psychic flash that it was more than just a vision. It wasn't just something in the future that might happen. It was something that had already happened to someone.

"Bad dream?" I shot out of the bed and onto my feet, eyes scanning the darkness for the source of the voice. It hadn't been for his nearly stark white skin, I never would've seen him.

"Leo?"

"Hey, there, sunshine," he said. He flicked on the lights, illuminating the room. When I blinked away the spots that flashed against my retinas, I saw him standing there, casually leaning against the wall.

"My parents are downstairs," I said. "They'll hear if anything happens to me." Leo's expression didn't even change. I didn't understand him. The day before, he had been raging like a madman, and now here he stood, completely calm. Something was very wrong about that. He walked across the room, almost leisurely, making his way to the other side of the bed. I shrank away a little bit as he approached. He stopped at the edge of the bed, directly across from me, and looked me dead in the eyes. I tried to look away, but something drew my gaze up into the deep black of his eyes. They looked...different, somehow. Usually, they were hard and impenetrable, like coal. But now, something was in them, something bright and strange, dancing behind his corneas. They resembled obsidian when it was still in the volcano, the light from the flames bouncing all over the glassy surface.

"Fire is light." I snapped out of it and focused on him.

"What?"

"Light burns away darkness." His expression was stoic, but he spoke with an importance, like he was giving a solemn decree.

"What are you talking about?"

"Here's what you know." He snapped his fingers and a fire blazed to life in the middle of his palm. I should've run. Should've screamed for help. Here was a murderer, who had already killed two people, holding a blazing flame in his hand, but I stayed where I was and stared into the fire. It looked nothing like the fire from the gym. It looked bright and powerful and warm, like the kind of fire people huddled around for warmth and protection from the cold. Yet, it also blazed with a passion that said it would rage and rage and light up the whole world. It danced wildly in Leo's palm, flicking its fiery tongues into the air with passion and power. It gave off a powerful warmth that licked my face and burned away my fear. Looking into that flame, I could totally understand how some people became obsessed with fire. Fire raged wherever it wanted. It did whatever it wanted and made no apologies. It didn't pause to consider its every little action. Fire was freedom.

Burn...burn it.... The fire whispered to me, a low whisper that carried so much authority and power. *Burn it away. Burn it away.* Burn what away? I blinked, and the warmth, the comfort, vanished. Leo no longer stood across from the bed. I was alone, and the flame had gone with Leo. Was that a dream? No, that didn't make any sense. I would've woken up in bed, but I was still up. And anyway, it hadn't felt like a dream. It had felt real. And at the same time, not real. *What the hell did I just see?*

***

I texted Nico to get Hayley and Natalie and meet me at Whitmore House the next morning at ten. I wasn't exactly sure what I was going to tell them. I knew I was going to tell them about the dream, but for some reason I didn't want to tell them about seeing Leo in my bedroom. Five minutes before ten, I was out the door. I wasn't even all that sure about the dream. I mean, what use would it have? Obviously Leo was the one who killed Fairchild. Who else would have wanted her dead? I suppose there could be any number of people, since I knew nothing about her personal life, but something about her didn't strike me as the kind of woman with a lot of enemies. A lot of annoyed students, sure, but not real enemies. So it only could've been Leo. But no matter how much I told myself that, I couldn't get rid of this nagging sense that that dream meant something important.

When I passed by Annabelle's house, I couldn't help but stop and look for a moment. I hadn't actually talked to her after I dropped her off, and I so badly wanted to. Hell, when I wasn't dreaming about horrible, gruesome death, I was dreaming about her. I tore my gaze away from the house and kept going to Whitmore House. When I got to the house, nobody was there. It felt weird, standing in the house, all by myself. This was the house that kids had to be dared to go into, the house that little kids walked by really fast so they didn't have to look at it. And I found myself raiding its cabinets. I had snuck out early, leaving no time for breakfast. The cabinet was stocked with beef jerky, which I suspected was Hayley's doing, and I found a cooler filled with low-calorie sodas, which I suspected was Natalie's doing. I grabbed a water bottle from the bottom and bit into a piece of beef jerky. Not bad. Making my way to the staircase, I took a look up.

"Hello?" I wondered if anyone had gotten here early and gone upstairs. I didn't get an answer, but then a thought occurred to me. *I'm not alone in this house.* I started up the stairs, the landing leading into the hallway I had sprinted down in a panic just the other day. Then to the bedroom. I pushed open the door, and there he was. Cam lying in the bed, right where I'd left him. It looked like they'd changed the linens, and given him a new, less sweat-soaked shirt, but otherwise, he was the same and asleep, the rise and fall of his chest being the only indicator that he was alive. With the pale skin, and the fact that he was almost entirely still, one could've easily thought he was dead.

I took a few steps forward, scared he might wake up and start wailing like a banshee. Natalie had said I'd overloaded him. That seeing my "supernatural aura" or whatever, had been too much for him, and he'd passed out. I felt a strong jab of guilt at that. Was I really responsible for what had happened to him? For what he looked like now? I took another step forward, and it was like stepping into a warzone. It felt like machine gun fire was being shot off all around me, each one striking me right in the heart, each one bombarding me with terror, misery, anger, bitterness, despair. Nothing could ever be right, not with this much badness in the world. I fell backward, and the chaos that had momentarily raged inside me stopped, and I felt okay. I felt traumatized by the force I had felt, but I didn't actually feel it anymore. Looking back at Cam, something seemed different about him. His hair looked darker, his skin more ashy and brackish, like the very air around him had darkened. I could sense his energy, similar to how I had Leo, but his didn't feel nearly as warm as Leo's. Leo had been like hot breath on my face, breathed out straight from his soul, sent out through the whole room. But Cam's was just a whisper that tickled my consciousness. If I had to put a word on it– gulp–I would have called it the breath of a dying man.

"Hello? Anyone here?" The sound of Hayley's voice downstairs snapped me into focus.

"Yeah, I'm up here," I yelled back before going downstairs. Hayley had arrived with Nico in tow. She had a coffee in one hand, Nico's hand in the other. "Hey," I greeted both of them.

"Coffee?" Nico held out a container of coffee cups that they had apparently gotten before coming. I took mine gratefully. We waited for a few more minutes until Natalie walked in, looking annoyed as always. Like she had better things to do than stop a murderer.

"Okay, what was so important that you guys had to call me here at this ungodly hour?"

"Yes, Daniel, pray tell," Hayley commanded. All eyes were on me. Hayley had dropped herself into the loveseat with Nico, who had his hand on her back, but wasn't as nonchalant as she eternally was.

Natalie had sat herself down on the arm of the couch and was looking at me with thinly veiled impatience.

"Well...I had this dream last night."

"That's it?" Natalie asked. "You made me get up at six o'clock to talk about your dream?"

"We got up at seven," Hayley pointed out.

"Do you think *this* just magically happens?" Natalie said, indicating her clothes and hair.

"Daniel," Nico said, before things could get ugly. "Go on."

"Right. I think I saw Ms. Fairchild the night she died. I think...I think I might have seen her die." A thick silence fell over us. Even Hayley looked dead serious. Natalie, though still looking like she didn't want to be there, didn't look as bored or impatient. I knew I had to keep going, so I told them what I had seen, sparing the bloody details, but keeping in the part where the culprit barely even touched her, and never hit her. Just put his hand on her forehead.

"What is that supposed to mean?" Natalie asked.

"He just put his hand on her forehead and she...she started dying."

"It definitely sounds otherworldly," Hayley lent, "but how could Leo do that? He's a pyro, he starts fires. How could he pull off something like that?" Nico didn't look like he had any answers. Natalie either.

"There was one other thing," I added. "I don't know if it's important, but he took something off of her wrist. I don't know what it was, she was too far gone by that point." Everyone's faces had turned sober. Hearing a first-hand account of Ms. Fairchild's death made it feel more real.

"So what do we do?" Hayley asked.

"It's obvious," Natalie said. "Danny Boy here needs to remember what Leo lifted off the body so we can figure out what he wants with it."

"I didn't even see him take it, I just felt it leave her wrist," I said. "I have no clue what it was." As soon as I said it, my hand twitched, and a surge of color exploded behind my eyes. My hand shot up to clutch my head, gripping it in both hands.

"Daniel?" Nico was next to me in an instant.

"Pen and paper, quick," I said. Hayley was up, searching through drawers for something, but they didn't really keep drawing utensils stocked. Natalie rifled through her purse before producing a napkin and makeup pencil. Good enough. I snatched it up and sketched the color out onto the napkin before the pain could get too horrible. Luckily, the drawing was small this time. And it wasn't a dead body. It was a rock.

"What the hell?" Natalie said. "This is one of your little predictions? It's a freaking rock." It didn't look like just a rock. There wasn't much shading, so I assumed it was light in color, possibly white by the looks of it. It was jagged, with sides and planes that couldn't have been smoother.

"It's that stone," I muttered.

"What?" Nico asked.

"The stone I found in your drawers a few days ago."

"You still have that thing?" Hayley asked. I turned toward her. "What is it?"

"It's some stone he bought at a fair when we were like thirteen. Some gypsy lady said it held mystical properties. But it never did anything for any of us, so we assumed she was just full of shit. Why'd you keep it?" Nico shrugged.

"Are you sure it doesn't have any properties?" I asked.

"Pretty sure," Nico answered. "Why?" "Cause when I touched it, I just kind of felt this...energy. And then I did a drawing, and touching it seemed to have triggered it." All three of them exchanged a look, something I didn't think was possible. Add that to the list of the impossible things that had happened to me in the last few days.

Finally, Nico said, "Maybe we should have you take another look at that stone." Hayley agreed, and Natalie only begrudgingly agreed to come with out of curiosity. Nico's house wasn't far.

***

Once inside, Hayley and I exchanged hellos with Mr. Marshall. Natalie stormed up to Nico's room with purpose, so we cut our pleasantries short and followed suit. When we caught up to her in the bedroom, I indicated the drawer where I had found the stone. I opened it, and sure enough, it was still there.

"It looks so normal," Natalie said. I looked over at her, but she was serious. It certainly didn't look normal to me. Physically, it looked like an average stone, but there was almost a strange glow to it. The very center of it seemed brighter than the outer shell, and its light spread out, giving it a faint shimmer. I could practically feel the energy humming off the thing. It was more powerful than what I had felt from Leo, and a thousand times stronger than Cam. Immediately, my hand reached out to touch it before Nico's hand clamped down on my arm, pulling it back.

"Careful," he warned, but Hayley pulled him back. He released my arm, and I reached out and stroked the glassy surface and all of its edges. I felt the energy funnel into my hand, sending electric waves thrumming as I curled my fingers around the stone.

Images flashed across my eyelids, only this time, they were in focus. A man in the café. Now he was outside the café. Now he was walking through the streets. Then he was pinned against the wall of an alley. Then he was on the ground, covered in blood, his eyes empty. I knew the man. Mr. McCall, Nico's boss. He was lying in an alley, dead. I dropped the stone, and I was back in Nico's room, everyone staring at me expectantly. My hand felt like it was burning where the stone had touched it. I needed to clutch the edge of the drawer for support.

"Daniel?" Nico said. "Are you okay?"

"No," I answered. "We need to go."

"What? Why?"

"Someone else is about to die."

Chapter XVIII
The Stakeout

"Daniel, where did this happen?" Nico asked as we all piled into his car. He floored the gas and pulled out of the driveway.

"Uh," I tried to recall the brief flash of images I'd seen. "It was in an alley, it looked late. It was dark out."

"Well we have plenty of time," Hayley noted, looking at the clock on the dashboard. "It's still only eight in the morning."

"I think it was near the café."

"You think?" Natalie said incredulously. "You need to be pretty damn sure."

"Café," I said. "I'm sure." Nico hung a left into the town square, parking the car outside the café. We rushed out of the car and flung open the doors to an almost empty café. I don't think I'd ever seen it less busy. There were a few people around, but it was nowhere near as crowded as usual. Usually, at this time, it was flooded with people needing their early morning caffeine shot. With two people dead, most people were too afraid to go into town. Mr. McCall was at the register, and he looked up when we walked in.

"Nico," he said. "What are you doing here? You're not working today."

"We just wanted to come and hang out for a while," Nico said calmly. He gestured for the rest of us to sit down, so we gravitated to the nearest table, forcing a calm and nonchalant look. We ordered some coffee and scones, hoping for an excuse to hang around so we could keep an eye on McCall. We didn't know how we were supposed to go to the police, and tell him I had had a psychic vision of him being murdered, but we figured between the four of us, we could stop Leo if he tried anything. Nico kept looking over to Mr. McCall, as if checking to make sure he hadn't dropped dead since the last time he looked. I knew it had to be nerve wracking for him. He hadn't known Fairchild or Angie, even though he felt bad for them, but this was someone he did know. Someone he spent nearly every day with since he was thirteen. When the girls stepped outside to scope out the alleys for the one I'd seen, I wanted to ask him if he was okay. Although, part of me knew how annoying that question was, so I thought maybe I should be quiet.

"No Daniel, not really," Nico said. I must've looked astonished, because he grinned a little and looked at me. "No matter how jumbled up your thoughts sound to me, when you hear the same one fifty times, it kinda clears up." I smiled nervously.

"Well, I just figured you're freaking out a little."

"Yeah, a little," he said. He was quiet for a moment. I didn't really know what to say or how to comfort him. Usually, it was him comforting me, so I didn't know how to do it the other way around. "We don't have to talk about it," he said. I was relieved.

"So..." I tried to look for something to talk about. "What about Natalie?"

"What about her?"

"How did you guys get close to her?"

"Close?" he said, eyeing me.

"You know what I mean!" I rolled my eyes.

"Yeah," he said. "One day, a couple of years ago, Natalie was still learning to control her gift. She had this big catfight in the middle of the hallway with some girl. She got so pissed off, her eyes were practically red, that she accidentally busted a locker door open. Without laying a hand on it. Hayley and me saw, so we went to talk to her after school. Of course she got defensive, since back then, she thought she was the only one, but then we showed her what we could do," Nico paused, reliving the conversation, "and she collapsed, crying. She was so relieved that there were others like her. We've been helping her ever since." I stared at him in disbelief. It was hard for me to picture Natalie breaking down and crying in relief. Plus, it was a far cry from how I had reacted. Of course, the circumstances had hardly been the same. But while it may have sounded out of character for Natalie, it was exactly what I expected from Nico. To go to someone who felt lost and reach out to them, make them feel accepted. Natalie may have repaid him with venom, but still. At least I understood now, why Natalie had been so concerned for Hayley in the guidance counselor's office.

"Why do you think Leo is doing this?" I asked without thought. Nico looked at me with confusion. "Do you think it has something to do with that stone?" I had been wondering why I had reacted so strongly to the stone, while the others claimed not to have reacted at all.

"I don't know, Daniel." He looked at me like someone learning new things about something they thought they knew everything about. Which, I guess, was how I was looking at him. We waited for a while longer, watching McCall and talking so he wouldn't get suspicious. The girls came back, and we set up an unspoken system where two of us would keep an eye on McCall, and the other two would go outside and keep an eye out for Leo. We traded out positions, though Nico never went on Leo-duty. He stayed firm, not taking his eyes off of McCall. Nobody argued his right to this. Somehow, around noon, I ended up outside with Natalie. Some kind of mistake must have happened to cause this, because being alone with Natalie certainly had not happened by my choice. I was supposed to watch out with Hayley, but then she went inside for a second and Natalie came out. Hayley was now inside talking to Nico, ignoring me when I glared at her through the window.

"You know," Natalie said when she caught me shooting Hayley an *I'm going to murder you* look. "If you're not happy, you can always go back inside and tell one of the love birds to put it back in their pants and relieve you." I grimaced.

"Sorry," I said. "I just wanted to…talk to Nico—"

"I know what you wanted," she cut me off. "Contrary to popular belief, I'm not an idiot, and I know how you guys feel about me. Trust me; the feeling's mutual."

I blinked, not knowing what to say. "I didn't think you were an idiot." This time, it was her turn to blink. She looked at me as if I had called her the greatest genius since Albert Einstein, but she said nothing.

"Well good," she said, finally. "Because…I'm not." I nodded, and she turned away. Why would Natalie think I thought she was an idiot? Now a bitch? Sure. A drama queen? Of course. A future stripper/hooker? Probably. But an idiot? I had seen no evidence of that. "God, why are we even here?" she said after a few minutes. "Leo's probably not gonna show."

"He is gonna show, I saw it," I said.

"Yeah, yeah," she said doubtfully. I furrowed my brow at her.

"I saw it."

"So you say…" My jaw practically dropped open. She thought I was lying? Why would I lie about something like this? And why was she being so sullen about doing this? Did she have something better to do than save a man's life?

"I know what I saw," I said. "And we need to be here. We're the only ones who know what's gonna happen and what Leo's capable of. We have to stop this." She looked at me with barely contained anger.

"I know that."

"Really, because it seems like you think being here is a waste of time." This time, the anger was not in any way contained.

"Where do you get off talking to me like that? You walk in here with your new powers and suddenly everything goes to hell, then you look down on me all 'holier-than-thou' and try and paint me as the apathetic whore! Well did it occur to you that maybe I'm not the terrible person everyone thinks I am?" She stared me down with those hazel eyes that were absolutely blazing with anger. "But no, just because Natalie is rich and pretty and has a lick of fashion sense, that means I must be some insensitive bimbo who will just let a man die! Well you don't know anything about me, so quit assuming you know anything and back the hell off!"

If she expected a reply from me, she was disappointed. If she really did want to save Mr. McCall, then what was with the attitude? She had been acting like it was some great cosmic injustice that she should have to stand out here with me and prevent a murder. Like the universe was being cruel specifically to *her* for putting her here...then it hit me. Natalie didn't think that stopping the murder was a waste of time. She was angry that she had been put in this situation. In the middle of this whole mess with Leo, and all the murders, and with these powers. And I figured that out because it was exactly how I felt. She hated these powers and the situation as much as I did. I'm not sure what shocked me more. The idea that Natalie wasn't a total bitch, or the idea that we shared something in common.

I wanted to say something to her, but, being me, I had no clue what to say, and I probably would've gotten tongue-tied even if I did. I thought about what Nico had told me about the day they became friends with her, but I didn't think bringing it up would be much help. So I stayed quiet. Natalie went in and Hayley came out to relieve her. We kept it up for a few more hours, with no sign of Leo. Eventually, I was back inside with Nico. He was texting his dad and I was keeping my eyes on McCall who was pouring some espresso shots, and when he looked up, I nearly jumped out of my chair.

His eyes had turned completely black. As in, bottomless pits of darkness, from pupil-to-eyelids, black. Like his pupils had grown to swallow the entire eye. He was speaking to a customer, but I could've sworn that he was looking directly at me.

"Daniel? Daniel!" I snapped back to Nico, who had clearly been trying to get my attention, but he stopped when he saw the look of utmost horror on my face. "What's wrong?"

I turned back to McCall, but the black eyes were gone. He

looked completely normal.

"Daniel, what's wrong?" Nico pressed.

"M–McCall," I stammered. "I saw...it was his eyes, they were black. Like, completely black."

Immediately, Nico's face went grim. "Are you sure?"

"That's not something you get wrong, Nico."

"Well what does that mean? Have you ever seen something like that before?"

"I don't know, I mean I—" I stopped. "Wait...I remember it happening once before."

"When?" he asked urgently, seeming uncharacteristically demanding. I hesitated before answering, because I knew he wouldn't like it.

"I saw it happen to Ms. Fairchild. The day before she died."

Nico turned downright grave at that. His eyes took on a stormy intensity, like storm clouds swirling and coalescing before a typhoon.

"But we're not gonna let that happen," I reassured him. "We had no idea about Fairchild, so we had no idea we needed to stop it. This time we will. I promise." I had no idea if I was doing anything to help him, but I had to at least try. After a moment, the grim expression faded and his face relaxed a little.

"Yeah, you're right," he said, smiling, though that intensity in his eyes had not vanished.

After a few minutes, there was a jingle as someone walked into the café. I turned to see Annabelle walking through the front door. My throat went dry, and my palms got really sweaty. I hadn't seen her since our disastrous date, and judging from the expression on her face when she saw me, she hadn't been expecting to see me here. But she wiped her face blank and went up to the register to order. Nico took notice and turned back to me.

"Something going on with you two?"

I took a deep breath before answering. "No, not at all," Nico cocked his head in doubt.

"Nothing?" I thought for a moment before realizing that if I told

Nico, he was least likely to push me about it.

"I'm not really sure, actually," I said. "We...we kind of went on a date yesterday."

"Seriously?" Nico said incredulously. "That's awesome, how did it go?"

I shot him a dirty look that I think conveyed precisely how I thought the date went.

"That bad, huh?"

"And worse," I added.

"Well, what happened?"

"I...I just screwed things up like I always do." I was technically still telling him the truth. I would've told him the whole truth, but Annabelle had told me those things in confidence and it wouldn't be right to go blabbing them to my friends. It's her past to tell, not mine, and I would respect that.

"I see," he said. "Well, do you want to go talk to her?"

"I–I don't know," I said. "I don't think she wants to talk."

"Daniel, trust me, that's exactly what she wants," he said. I looked into his liquid silver eyes, and maybe saw just a glint of mischief.

"Are you reading her mind?" I asked. He winked. Biting my lip for a moment, I got up and walked up to the register. "Hey," was all I knew to say when I got to her. She only looked up for a second.

"Hey," she said blankly. I stood there uncomfortably. I looked back at Nico, and he gave me a nod of encouragement.

"So are we always just gonna greet each other with a single awkward syllable?"

"Are you always gonna blow me off every time I get close to you?"

I didn't answer that. I just went silent for a moment and stared down at my shoes. When I looked up, she was looking straight ahead.

"So, what're you doing in this ghost town?" I asked, nodding toward the vacant square outside.

"Just getting some coffee," she answered. She was still refusing to make eye contact.

"Hey, listen—"

"Okay," she interrupted. "Here's the thing. I know you've got this whole shy, mysterious, secretive thing going on, and that's great. We met, you were nervous and cute in a charming way, then we talked, we hit it off, and I thought there was something there. Then we take a late night walk underneath the stars, we almost kiss, and you blow me off. I don't see you for two days, and when I do, you're running away from me like your hair is on fire. Then the next day, you ask me out, we go for ice cream, I tell you something *unbelievably* personal about myself and we almost kiss, again, then you back off, *again*. So...what the hell?" "I...I don't know, I..." I genuinely had no clue how I was supposed to answer that. Especially the "almost kiss" part. Was that what had happened? And had I really been *charming* when we met? This was so far out of my comfort zone, it's like we were on a different continent.

"Cause if you're not interested, I'd really appreciate you telling me, and if you are, then same thing. But just stop going back and forth between the two and tell me." Not interested? Oh God, if she only knew how far away that was from the truth. Even in the panic and confusion of this moment, I still couldn't help but be entranced by her. I brought my eyes up to her gorgeous, chocolate ones. I could stare into them forever and never reach the bottom. Her hair caught the sunlight perfectly coming in from the window, framing her and giving her an almost golden outline. If I could've drawn her right then, I surely would've been capturing the image of an angel. I don't know how to describe how I felt, all I knew was that this girl standing in front of me was beautiful, and artistic, and being around her made me feel at peace, yet also made my heart race faster than it ever had, and even though I'd only known her for a week, I didn't want my life without her in it.

I probably should've said all of that. But when I opened my mouth, I simply couldn't force the words out. To say those things, to even attempt at telling her how I felt about her, would be to expose a part of myself I didn't know was there myself, and a part I didn't know if I was capable of showing. To anyone. I wanted to. I really did. I just didn't know *how*. So I said the only thing I could.

"I'm sorry." She looked at me with such a look that for a second, I wished Leo had taken me out in that fire. Before she could say anything else, the barista came back and handed her a paper bag and a coffee. She took it and looked back at me.

"Me too," she said, before walking out of the door. *There goes my angel,* I thought. Trying hard to stop the ache in my chest, I sat back down across from Nico. He looked at me like he always did, with caring sympathy and worry.

"I'm sorry," he said. I didn't say anything, just watched through the window as Annabelle walked to her car, got in, and drove away. "Daniel?" Nico said, breaking me out of my reverie. "Are you gonna be okay?"

"Let's just watch your boss," I muttered. For the next few hours, we sat in silence and kept a close eye on Mr. McCall. Like hawks. If the man so much as sneezed, we were there to see it. The girls returned not long after Annabelle left. Hayley was, of course, inquisitive on why I was so silent, but Nico got her to drop it, though I suspect she forced him to tell her telepathically, because she kept looking back at me with sympathetic eyes. Natalie, on the other hand, didn't seem particularly interested. When the clock struck three-thirty, Nico had to start his shift, so it was just the girls and me, although at this point, I really didn't care. Plus, nobody was there, so Nico didn't have to do much. We waited for hours more, and by five o'clock, everyone was restless. Natalie had satisfied herself with texting her popular friends, while Hayley had taken out a piece of paper and scissors (I don't want to know where she got those) and occupied herself by making paper angels. I, on the other hand, didn't take my eyes off of McCall. Whether or not I had my vision because I was "meant" to save him, I had predicted Fairchild and Angie's deaths, and I had done nothing to stop either of them. I wasn't going to make the same mistake this time. Plus, it gave me something else to focus on. When it finally reached six o'clock, Natalie was fed up.

"Okay, how much longer are we gonna stay here?" she asked.

"As long as it takes," Nico answered.

"We have been here all day," she said. "For ten hours, we have sat here watching that man, and nothing has happened. Not so much as a paper cut, so can we assume that Daniel's vision was bogus and go home?"

"It wasn't bogus," I said. "It was late when it happened, so it could still happen tonight."

"Great," Natalie said, throwing her arms up in the air. "So we're gonna stay here all night, then?"

"If that's what it takes," Nico said calmly.

"But—"

"We are not leaving," Hayley exclaimed. "We are going to stay here as long as it takes, to save that man's life, but if you want to keep being like this, you can go home if you really want."

"Guys," Nico said. "Can we please not fight? We're all gonna stay here for as long as we have to."

"And who exactly put you in charge?" Natalie asked.

"I never said I was in charge," Nico said.

"Oh really? Well with the way you've been barking out orders, you'd think you were a freaking emperor."

"Can you back the hell off?" Hayley scoffed protectively.

"Don't talk to me like that, skank," Natalie snarled. I felt like I was seven years old again, listening to my parents yell at each other. I couldn't stand listening to it, so I got up, telling them I had to use the bathroom. It wasn't a far cry from the truth. We had been here for ten hours, and I had drank four cups of coffee. After I relieved myself, I took a little longer than necessary to wash my hands, because I really didn't want to go back out there. When I finally looked up in the mirror, I saw something on the walls that hadn't been there a moment ago. Him. The mysterious-always-has-his-back-to-me-disappears-when-I-look-away guy. True to his name, he had his back to me, but he seemed to be staring at the wall.

"Who are you?" I asked. "What do you want from me?!" He gave no answer, no indication he'd even heard me. I walked forward and tried to see what was so special about it, but it appeared to be just a wall. But as I took another step forward, it started to change. Writing began to appear on the wall. Blood red writing. It almost seemed to come *from* the wall, as if bleeding out of it.

"Lies plague the beaten path, but rivers hold clear truth. Your trust is misplaced."

It made no sense, but I didn't have time to ponder it, because I heard a loud scream from outside. I ran out and saw Nico standing with the door to the back room open. Natalie stood by her chair, one hand covering her mouth, eyes wide open in horror. Hayley was next to her, staring into the door with thinly veiled shock. I ran next to Nico, and saw exactly what they were looking at.

"No," I muttered. Mr. McCall was lying there, blood-soaked, his skin paled to ivory. There was a sink in front of him, spilling over water that had mingled with his blood, leaving it red. I looked over at Nico, whose expression was of pure shock. "Nico," I said, trying my best to sound comforting. He closed his eyes in a way that I recognized well for all the times I had done it. He was trying to blink away tears. When he opened them, I was shocked by what I saw. Anger. Rage. Nico was mad. The concept was amazing to me, because I had almost never heard Nico even raise his voice, and now he looked absolutely murderous. But right then, there was a sound like a door closing from the side of the room. I turned and saw a figure disappearing behind the door.

"Hey!" I shouted. "Stop!" I shot off running, ignoring the sound of the others calling after me. The door led into an alley, and I saw the figure running toward the end, where there was a gate that lined the backs of the surrounding buildings. "Stop!" I shouted again, taking off after him again. It was too dark to see who it was, but it looked like he was wearing a hoodie. He was fast, but so was I. We hit the gate and he turned left, across the back of the building. The space was a good yard wide. I was beginning to close the gap between us when a set of surprisingly strong arms grabbed me and pulled me back. "Hey!" I struggled against whoever had me.

"Calm down," an irritated voice grumbled in my ear.

"Leo?" I exclaimed, successfully shoving him off. He didn't try to grab me again, and I almost called out for help, before something occurred to me. "Who was that?!" I demanded, pointing after the guy who had fled.

"That," he revealed, "was who you're really looking for." I could've pretended not to know what he meant, but there was no use anymore.

"The killer," I said quietly. Leo didn't answer, but his silence spoke volumes. I closed my eyes and steadied myself. "Who is it?" When he opened his mouth, he was cut short by the sound of a police siren. One of the others must've called the police, and their headquarters was just down the block. I looked back at him. If the police got there, they would question the others, and might say Leo had killed McCall. And then they'd come out to find me.

"We need to talk," he said. I nodded in agreement. "Tomorrow, the school." He was gone, leaving me standing alone in the chilly night.

Chapter XIX
A Heel-Face Turn

I was right. The police questioned all four of us. Our statements uniformly dictated that we felt cooped up at home so hung out at the café all day. It wasn't a lie. And the only person who would be able to corroborate how abnormally long we had been there was dead. When they asked me if I had caught a glimpse of the killer's face, I said no, and gave extremely vague details about his build. Even though the others were confident Leo had done it. I couldn't directly contradict them, especially since I still wasn't a hundred percent positive that he was innocent.

While they were talking to police, I caught notice of the town coroner. He was taking away the gurney, covering a large form with a sheet. I stopped midsentence when I saw it. Some blood had soaked the white sheet, leaving red blotches all over it. The others saw it too, and we all stopped as he was rolled past. I felt a stab of guilt. This was my fault. I had the vision; I was supposed to stop him from dying.

I looked over at Nico and could still see that frightening anger. Hayley had her arms around him comfortingly, but I think she was probably looking for some comfort too. I saw tears glistening in Natalie's eyes. I couldn't help but think that she didn't belong here. She was a rich, pretty girl; she wasn't supposed to be here. None of us were. We were just kids for god's sake. I was sixteen, and all the others were the same age as me, give-or-take a few months. We shouldn't be staking out a murder. How could it be possible for people so young to have seen something like that?

When they were done with us, our parents were waiting to take us home. Mr. Marshall was standing by Nico's car, waiting for his son. Hayley's mom was with Hayley's little brother, Justin...or Zac. Whichever one it was, he was jumping up and down, trying to get a look at the crime scene. I don't know who was picking up Natalie, but from the fact that she looked sixty and was wearing an apron, I'm assuming it was her maid. I couldn't believe her parents weren't there to get her. All of the other parents were waiting nervously for their kids, or else demanding to see us at once. My own parents were anxiously waiting for the detective to release me. When I joined them, they swarmed me with questions and hugs. I got in the car and looked back at the café. There were now squad cars covering the place, and bright yellow *Do Not Cross* tape blocked off all entrances. One more place in town that was now a crime scene. I silently cursed the darkness for doing this to us.

***

The next day, I woke up praying that last night had been nothing more than a dream. That hope was crushed the second I walked downstairs and saw the somber look on my mom's face.

"Good morning," she said.

"Where's dad?" I asked. She looked up from the French toast she was making.

"Still asleep," she replied. She opened her mouth to say something else, but I was gone. I marched into my parent's bedroom, closing the door behind me. My dad was at the dresser, wearing only pajama bottoms, though I'm assuming he was searching for a shirt.

"Hey," he said when I came in.

"Hi," I said quickly. "Um, do you remember a few nights ago, when you told me I had some...special gifts?" His expression turned serious as he sat down on the bed.

"Yes," he said.

"Well, what did you mean by that?"

I got the feeling he was considering his words very carefully. "Daniel, do you know where the name Cohen comes from?" I shook my head. Like my first name, I had never given my surname any thought. "It refers to a child or descendant of Aaron, the prophet." Prophet. Kind of like Daniel.

"Uh huh," I said. "But you said...you said special. Like...different?" I wanted to know why I had responded to the stone when the others hadn't. My dad looked me in the eyes, his opalescent blue locking with mine.

"Yes," he said. "Different." I was about to ask him how, but my mom called from the kitchen that breakfast was ready. I wanted to yell that I wasn't hungry. "Trust yourself, son," he said. "Trust your instincts. They won't let you down." That's all I got from him. Again.

***

I scarfed down some French toast before I told my parents that I was going to check on Nico. In reality, I drove to the high school, where Leo had asked to meet. True, it may not have been wise to rendezvous with a suspected murderer with powers over fire, at the site of two of those murders, all by myself. But it wasn't like I could invite someone to come with me. Everyone was convinced that Leo was the one killing people. I still wasn't completely sure that he wasn't, but I knew I needed to find out somehow, and something about that fire from my dream...I just needed to talk to him. Still, I was careful to make sure my phone was on and ready to dial 911.

When I pulled into the student parking lot, the school was deserted. Even more so than it would usually be on a Saturday morning. Usually, there would at least be teachers here grading papers, or students coming in for Saturday detention. But the parking lot was completely vacant. Driving through town hadn't been much different. Usually, there were people outside milling about in the square or outside shops. But today, the entire town had shut themselves inside. Most of the stores had closed down for the day, and the café was still taped off as a crime scene. It had felt like a ghost town straight out of a horror movie. I half expected someone to peak through the blinds, then snap them shut when I noticed.

I walked the school grounds. Leo hadn't actually said where we were supposed to meet, so I was hoping I could find him, wherever he was. As I approached the Chemistry Lab, I saw that one of the doors had been propped open with a rock. I raised an eyebrow and looked around, but there was nobody in sight. Technically, it would've been illegal for me to walk into the school when nobody was there. Breaking and entering, or something like that. But...well, nobody was there. Slipping through the open door, I saw that the stairs where Ms. Fairchild had been found were still taped off. I suspected the old gym was too. There was absolute silence in the halls. So quiet, that every step I took sounded like a thunderclap echoing down the hall. I reached windows that overlooked the courtyard. In the distance, I saw that the entrance to the old gym was indeed barred from entry. Not that anyone was likely to go in. It was nearly burned to the ground. The walls were blackened and scorched around the brick, and the wood was charred.

A sound behind me sent me spinning around to see Leo striding toward me. I steeled my gut as he reached me.

"Hey," I said. "So why did you want to meet here?"

"Less people around," he said, as if we were under surveillance. He nervously took out a cigarette and bent over to light it. I crinkled my nose in disdain. I couldn't stand the smell of cigarettes. I didn't even get why people smoked them. I mean, they smell awful, they're bad for you, and you don't even get a high off of it. But I said nothing. Once it was lit, he took a puff of it and blew smoke out of his mouth. "Okay, the first thing you need to know is, I may not be a killer, but I'm also not a nice guy, so don't get confused." *Gee, you're so welcome for covering for you with the cops. No biggie.* In my imagination, I said all of that out loud.

"Okay," was all I actually said. "So what all do I need to know?"

"First of all, you don't know half of what you think you know."

"Well that would be where you come in," I said. "Do you know what we are, what this *mana* is?"

"Well...I don't know the official term. I've heard us referred to as star children, spirit walkers, earth bound. Supposedly we have a strong connection to the Spirit Realm that allows us to use these powers." Something about the last one stood out in my mind. Earth Bound. It seemed to click in the same way that *mana* had.

"And *mana*?"

"*Mana* is the universal energy that flows through both the Earthly Realm, and the Spirit Realm. Because we're connected to both realms, we can use it to fuel our powers."

"Okay, you keep talking about this Spirit Realm, and the Earthly Realm, and it's all sounding really..." I didn't finish. He reached forward and grabbed me by the arm. My first instinct was to jerk my arm back, but then he closed his eyes and I felt something pass through his hand into my arm. It was like the feeling of standing outside in the summer breeze, mixed with the sound of music pumping through your head and blood coursing through your veins. It made me think of the rush you get when something sudden happens in a horror movie, the rush of adrenaline that spikes through your brain. It was radiant and brilliant and made me think of thrill and joy and euphoria. It was pure life. Then he took his arm back, and the incredible rush of life was gone, but I could still feel faint traces of it, blowing through the air and through the soft grass outside.

"Okay then," I said dreamily. "That was interesting."

"That," Leo said, "was *mana.*" I understood now why Nico and Hayley hadn't been able to explain the extent of our powers. What I had felt was inexplicably incredible, and I had no doubts that it could do some amazing things.

"Okay," I said, nodding, still a little high on the feeling of the *mana* running through me. "How do you know all of this?" He reached into the pocket of his jacket and grimaced a little. It wasn't a far cry from his usual expression, but it struck me as odd. He pulled out a small leather-bound book. It looked old and weathered, with the edges frayed and stray pages sticking out. On the cover, in glossy print, were the words *Libro Animo.*

"Book of Spirits," he clarified. "I learned it all from this."

"Where did you get that?" I reached out to touch it, but he pulled it back and placed it tenderly back in his jacket.

"My parents left it to me." Leo was looking away, and it struck me that maybe there was a reason Leo was always so sullen and angry. It didn't look like he felt like discussing it though, and I probably wouldn't know what to say, so I changed the topic.

"So the killer, he's one of the Earth Bound?"

"Yes," he said.

"And you're telling me all of this why?"

"Because you're different," he answered simply. I waited for him to elaborate, but he didn't.

"Different how?"

"You're...more powerful than others."

"Powerful?" That made no sense. How was I more powerful than the guy who could control fire?

"It's your drawings," he said.

"Wait, how do you know about the drawings?"

He shrugged. "I've got my ear to the ground. The drawings, they're...unique. I've never heard of anyone being able to do something like that. I think he wants to take it from you."

"Wants it? You mean...he can just...take it?"

"It's a simple manner of draining your *mana*." I thought back to the way he had seemed to drain the life out of Fairchild. And judging by the condition of her body, he had done the same to Angie and McCall. Looking for Earth Bound. Leo seemed to take note of the shocked look on my face, and he must've interpreted it as disbelief.

"Look, you can believe whatever you want."

"No, I...I believe you. It's just hard to think of myself as powerful."

"Well get used to it," he said. "It's the only reason I'm here."

"Wait...you moved to Spirit Ridge...to find me?" He nodded, his face remaining sullen as ever. "Why? How did you even know where to find me?"

"It's easy to track someone down," he said. "Especially if you're one of us. And as for why; to protect you," he answered simply. "You're important Daniel. I don't know why or how, but you're important."

"And who told you that?" I asked incredulously.

I waited for an answer, but then it dawned on me. His parents. They must've told him. Sent him here to protect me before they died. How they knew was a question for another day.

All of this talk about how I was so special and important, it didn't feel right, made me uncomfortable. How could I possibly be so important? "Okay then," I said, deciding not to voice those thoughts. "So you said you're not the killer. I believe you. So...who is it?"

"I don't know yet," he responded. "All I know is that he's very powerful." Great, even Leo didn't know who the killer was.

"Awesome," I muttered.

"Hey, I don't see you contributing." I looked over at him. Not contributing? Didn't he just say that I was in the center of all of this? And did he have any idea what it took for me to come out here today? I felt irritation at his crack, and that irritation grew to anger. After everything that had happened to me over the last week, I really didn't feel like being insulted by a broody, antisocial jackass like him.

"Well, I don't really think that nearly getting me killed in a fire goes far in the way of protection, do you?" His eyes narrowed dangerously at me, but I stood under his gaze.

"Watch it," he said.

"I'm just saying that if I'm so special and powerful, it's not really living up to your potential to nearly get me killed."

"Listen you little punk," he snarled.

"What? Are you gonna hurt me?" He growled in fury and looked like he very much wished he could hurt me. But he restrained himself.

"Look, let's just focus on finding out who the killer is."

"Great, so he's—" I was stopped short when my cell phone went off. "Hang on," I said, answering the phone. "Hello?"

"Daniel?" It was my mom. "Where are you?"

"I'm with Nico," I lied.

"Really? Interesting, since Mr. Marshall is right here, and he says he hasn't seen you all day." I bit my lip in anger. *Damn it.*

"Okay, fine, I'm..." I struggled for a lie to tell her, but nothing came to mind.

"You're coming home, right now." I sighed.

"Okay," I said. She ended the call.

"What?" Leo asked.

"I have to go. I told my parents I was with Nico, they know I'm not, so now they're freaking out."

"Now? What about the killer?"

"We'll talk later," I said. "If I don't go see them, they'll probably start thinking I'm dead."

"Fine," he said. "Tonight, back here." I nodded before starting to walk away. "Daniel, wait."

I stopped and looked back at him. "What is it?"

"What do you know?" he asked.

I stared back at him, at the menacing position and the terrifying black eyes and...I knew. I remembered what my vision of Leo had said. *Here's what you know.* With that flame, he showed me what I already knew. What I had always really known. "I know you didn't kill those people."

He nodded, and I turned and went back through the hallway back to my car. As I cranked the ignition, I saw Leo still standing by the steps. I wondered if he would be going home. Despite his attitude, I felt some pity for him. My parents may have been unbearable at times, but I couldn't imagine not having any at all.

***

The drive back home didn't take long. The town was no less deserted the second drive through. When I pulled back in the driveway, my mom immediately marched across the driveway, nearly pulling me out of my car by my hair.

"Where were you?" she asked furiously.

"Mom, it was nothing."

"Nothing?! People are dying out there, and I didn't know where you were!" Her voice was thick with tears, mingled in with the fury.

"I'm sorry," I said. "I'm sorry!" She pulled me into a tight embrace. I felt her tears wetting the back of my shirt. "I'm okay, mom, I'm fine." Behind her, I saw my dad and Nico's dad watching us. I made eye contact with my dad, who nodded at me. When my mom finally released me, she took me inside. To my relief, she didn't ask where I had gone, but she didn't sound eager to let me leave the house again.

When my mom was talking to Nico's dad, I took mine aside. "Okay, I need to hear it," I said. "Do you know that I'm...that I can...do you know—"

"Yes," he said. "I've known ever since you were born." I took a minute to soak that in. Part of me was relieved that my suspicions were finally confirmed, but another part only had more questions.

"And does that mean that you are..."

"Yes," he said. I let out the breath I hadn't known I'd been holding.

"Why? Why didn't you tell me?"

"Because that isn't the kind of thing you throw on your son until he's ready."

"What, and I'm ready now?"

"Well, circumstances being what they are, I didn't really have much of a choice. I wanted to wait until you were eighteen and tell you myself."

"And if I found out before then?" He didn't have an answer for that one. I found myself reexamining my entire childhood, trying to find indicators that my father was one of the Earth Bound. Then one hit me. A terrible one. "Is that why you didn't want to send me to a specialist? When I was a kid."

"Daniel...I knew what you would have to go through in your life. I figured..."

"I needed to toughen up," I finished. Normally, I would never have said that out loud, but I was still running off of adrenaline from my conversation with Leo.

My dad looked at me with sorrow. "I'm sorry."

"Whatever," I said, walking away into the kitchen. Mr. Marshall was there alone now. My mom had gone back into the living room. I opened up the fridge, hoping we had some sodas, when something hit me. "Um, Mr. Marshall?" Nico's dad turned around. "Where's Nico?"

"Oh. He's with Hayley." I nodded. It made sense that after what we had seen last night, Nico and Hayley would want to be together. I wondered if, under normal circumstances, I would be with Annabelle right now.

"What the hell are you talking about?!" my mom shouted. I turned toward the sound of her shout.

"I'm just saying that we shouldn't be too hard on him," Dad responded.

"Too hard?! He lied to us! Refused to tell us where he was going, and went off God knows where! He could've been killed!" I looked around the corner into the living room. My parents were facing each other, anger plain on my mother's face.

"But he wasn't! He's fine."

"This time!" "Well maybe you should have a little more faith in him!"

"What are you trying to do?!" "I'm trying to trust our son!"

"He's sixteen years old!"

"Sixteen, Grace, not seven! You can't keep protecting him

forever." My mother didn't notice, but the last part sounded more like Dad was trying to convince himself.

"I am his mother, I sure as hell can. And if you were going to act like a father, then you would be too!"

"So now this is a question of whether or not I'm a father?!" I hadn't seen my parents argue like this since I was seven years old, and it didn't bring back happy memories. Especially since, once again, they were arguing over me.

"You know what? Maybe it is."

"Oh for God's sake!" my father exclaimed, throwing his hands in the air.

"What do you want me to think, Nathan?! Our son witnessed a murder last night, and now he goes off somewhere and doesn't tell us where, and you're acting so calm about it, what do you want me to think?!"

"I want you to think that Daniel is a big boy, and he is capable of taking care of himself!"

"Guys," I tried to cut in, but my mom bulldozed over it.

"So that means we should let him go out somewhere where a killer is running around and just be okay with it?"

"Guys, stop!" I shouted. They snapped out of their argument, turning back to look at me.

"Daniel, honey, go back in the kitchen," my mom said.

"No," I said. She turned her eyes back on me.

"What?"

"No," I repeated. "You guys need to stop." She looked at me like I had spoken a foreign language. "Just stop." She looked over at my dad with a look I had never seen her give anyone. It made me want to cry seeing her give it to my dad. Then she turned back to me, her expression going gentle.

"Honey, I've been thinking," she said. Not *we've* been thinking. Like she was a single parent. "I think we should try and go see Dr. Farrell again."

"Mom, that guy is an idiot," I said. "He can't do anything for me."

"Well," she said. "I already spoke to him on the phone. He thinks it would be a good idea for us to go somewhere else for a while." I stared at her, sure I had imagined what she had said. After a second, I blinked.

"What?" I asked blankly.

"Grace, I have a job. We can't just—"

"Not forever," she said hastily. "Only for a few months...maybe a year, while things settle down. Just Daniel and me." It settled in what she was saying. She wanted to move me away. To leave Spirit Ridge. For a second, I thought for sure that she had gone insane, and that someone would tell me that this wasn't an actual plan. But nobody spoke up. Everyone kept staring at me.

"Wha–but...we can't leave. It's Spirit Ridge."

"Daniel," she began, but I wasn't done.

"I've spent my entire life here, my friends are here, Nico and Hayley..."

"You would still be able to talk to them."

"What, on Skype? Postcards? No, we can't leave, we can't!" Panic rose in my chest, suffocating me. My dad sunk into the couch with his head in his hands. No way could we leave this place. I couldn't let such a thing happen, I couldn't!

"Daniel, I know that this probably doesn't sound—"

"NO!" I shouted. "No!" I took a step back from her, before turning on my heel and running out the front door.

Once I was in the Honda, I slammed the door and peeled out of the driveway. I didn't really know where I was going, but I couldn't be there. I just couldn't. I mean, move away from Spirit Ridge? That's insane. That's so beyond insane. To move to a new town, completely start over? Making friends here had been hard enough, but trying to do it again, in a town where nobody knew or heard of me? No way. The hysteria my mom had caused me made it so I wasn't really aware of where I was driving until I got there. When I stopped the car, I found myself back at the art studio.

I stepped out of the car, staring up at the familiar building. I hadn't gone inside since the day I drew Fairchild's death. The drawing that started it all. Ever since then, this place didn't feel safe anymore. It used to feel so isolated and impenetrable, like none of my problems could reach me up here. But the darkness did. It penetrated my safe place and contaminated it. I only went there because I was desperate; it was my only hope. Somehow, the place now seemed looming and threatening. I touched the handle of the door, choking back the fear, and pulled it open.

As always, the smell of acrylic paint and dust hit me, but it didn't smell as comforting as it usually did. Walking inside, I didn't feel the weight drop like normal. My worries were dragged inside with me, like a ball and chain attached to my leg. Everything looked different. The dust coated floors looked dingy and mysterious, and the paint splatters all over the floor looked to me like blood. Then I came to the easel and saw, to my surprise, that the drawing was still there. The pure-white steps, tainted with blood, with a hand lying over, insidious darkness looming over it. A bitter, hateful resentment welled up inside of me, spreading until I stared at the drawing with pure hatred. If it weren't for that drawing, none of this would've happened. My life would still be semi-normal. I would be cowering at home like everyone else in town, blissfully unaware of what was really going on. I would never have been in that fire, wouldn't have been there when Mr. McCall died. I wouldn't be trying to catch an all-powerful murderer, my mom wouldn't want to move me away, and my parents would still be tolerable.

The same anger from the school rose in me, as I grabbed the drawing, crumpled it up, and threw it across the room. I angrily flipped through past drawings. Had any of these come to pass, and I just didn't notice? If so, I decided, I didn't want to know. I didn't want to know anything. I threw them all aside. Before, I had wanted answers; I had wanted to know what was going on. Now I regretted ever having found out. I wished I could've let it go. I wished I couldn't know what was going to happen. I wished I didn't know.

I tore away a drawing from a few years ago and behind it was just a blank page. I stared at it for a second. At the vast empty landscape, and my mind started filling it with colors, mixing and shaping themselves into something more.

No, I thought. *Not again.*

I felt the drive, the need, rage inside of me once again. Only this time it was different. More powerful. The swelling of importance inside was like no other drawings I had done. It filled me to the brim and seized control of every muscle in my body. I grabbed hold of a pen, put it to paper, and drew. I drew and I drew and when I was finished, I grabbed another sheet of paper and started another one.

I drew like I was possessed, finishing one and then jumping into another. I lost count of how many drawings I did. It was like time ceased to exist and there was only me, my pens, and this driving force that had taken over. I was no longer in control. The power was. And it wanted very badly to show me something.

Eventually, the feeling ebbed and lessened, until I was pulling a very sore hand away from another completed drawing. Wiping sweat off my brow, I looked outside to see that night had fallen. How long had I been here? Hours, clearly, but was it even the same day?

Hesitantly, I turned to look at the drawings. I had hung them all up on easels so that I could look at them all at once…and they were not pretty.

One of them showed some kind of hallway. I couldn't tell what it was, it was pretty generic. Wherever it was, there were three people in it. A brown-haired boy, a blonde girl and a black-haired girl. Me, Natalie, and Hayley. And we were running. From what I couldn't tell, but I could feel fear resonating from within the page.

Another one depicted us in a chapel setting. And it was coming down in flames. There were two people standing near the exit, with one approaching them from the altar. I couldn't make out any faces, so I turned to the next.

A pair of eyes. Completely black. Not a trace of pupil, iris, or humanity in them.

The man I keep seeing. The one whose face I never see. He stood against a white background, but this time his head was turned ever so slightly, as if about to turn around.

The darkness, swirling, storming, preparing to strike.

"Daniel!" I froze at the sound of my name. I turned to see Hayley standing at the door.

"Hayley?" I said, astounded. "What are you doing here?"

"Your mom called me," she said. "She told me you ran out, we've been looking for hours. What's up?"

"How'd you know about this place?"

"Oh, I've known about this place for years," she said. "Things are different on the astral plane, sometimes you end up places you didn't mean to go."

"But...but this place is mine," I muttered. "It's mine, no one knows about it."

"Well, sorry to break it to you, but 'no one' doesn't mean what it used to." She sounded nonchalant, as always, but she didn't understand what a big deal this was to me. This place had always been only mine. Nobody knew this place was here. At least, they were never supposed to. That's what made it safe, that no one would ever look for me there. And Hayley had found it by astral projecting. By using her *power*. Bitterness once more reared its ugly head.

"So you projected here before?" She nodded. "How much?"

She shrugged. "I don't know. Like I said, it's different on the other side."

"Great," I said, throwing my arms up in defeat. "That's just another thing that this took away from me."

"What are you talking about? Are you okay?"

"Why does everyone always freaking ask me that?!" I shouted. "Everyone is always asking 'are you okay?' 'Hey, Daniel, are you okay?' 'You okay, Daniel?' Well you know what, Hayley? No! I AM NOT OKAY!"

"Hey, calm down." Hayley came over to me. "What is the matter with you?"

"What's the matter is these damned powers ruining my life!"

"Okay, I get that you're upset about Mr. McCall, about Annabelle being mad at you, but that doesn't give you the right to start using your gift as a scapegoat."

"It's not just that, it's everything! It's everything in my life that's been destroyed by this *thing* inside me!"

"Oh come on."

"Do you know what my dad told me today? That the reason he didn't want to do anything about my condition was because he knew what I was. And he thought that with that to deal with, Asperger's was no big deal! That's why my parents fought, Hayley. My parents would still be happy together, if I was just normal!"

"Well, you're not!" she shouted. She turned my head toward her, forcing me to make eye contact. "You're not normal. Never have been; never will be. But guess what? None of us are!"

"It's different!" I yelled. "It's different for me, cause apparently, I'm 'different'."

"How?"

"Look at what's happened Hayley! This killer came after me in that gym fire. I reacted to the stone when you guys didn't, Nico can't read my mind correctly. And..."

"You're an Aspie," she finished. "Oh my god, Daniel...you know that old song is getting really tired."

"What?"

"Do you think you're the only one with problems? You know, there are people with your condition who are a lot worse off than you."

"Worse off?" I asked. "What are you trying to say?" "I'm trying to say that you've got it easy. Do you know that some Aspies have to practice in front of the mirror just to be able to start a conversation? Not carry one on, but just start one. You've got it a lot more mild than them and yet you still whine and bitch about it."

"Oh my god," I said. I couldn't believe what I was hearing. "You...how can you even—"

"What?" she challenged. "Do what? Take away your excuse?"

"Excuse?!" I said incredulously. "Excuse for what?"

"For acting like a little beaten down puppy, that's what!"

"Okay, you're not making any sense."

"Look, for as long as I've known you, people have been cutting you slack because of your condition. If you say something wrong, they think, 'Oh, he's an Aspie, it's all good.'" I stared at her uncomprehendingly.

"What, so that's why you're always so blunt? It's, what? Tough love?"

"Damn right!" she shouted. "I'm not buying into your act, and I'm not gonna play along with it either."

"What act?!"

"The weak little kid act. You put up this weak face, so people feel sorry for you and don't try to push you. But I don't buy it. You're nowhere near as weak as you make people believe."

"You don't know me," I muttered.

"Stop mumbling!" she screamed. "That's always what you do! Someone tries to see something other than the act, you just mumble some apology or half-assed defense, or else you act like a smart ass."

"You don't know me," I said, more clearly.

"Yes, I do! I know you're not that weak. You're tough. Nobody, as weak as you believe you are, would have stood up to Leo like you did. Nobody that weak would have gone and staked out a murder victim because he thought it was his responsibility to save him. Or would've gone chasing after a psychopath because he needed to be stopped."

"I never said to anyone that I was weak."

"You don't have to. You made yourself believe that when you were diagnosed so you would have an excuse not to deal with it. So you could hide behind that. That's all you've ever been doing is hiding! Hiding behind your condition, and now behind your gift, all so you don't have to admit that you're just *scared*."

"I am not hiding behind anything!"

"Yes you are, and if you could find half the courage that I know is in there, you'd be able to admit it."

"God, you are unbearable," I said.

"Why, because I don't put up with your crap?"

"Because you act like it matters!" I was done with this. Years of holding in everything, and it was all spilling out now, regardless of whether or not I wanted it to. "You say that I put up an act, but I'm not alone, because you're the one who *acts* like you actually care!" Now it was her turn to look confused.

"What are you talking about?"

"I'm talking about the overkill. Poking fun, giving helpful suggestions when Nico is around, all that is fine. But trying to force your self-help lessons into my head? It's overkill! When Nico isn't here, you no longer have to pretend you're my friend!"

"Wait a minute," she said. "You seriously think that the only reason I'm your friend is because of Nico?"

"Yeah, you know what, I do! And I'm so done pretending I'm completely oblivious, when we both know that you never would have acknowledged my existence if you hadn't met him!" Hayley, for once in her life, looked speechless. We must've stood in silence for over five minutes before she opened her mouth.

"You're right," she said. Now I was the one who was speechless. I had expected a little bit of denial, at least a weak argument. "You're completely right. If Nico and I had never started dating, I probably never would've even known you existed. I mean, nobody ever really has reason to notice you until they're introduced. Probably the only people besides me, Nico, Natalie, and Leo who even know you're name are the people who heard it during roll call. You hide yourself away so nobody sees you, and it works. Nobody ever notices you. And for some reason, you feel you have the right to complain about it. To complain that you don't have any friends, when it's your choice to avoid basic human interactions."

"It is not my—" I started, but Hayley was on a roll.

"Oh, are you about to blame it on the Asperger's again? Because you have no right to that excuse because you don't even try and make it better. You're scared, and you can't even see how much you've grown because you keep clinging on to what used to happen when you were seven years old!"

"I'm not clinging! I'm...I'm..."

"Yes you are! You developed so much fear, and now you hold on to it so tight you can't let go."

"That's not true!" I said. "I'm just—"

"What? What are you doing? Do you need time to come up with a new excuse now that I've challenged your original one?"

"I—"

"You're not seven years old anymore, Daniel. You're sixteen, and you need to have just a little faith in yourself. You need to learn to see all that greatness inside of you that we see."

"It's not there!" I shouted. "Whatever you all think that you see inside me, it isn't there, understand? It never has been, it never will be. I'm not powerful; I'm not great; I'm just Daniel."

"Well, you know what? Just Daniel needs to man up and realize that he's a pretty kick-ass dude. Because if you can't stop believing that you're hopeless, then you really are."

"SHUT UP!" I shouted at the top of my lungs. "SHUT UP!" The echoes of my shouts were pierced by the sound of Hayley's ringtone. She held my stare for another moment before pulling her cell phone out of her pocket. She looked at the caller ID before looking back up at me.

"I'm not done," she said before she answered the phone. "Natalie, is this important?" Hayley listened for a moment before her face morphed into a look of horror. "What?! Are you sure? Well what happened?"

"Hayley, what's going on?" I asked. She put up an impatient hand to silence me.

"Okay, we'll be right there," she said. She hung up the phone frantically and looked back up at me. I saw another look that I've never seen on Hayley before. Fear. She looked terrified.

"Nico's gone," she said. Immediately everything from half a minute ago vanished.

"What?"

"He's gone! Natalie can't find him anywhere."

"His dad told me he was with you," I muttered. "When you showed up without him I thought you had split up to look for me." Slowly, she shook her head.

"I haven't seen him all day," she said. I felt my chest constrict as if trying to crush my insides, and for a second, I couldn't breathe. I turned to look at the last drawing I had done. I hadn't had time to look at it before Hayley came, but now I saw it. My stomach dropped out of my body. It was Nico. Nico, laying face down on the ground, his silver eyes staring straight ahead, but not really seeing a thing. His warmth extinguished.

"We need to go," I said to Hayley. "Now."

Chapter XX
Dreams Do Come True

We ran outside and head straight for Hayley's car. She jumped into the driver's side, but I stopped when the tires caught my eye. She didn't see it, but I had an artist's eye for detail.

"Hayley," I called. "Look."

"What?" she yelled running out to where I was. "What are you doing?"

I pointed at the tire, and she looked back up at me in horror. The tire was slashed. The rest of her tires were probably the same.

"Who could've done this?" I asked.

"Who do you think?" she responded. She turned and screamed. "Leo! Leo you bastard, we won't let you do this!"

"Hayley," I said, trying to calm the growing panic in my chest. "Hayley, Hayley, calm down. We'll take my car." Stupid thought, since my tires looked just like Hayley's. Whoever did this really did not want us leaving.

"Dammit!" Hayley screamed. "Come on, we'll have to huff it."

We followed the tire-track-path left by our cars, through the woods, moving as fast as we could. Neither of us spoke, but it was clear what we were both thinking. It's just that neither one of us were willing to say it.

Hayley may put on a brave face a lot, but if there was one thing I knew for sure about her, it was that she was in love with Nico, and the thought of something happening to him was scaring the hell out of her. I couldn't say I was feeling much different. I couldn't banish that image of him lying on the floor, taken away from us. I wouldn't be able to handle that.

"Nico's gonna be okay," I said, more to myself than to Hayley.

"Of course," she said. "He's probably…at the café."

"The café is closed; it's a crime scene," I pointed out.

"Right," she said. "Still…I'm sure he's fine."

"Uh huh," I said, nodding. "What if Fairchild had a stone? Like the one Nico had?"

"Daniel—"

"What if it was a small one, set into a bracelet? That could be why I drew it. If those stones are tying everything together…Hayley, Nico has a stone."

"I know!" she shouted. "Don't go there Daniel."

"Sorry," I said.

"Nico's *fine*," she stressed. Then, under her breath, "I'm gonna kill Leo." I didn't respond. I hadn't said anything yet about not thinking Leo was the killer. Hayley would think I was crazy. But if we couldn't find Nico, Leo would be the first person she would want to go to, and that would be wasting precious time.

"Hayley, what if we've got some things wrong?"

"What?"

"Some of the things we've assumed…well, what if they're wrong?"

"Like what?"

"Like…I'm just saying we need to be sure about everything before we go charging in anywhere."

"Daniel, you're not making any sense," she said impatiently.

"It's just…certain doubts I have…"

"About what?!" "Leo!" I snapped. God, my self-restraint was jumping out the window.

"What about Leo?" she said. "What, doubting that he's the killer? Daniel that's crazy!" "Is it though? I mean, we just assumed that Leo was the one killing people."

"Well yeah, unless you know someone else who can start fires with their mind?"

"Maybe..." Hayley looked at me incredulously.

"Daniel, what aren't you saying?" I hesitated for a moment.

"Let's just find Nico; then we'll worry about it."

"No, we'll worry about it now!" she yelled.

"Hayley—"

"Daniel, talk," she ordered.

"I talked to Leo, okay? I met up with him at the school today."

"Are you insane? You went to talk to him *alone?!*"

"You provoked him into setting a librarian on fire."

"More proof that he's a psychopath!"

"He's not!" I was shocked at the amount of certainty in my voice. I realized with startling clarity that I was one hundred percent sure that Leo didn't kill anybody. That everything he said in the school was true. "He's not the killer. I don't know who is, but it's not him."

"And this killer just so happens to have powers as well, does he?"

"Yes, he does," I said.

"Daniel, Leo is lying to you!"

"Well if he wanted me dead, he would've killed me earlier today. He never would've gotten a better opportunity, but I'm still here, so clearly he doesn't want to kill me."

"Never try and apply logic to *insanity*."

"Why is it so far-fetched?"

"Because it just is!" she said. Her cell phone rang again just as we made it to time square. She growled in fury before answering it. "What?! Natalie, we're on our way. We'll meet you at the house in five minutes." She hung up the phone. Both of us were scanning the entire area closer than detectives, trying to find some hint of sirens flashing, or police tape going up to indicate the unspeakable had happened. Night had fallen, and if there had been anyone out this afternoon, they were gone now. Somehow, the night made the deserted streets feel even emptier. The black sky made the silence even more imposing. I could see the foggy mist of my breath in the cold air, and every step we took felt like it could be heard miles away.

"I'm not crazy," I said.

"Maybe not, but you are stupid," she replied. "Whatever game he's playing, Leo is lying to you."

"Does Leo strike you as the kind of guy to play games?"

"How do you know anything about Leo?"

"I... I don't know," I said. "I got the feeling he was telling me the truth."

"So now you're the psycho-whisperer? Tell me, who does Leo say the killer is?"

"He doesn't know," I answered. She scoffed.

"How convenient."

"But he does know that the killer is an Earth Bound."

"A what?"

"That's what we are; that's what it's called," I explained.

"Did Leo tell you that?"

"Okay can you stop being stubborn for half a second and listen to me?"

"Okay fine. Let's say Leo isn't the killer. Let's say that he knows the word for what we are just because he does, and let's say someone else is killing people. They just happen to be an 'Earth Bound'?"

"Well actually—"

We jumped, as headlights flashed and sped toward us. "Hey!" I think she expected to see Leo, and I expected to see the figure in the hoodie, but we were both surprised.

"Annabelle?" I was startled by the onslaught of jet-black hair in my face as she jumped out of her car and threw her arms around my neck.

"Oh my God, I'm so glad you're okay," she said in my ear. I was barely aware of the rest of the world around me. Part of me was shell shocked, while another part was too blissed out to care. Her hair smelled strongly of strawberries, and the scent was so sweet and was making my brain fuzzy. "Your mom called me and said you'd ran off and that it'd been hours, and with everything that's happened…"

"You were worried?" I asked once I regained my ability to speak.

"Yeah," she said.

"Wait, where did my mom get your number–" I turned to Hayley.

"Okay yes, I gave it to her, but we don't really have time for that now do we? And you," she pointed at Annabelle. "If I wasn't in a massive hurry, I would so bitch you out right now."

"Wha—"

"You have the nerve to say that Daniel closes himself off around you? I've never seen him more open than he is with you."

"I really don't think that's any of your business," she said.

"She doesn't care," I said.

"Listen to me," Hayley said. "This boy is head over heels in love with you." She pointed at me and I wanted to sink into the ground. "And if you're really too blind to see that, then there is something seriously wrong with you, and admit it or not, you can't stop looking at him either, and I would go into more detail, but as I've said, I'm in a hurry, so let's go Daniel!" She grabbed me by the arm and started pulling me along the street again.

"Hold on!" Annabelle yelled. "I want to talk to you."

"What didn't you understand about 'in a hurry'?" Hayley said, pushing ahead of her.

"I'm sorry," I said. "But we have to go."

"Please," she said. "I need to say something." She looked me straight in the eyes, and I found myself unable to form the word *no*.

"Go ahead, Hayley, I'll meet you there in a few minutes." Hayley looked like she wanted to argue, but her haste to find Nico won out.

"You get five minutes," she said before running off. I grabbed her by the wrist and pulled her in, dropping my voice to a whisper so Annabelle couldn't hear us.

"I drew something before you found me. There was some kind of chapel, and it was on fire. Find Natalie and check the churches."

She pulled back, nodded, and took off. And I turned back to Annabelle.

"Okay, so..."

"Okay," she said. "I know that it's none of my business, but today I didn't know where you were, nobody knew where you were, which shouldn't have been so scary, but it was. And now, here I am standing in the empty streets where a serial killer has been running around, and I know you have the whole mysterious, shy thing going for you and all, but I kind of get the feeling that you keep a lot of secrets, and I've never been a fan of secrets, and even though I can't expect you to spill your guts to someone you just met a week ago, I feel like you're keeping me at arm's length, but I also get the feeling that you do like me, and I don't understand any of it." She finished, letting out a deep sigh. I stood there for a second, stunned.

"You just rambled..." I said.

"Excuse me?"

"Nothing, it's just...I haven't heard a ramble like that since...well, me."

"Seriously, you don't seem like the type to ramble. I basically get one to two word responses most of the time."

I laughed. "Now, but, when I was little...wow."

"What happened?" I stayed silent. I had yet to tell her about my condition and this didn't seem the time to get into that. When I didn't answer, she just nodded. "You won't tell me? Of course."

"I'm sorry, it's not that I don't trust you...it's something that's kind of complicated."

"I'm a good listener," she said.

"I don't have time," I said. Nico could be anywhere, and at the back of my mind, I knew it was stupid for me to even be standing here talking to her.

"Why not? What is so important?"

"I can't tell you," I said sadly. I couldn't help but think that she still looked like an angel.

"I know I'm practically a stranger to you, but—"

"I know," I said. I knew exactly what she meant. "But I can't."

"Fine," she said. "Then I can't either. I can't waste any more of my time, because it's clear that's what I'm doing." She started to get back into her car.

"Annabelle," I called after her. "Don't go." I ran up to her, turning her around to face me. I knew I shouldn't be asking her to stay. She should leave. I should go meet up with Hayley and Natalie so we could find Nico. I needed to find him and make sure he was okay, and she needed to leave because it wasn't safe to be around me. But regardless of all of that, I needed her to stay. It was crazy and stupid and irrational, and I couldn't think of a single logical reason that she should stay, but all I knew was I couldn't bear the thought of her giving up on me. "Please don't go."

"Daniel," she started to say. I couldn't think of anything I could say to make her stay that wouldn't make her think I was insane. But as long I was doing irrational things, I did the first thing that came into my mind. I pulled her to me, and I kissed her. My lips just barely brushed hers, but in the brief second, I felt an explosion in my chest that sent waves of electricity coursing through my limbs, eradicating every thought in my brain.

She pulled back and looked at me, her face reflecting everything I felt. Just like with Cam and Leo, I could feel passion radiating off of her and off of me too. I stared into those gorgeous brown eyes and I lost myself. Before either of us could say a thing, she put her arms around my neck and pulled me to her. I don't remember a time in my life when I felt anything even close to this. Close to the strawberry scent of her hair, or her breath that tasted like cinnamon in my mouth. It was like when Leo showed me his *mana*, but ten times more intense. I brought my hand behind her head and pulled her so close to me that I could feel her heart beating in perfect harmony with mine. That same fire from the other night enveloped us, circling us closely, pulling us together, making me feel warm and safe, while at the same time making lightning crackle through the air. I could've stayed there for the rest of eternity, in that spot, kissing her.

But then, all too soon, we broke apart. I wanted to stare at her forever, for the image of her to never leave my mind. Should've known I wouldn't get my wish. Her image was interrupted by a flash of images barging, uninvited, into my eyes. "No, no, no, not now," I muttered.

"What?" Annabelle said, but I didn't have time to answer. The pain was already beginning to mount.

"Do you have any pens?" I asked her.

"Wait, what are you—"

"Pen, pencil, paints, anything." She dug in the front seat for a moment. She emerged with a sketchbook, a pencil, and a confused and somewhat frightened look on her face. The pain in my head was rising faster than it had before, and I pushed on my temples.

"What's wrong?" she asked.

"Just give me the—*ugghh!*" A jolt of pain shot through my head, urging me to get the images out. I felt my knees buckle, and Annabelle was there, trying to help me up.

"What is happening?" She sounded scared now, but I grabbed for the sketchpad in her hand. I opened it to a blank sheet, took the pencil and set it to the paper. Immediately, my hand started moving, tracing lines across the paper, drawing away the pain. "Daniel?" she sounded really scared now.

"It's okay," I tried to sound reassuring as my hand did the work. "I'm okay." My hand flew across the page, taking a few finishing strokes to complete the drawing. I eagerly examined the image. It was a road. I couldn't tell where; there were no road signs or land markers anywhere. I could see the corner of a sign at the edge of the drawing, but I couldn't make out what it said. "It's not enough," I said.

"What is that?" she asked.

"It's not enough!" I ripped out the sheet and crumpled it up. I put the pencil to the sketchpad again, willing my hand to draw more, to show me where it was. Where Nico was. But no more images came. My hand was still. "Damn it!"

"Daniel, what is going on? Why did you draw that? What happened to you?" I didn't have time to answer her questions. The fact that I had drawn something meant that I needed to see something. Meaning Nico could be in danger. Which meant I needed to figure out where. I needed help.

"I need help," I said. "Can I borrow your car?"

"What? Why?"

"Trust me, I need to get somewhere fast." She opened her mouth to ask more questions, but I cut her off. "Please. This could be life or death." I could tell by her expression that I was scaring her, and I hated myself for that, but if Nico was in trouble, then I had to find a way to find him. And I didn't have any time to waste by walking.

"Okay," she said. "But I'm coming with you."

"What? No."

"You want my car? I'm coming with you." She still looked scared and confused, but there was a determined set to her jaw. The thought of taking her with me to try and stop a psychopathic, super powerful, murderer didn't sound like an option to me, but I couldn't take my car, and I didn't have time to argue.

"God, fine," I said. She nodded, handed me the keys, and ran over to the car. I jumped into the driver's seat and jet down the road as soon as Annabelle was in the other seat. The drive wasn't far to get to my house.

"Why are we at your house?"

"Please don't ask questions." I jumped out of the car and ran into the house, Annabelle following behind me. I threw the door wide open and started looking frantically through the room. "Dad? Dad!"

"Daniel?" my dad came around the corner into the kitchen. "Where have you been? Your mother is riding all over town looking for you! It's almost eleven—"

"Nico's gone," I cut him off. "Someone took him." His face turned somber.

"Who?"

"I don't know, but I drew this." I took the drawing out of my pocket, unfolded it, and held it out to him.

"Not very precise," he said.

"No, not really," I replied. Annabelle had come in behind me, and my dad took notice of her. He raised an eyebrow at me.

"Daniel."

"Look, I know, but I didn't have a choice. Can you find him or not?"

"How would I be able to?"

"You're a seer, right? Like me?"

"Hold on," Annabelle said. "What?"

"No," dad said. "I'm not a seer."

"But, I thought—"

"*Mana*'s work doesn't always make sense, son."

"What?" Annabelle and I said in unison.

"What is that supposed to mean?" I asked.

"It means you're special, even amongst the Earth Bound, and you can do things that we can't."

"Like my drawings and my dreams?"

"Yes, and more."

"Daniel," Annabelle said.

"I swear I will explain everything, but I just don't have time right now." I could see that she didn't understand any of this. She was scared after seeing me draw that, and now she was hearing all of this about visions and seers, and it was freaking her out. Just like with Cam and with Leo, I could feel all of that fear and confusion radiating off of her. But I could also feel that she wanted to trust me. Ask me how I knew these things, I have no idea, but I did. Slowly, but surely, she nodded. "Okay," I said, turning back to my dad. "So if you can't have visions, how do we find Nico?"

"Simple," he said. "You need to have a vision."

"Dad it's not that simple, I can't have them on command. In fact I can barely have them at all, I've only had one once, and that was with a kick-start."

"What kick start?" he asked.

"This stone Nico had." He turned thoughtful for a second.

"I think I can give you something almost as good," he said. "Follow me." He turned and walked out of the kitchen. Annabelle and I followed him as he went upstairs and went into my room.

"What are we doing in here?" I asked.

"Shh!" he said. He was standing in the middle of the room with his eyes closed.

"What is he doing?" Annabelle asked.

"No clue," I answered. Abruptly, he opened his eyes.

"Okay," he said. "I think I know who this killer is."

"W–what?" I stuttered. "What do you mean you know who he is? All you did was stand there with your eyes closed."

"I've just convened with the spirits."

"Spirits?" Annabelle asked.

"Yes," he said. "They haven't been particularly talkative lately, but I guess desperate times…"

"Wait, spirits?" she said. "As in like…*spirits*?" She turned to me, but I just shrugged impatiently.

"Don't look at me."

Dad groaned in frustration. "God I wish they would've let me teach you. Okay, the point is, they think that this killer, may be one of them. A spirit."

"What?" I asked. "But…but Leo said the killer was one of us. An Earth Bound."

"He is," dad said.

"Okay, dad?" I threw up my hands to stop him. "I don't have time for this. What the hell are you talking about?"

"God, this is frustrating," he said.

How do you think I feel? I thought.

"Okay…" Dad said. He scanned the room before lunging at my

desk. He went to my stack of art supplies and grabbed two sheets of colored paper, one red and the other blue. "There are two separate realms of existence, both existing on top of each other, overlapping." He placed the papers on top of each other and held it up so that only the red paper showed. "The Earthly Realm, where humans, animals, everything that normal people see, exists. The red paper. Then there is the Spirit Realm." He flipped it over to the blue side. "Where the spirits reside. Spirits of nature, spirits of the dead, and the primordial spirits who rule over it all. They're blue. But the Earth Bound..."

He held the two sheets of paper up to the light. The beams shown through the overlapping sheets, causing the ocean blue and cardinal red to blend together into a royal violet.

"We're purple," he said. "We exist in both places. That's why we can do what we can do, see what we can see."

"Okay..." I said, wishing he would get on with it so I could find Nico. "But what about the *mana?*"

"*Mana* is like...it's the glue. It adheres the two worlds to each other, binds them together. Since it runs through both worlds, and we exist in both worlds, we have *mana* running through us."

"And that's why we have our powers."

"Yes," he said.

"Okay, but what about the killer? What does he have to do with it?"

"The killer, the spirits say, is a spirit. He's dead, but they think that when he was alive, he was an Earth Bound. Our state of existence works both ways, Earth Bound who are alive can interact with the Spirit Realm, and those who are spirits can interact with the Earthly Realm."

"Wait so..." I tried to work through what he was saying. "You're saying that this killer... is a ghost?"

He shrugged. "If you want to put it that way, yeah."

"But what does he want?" Annabelle spoke up. "Why is he doing this?"

My dad didn't speak, just shot a grave look at me.

"Me," I said. "He wants me. He wants to take my power."

"I think so, yes," he said.

"But why all of those other people if all he wanted was me?"

"I don't think he was sure it was you he was after," dad said. "He needed to read your aura to find out, and I..."

"What?" I asked.

He hesitated for a moment, and I could've sworn the look on his face was something like...guilt.

"I've been hiding your aura from him so that he couldn't find you."

"You...you what?"

"I hid you from him," he repeated. "Suppressing your aura so he couldn't find you. And because of that he killed all of those people trying to find the Earth Bound he wanted."

I was silent for almost a whole minute. My dad looked down morosely and I could feel his pain. "That's not important," I said finally. "What's important is I need to find Nico. So did the spirits happen to mention anything on how to have a vision?"

"Oh right!" he said, looking up. "You're blocking yourself."

"What?" I asked.

"You're trying to keep your gift at bay, and so it manifests in your drawings."

"Wait, I thought I was *supposed* to draw it."

"Does it hurt you?" The question was pretty off-putting.

"What, drawing the future?" He nodded. "Well, a little." Annabelle raised an eyebrow. "Okay, a lot. But only until I let it out."

"And it gets worse the longer you hold it in?"

"Yeah," I answered. "Why?"

"You're blocking yourself," he said.

"What does that mean?" I asked, getting frustrated.

"You're rejecting your gift, trying to keep it all pent up inside and restricted, and it needs to find a way to let itself out. That's why it has to fight its way out. That's why it hurts you, because it wasn't meant to have to restrict itself, and it's supposed to be able to work itself freely. Drawing is your means of release, so your gift uses that to release itself."

"So…to have a vision and see where Nico is…I have to…"

"Figure out a way to let your gift come out freely."

I scoffed in desperation. "And how the hell am I supposed to do that?!" This time, he looked at a loss.

"Let it in?" Annabelle said. "Find a way to relax. Open yourself up." I looked at her. She was looking at me like she was seeing me completely differently. I wasn't sure if that was a good or bad thing. But what she said sparked a thought. A memory of a dream that had come to me before any of this.

"That's it," I muttered.

"What?" Dad asked.

"I need to sleep."

***

I lay down on my bed, having already explained my plan to my dad and Annabelle. Telling it to Annabelle had required giving a Cliffnotes version of the whole Earth Bound, *mana*, killer thing. She had looked doubtful, but at least she seemed more at ease and less confused. She was looking at me with concern now as I lay myself down.

"Are you sure you'll just fall asleep?" she asked.

"Yeah," I said. "The last time I needed to know something, sleep came to give me answers. It'll do it again."

"Daniel," Dad said.

"Dad," I cut him off. It wasn't like I hadn't had doubts. If I did this, I knew there was no going back. That I would be like this forever, and there would be no taking it back. But Nico was in danger, and right now, that was all I cared about. "You told me to trust my instincts. This is what my instincts are telling me. I know what I have to do." He nodded and smiled at me.

"Good luck, son," he said. I nodded and felt my mind start to go fuzzy as sleep engulfed me. Before I knew it, I was there again. Standing before that pure white, glowing door, surrounded by black. The shadows were curling themselves around my body now. Their cold, evil touch made me feel like I was dying. But I needed to get to the door. I wouldn't let them stop me this time.

I took a step through the shadows, and it felt like I was wading through ice water. Cold, sinister, lifeless water. Another step took me through the last of the smoky tendrils, and brought me to the door. Its glow was truly amazing, and I could see the gilded doorknob was still there, with the eye design crafted into it. Quickly, I grasped the doorknob, but the fear crashed into me again. That terrible sense that if I opened this door, something awful would happen. But something truly awful would happen if I didn't. Summoning up my courage, I wrenched the door wide open. Insanely bright, golden, white light streamed in through the door, burning the darkness away in seconds. The light shone on every surface of my skin, and I could feel it infusing its power with every particle of my being. The light soaked itself into me, becoming a part of me, shining itself straight through to my soul. Then I wasn't near the door any more. I was in an area I knew well. The long-term care facility of the hospital. I was in the waiting room.

There was practically nobody there. Now that was strange. However empty it was outside, there should've been more people. There wasn't even a nurse standing at the check-in desk. I looked down the hallway leading to the bedrooms, and instantly I was standing outside a door, looking into a room. There was a woman lying in the bed, hooked up to a monitor, IVs poking out of her at various places and angles. She lay unmoving, with someone sitting in a chair by her bedside. A blond haired, wiry someone, with his hand wrapped around hers. And there was another someone there too. Someone with mahogany hair and a hidden face, peeking around the corner of the room. Then I was back in my bedroom, jerking awake. I shot up out of the bed, sending Annabelle and my father, who had been leaning over me, flying backwards.

"What?" Dad asked. "What happened?"

"I know where Nico is," I said. "We don't have much time. We have to hurry."

Chapter XXI
The Darkness

My dad and I ran downstairs and I jumped into Annabelle's car. I looked back at him, but he didn't get in.

"What are you doing?" I asked.

"I can't," he said. He had that look in his eyes again, the one I had seen in the dream. That sad, helpless look. "I can't come with you."

"What are you talking about? I need you."

Pain and frustration were coming off of him in waves. "This is *your* fight. Your battle. I can't interfere. It was all they would let me do to hide your aura from him. I can't fight this for you." Looking into his eyes, I knew he was right. For whatever reason, he couldn't come with me, and I didn't have much time left to get to Nico.

"It's okay," I said. "I'll be okay."

He nodded, before his eyes moved and fixed on something behind me.

"Daniel, she's not going either," he said. I looked beside me and saw that Annabelle had strapped herself into the passenger's seat. She looked at us like a deer caught in the headlights.

"Of course I'm coming," she said.

"No way," I said to her.

"Yes way," she countered.

"No you're not, it's too dangerous."

"And it isn't dangerous for you to go?"

"I'll have Hayley and Natalie with me," I argued.

"So it can't hurt to have me there too," she countered. She leaned in closer so that my dad couldn't hear her. "I took self-defense lessons when Jesse was following me, I can handle myself."

"I don't think Tai kwon do is gonna do much against a malevolent spirit," I hissed. "Annabelle just...please stay here with my dad. I need to know you're safe." She looked like she wanted to argue some more, but she knew we didn't have much time to argue, and knew that I wouldn't be letting her go.

"Be careful," she said. I nodded.

"I will," I said. "Don't worry. I'll be back." She nodded before unbuckling herself, stepping out, and closing the passenger side door. I put the car in reverse and left Annabelle standing with my dad, both staring after me. As soon as I was out of the driveway, I picked up my phone and dialed Hayley's number. She picked up on the first ring.

"Daniel? Where the hell are you? We checked almost every church in town—"

"No time, I had another vision. Nico is in the hospital, in his mother's room. I think the killer was there with him, and it didn't look like Nico knew he was there, so he's in big trouble. Just get Natalie and meet me at the hospital, fast!" I hung up the phone before she got the chance to say anything else. The drive to the hospital was fairly short, especially considering the perfectly illegal speed I was going.

When I pulled up to the entrance, I didn't have any time to waste. They wouldn't be far behind me, and I didn't have the time to wait for them. I ran up the staircase, taking them two at a time. I burst out of the door to the third floor landing, sprinting down the hall. Just like in my vision, there was nobody there, but unlike it, there was nobody outside the room either. When I got to the door that Nico's mother was behind, I saw that it was closed. Running up to it, I yanked as hard as I could on the door handle, only to find it was locked. Fear coursing through me, I pounded my fist on the door as hard as I could.

"Nico!" I shouted. "Nico are you in there?" There was no answer from the other side. I knew I had the right room. God knew I had found Nico visiting enough times to know where the room was. I pounded on the door again. "Nico! Nico answer me!" I yanked on the door as hard as I could, begging it to open, but to no avail. As I pulled back to bang on it again, a chilling, creeping sensation snaked up my spine. Like frigid fingers brushing the back of my neck. It was the same sensation from my dreams, feeling that horrible darkness brushing up against me. It froze me in place and sent my heart hammering in my chest.

I turned to look down the hallway, but what I saw struck such fear in me that nothing from the past week could compare. It was depraved and evil and sinister. It had no form, hovering above the ground, a fog of pure shadows and darkness. *The* darkness. Right in front of my eyes. The evil darkness that had haunted my dreams and infiltrated my life was creeping its way through the hall toward me. I could sense its evil emanating from it like a horrible wave, a coldness. The sight of it provoked a terrible, awful choking sensation. What I was seeing was pure evil. And it was moving like a mist toward me. I wanted to run. I wanted to run far away from this thing. But Nico was in there, and I couldn't leave him. Wrenching myself out of the paralyzing fear, I threw my entire weight against the door. Pain coursed through my shoulder at the impact, but I ignored it and threw myself against the door again, begging it to give.

Daniel, Nico's voice penetrated the cloud of terror swirling in my mind. I stopped my assault on the door.

Nico? Then I remembered that it was hard for him to hear my thoughts. I focused my thoughts as best I could and pushed them out, praying he would hear them. *Where are you?* It took him a second to answer.

I'm okay, just run.

But—

Run, Daniel. RUN! I looked back at the smoky cloud moving toward me, and I decided not to argue. I ran.

***

I ran down the steps, and I don't remember ever running so fast in my life. But when I hit the second floor landing, I collided with someone. I kept from falling, to see Hayley standing there, her hair covering her face. Natalie stood next to her, looking frightened but determined.

"What are you doing?" Hayley asked, brushing her hair aside. "Where's Nico?"

"Run," I said.

"What?" Natalie asked.

"Just run!" I grabbed them both by the arm and started pulling them down the steps. I sprinted into the lobby of the hospital and made for the automatic doors. But I was stopped when I ran face-first into the glass doors. "What the hell?" The doors were supposed to open automatically, but they were staying shut. I tried to pull them apart by force, but they wouldn't budge. I turned back to the girls. "It's locked."

"What," Natalie said, "is going on?" I looked back toward the hallway. We had no time to try and pry the door open.

"We need to run!" I said frantically.

"Where is Nico?!" Hayley urged.

"He...he was..." I was cut off by the sensation on my back intensifying. "Run!" I yelled, pulling them to the hallway leading straight out of the lobby. It led to the adjacent hospital's emergency room check-in. Like the rest of the town, nobody was there. And this late at night, they would probably all be asleep. I didn't think they would be waking up until he wanted them to. I ran to the ER exit, but like the other one, it was mysteriously stuck. "He's not gonna let us out," I muttered. I got the feeling that our powers wouldn't be able to open the doors.

"What do we do?" Natalie asked. They were both looking at me anxiously, like they expected me to know.

"I...we..." I stumbled for something to say, trying desperately to figure out how we were going to get out. I brought my eyes to theirs, but their eyes had gone wide. They were staring at me in horror. "It's okay," I said, trying to sound calm. "We just need to—"

"Daniel," Hayley said.

"What?" She pointed at something behind me. I turned around and realized that their stares of fear hadn't been toward me. They had been toward what was behind me. The transparent glass doors had gone completely black. The darkness was outside now, covering the doors like a blackout, ensuring that we were trapped. It was so thick and encompassing that I saw nothing outside, only the suffocating darkness. It was closing us in.

"What is that?" Natalie said. Before I could answer, there was a shift on the floor. The darkness had started to seep its way underneath the doors, drifting quickly toward us.

"Run!" I shouted. I turned and pushed Natalie and Hayley in front of me as we sprinted off down the hallway. It was lined with examination rooms. I could sense the darkness gaining on us. It was chasing at our heels. I put on another burst of speed. I had to think fast. There had to be some way to get away from that thing. Looking ahead of us, I saw that the hallway ended in a set of double doors with EMERGENCY written across. We burst through them, slamming them shut behind us. I searched the room for another exit. There was an operating table in the middle of the room, chrome table set all over with shiny metal instruments carefully arranged. But no exit. We were trapped. "Bar the door," I yelled, though I didn't know what good that was going to do against this thing. Natalie grabbed a broom lying on the floor and stuck it in between the door handles. We backed away from the door. It didn't move, there was no indication from the other end that anyone was trying to get in.

"What's happening?" Hayley whispered. "Is it gone?"

"I don't know," I answered. I took a tentative step toward the door. Nothing happened, so I took another step, and that cold, morbid feeling crept up again. The broom in the handles began moving to the right, completely of its own accord. "No!" Natalie ran up and locked her eyes onto the broom. It stopped and started moving back into place, but then stopped again. They seemed to be locked in a struggle, both trying to move the broom a certain way.

"I'll hold it, find a way out of here," she yelled back at us.

"You heard her," I said. "Hayley, help me look." Hayley didn't move. She was staring at the broom and at Natalie. "Hayley!"

"That thing...how could Leo do that?" she said.

"He can't," I replied. She looked over at me.

"It's really not him." I shook my head. "Then who is it? *What* is it?"

"I don't know," I answered. "But if we don't move, whatever it is, is gonna kill us." She nodded and started around the room. We tried to find some kind of exit, but the room was only so big, and there were only so many places to look. Meanwhile, Natalie had started to sweat with the effort of keeping the broom in place. Her jaw was clenched in determination, but it was clearly taking its toll. She wouldn't be able to hold out much longer.

Suddenly, there was a loud crash on the door, like it had given up trying to get the broom out, and was now going for breaking it in half to get in. There was another crash, and another, but from the look on Natalie's face, he was still working on the broom. I didn't stop to think how he was doing both, I just kept searching the walls for a door, or an exit. But nothing. I looked back at Hayley and saw that she had found the same.

"We're trapped!" she wailed. "We can't get out!" Natalie's face was rapidly reddening from the strain. I had to find a way out of here. Desperately, I reached out my mind, trying to find Nico. *Nico where are you?* I focused all my energy on making the thoughts clear to him. I didn't get an answer, so I thought maybe it wasn't clear enough. Straining my mind, I conjured up a thought and pushed it out with all the power I had. *NICO. HELP.* I could practically hear the thought echoing throughout the ether or the void or whatever it was. There was no way, I thought, that Nico hadn't heard that. No way it wouldn't be audible to him. I waited to hear him respond, to hear his voice enter my mind. But there was nothing.

Terrible fear shot through me. What if he couldn't hear me because he couldn't hear anything anymore? My heart sank at the thought, and frantically, I pushed out my thoughts with all I had, begging Nico to hear me and to respond. To give me some indication that I hadn't been too late. That that horrible thing hadn't taken away the one person who'd always been in my life. *Come on Nico. Please hear me. Please God hear me! Answer me Nico!* But Nico remained silent.

Feeling as though I couldn't get enough air in my lungs, I felt myself fall against the wall, and it was all I could do to keep from sinking down to the floor. This couldn't be happening. It couldn't. Looking around, I saw that Hayley was looking at the door in absolute terror, totally helpless. How could it be possible that the day had come that Hayley Rutter looked helpless? And Natalie. A rich girl from Wind Eye Hills, standing strong against an inhuman force, pouring all of her strength into keeping us alive. A distant part of me was impressed by her in that moment. Impressed by the powerful way she stood, unmoving. The determined set of her jaw and the stubborn clench of her shoulders. What a piece it would be to draw her right now. The rich girl rising to the challenge and showing her true inner strength. That's how I would've drawn it.

Only real life wasn't like that. In real life, I could see Natalie's knees beginning to buckle, the pale gray pallor creeping into her creamy skin from all the exertion, the sweat pouring down her face. It didn't seem real. *How had we ended up here?* It didn't seem possible that we could've fallen so far in just a week. I felt a surge of anger at the shadows behind those doors. We didn't deserve this. I had been cowering in fear my entire life, but Hayley and Natalie hadn't. They deserved better than this. They did not deserve to die. It was *me* the darkness wanted. It was *me* it had wanted all along. Unbridled fury rose at the thought of Ms. Fairchild, Angie, Mr. McCall, Nico...*Nico.* All the victims who had fallen on my account. It wasn't fair for them to suffer because of me. Where did this thing get off?

I moved toward the door. It was banging furiously, and every bang fueled my rage. I grabbed hold of the broom and threw it aside. This bastard was not going to keep hiding behind his shadows. If I was going to die, then dammit, he was going to look me in the eyes. Before I even touched the door, it swung open; the hall was empty.

"Really?" I shouted. "I come out to you, and you're gonna hide? Come on! It's me you want, right? Well come and get me!" For a moment, there was silence. Hayley and Natalie surely thought I had gone mad, which perhaps I had.

"Daniel," Hayley said, but she was cut off by a sudden blackness. The fluorescent lights overhead flickered, then flickered again, in a classic horror movie fashion. Something about it was startling familiar, though I couldn't place what it was. But it bothered me. The lights continued to flicker, and the familiarity of it was grating at the edge of my subconscious, and it was driving me insane.

"Stop it," I commanded. "Stop it!" It wasn't making me mad so much as scaring me. It shouldn't have been. I had never thought that it was scary when lights flickered in movies. It seemed so passé and it had never quite accomplished the eerie atmosphere it was probably intended to create. Even now it wasn't eerie, but something about it shook me down to my core. It was like seeing the sunlight moving to cast its light on something truly terrifying. The flickering wasn't the terrifying part; just what it was shining light on. But I couldn't figure out what that was. "STOP IT!" The air exploded with the sound of shattering glass, and I reflexively ducked down.

I felt a rain of glass hit my back and was thankful for the sweatshirt I had on that offered an extra layer of protection. When the rain ended, I looked up and saw that every light bulb in the ceiling had broken into a million pieces, showering the floor with shards of glass, and casting the hallway into darkness. Natalie had fallen to her knees from exhaustion and Hayley was there beside her. Since Natalie was wearing a silk top, Hayley seemed to have ducked over her, her leather jacket shielding the both of them. They were both looking at me with something I had never seen before, and couldn't quite identify. Their eyes had gone round, and their mouths were slightly open, but I couldn't tell what they were thinking.

"Okay," I said. "Let's go," They both got to their feet, and Natalie wobbled unsteady, but Hayley let her lean on her for support. Together, we made our way to the door. I walked numbly, confused but not knowing why. I should have been sad. I should have been devastated. Nico was.... I couldn't even bring myself to think the word. But I knew I should feel destroyed because of it. But all I felt was confused.

When we came up to the glass doors, I could once more see the outside. The darkness seemed to have receded, but when I walked up to the doors, they still didn't slide open like they should've. Brow furrowed, I wedged my fingers in between them and pulled, but they didn't move. I took a step back from the doors. Looking back at the girls, I saw that they shared my apprehension.

"Why aren't the doors opening?" Hayley asked. "I thought it was gone."

"So did I," I said. I looked all around the room, and that sinister chill had disappeared. The darkness was no longer with us. Something had driven it away, but something was still keeping us locked inside.

Daniel? My head shot up at the voice that echoed in my head.

"Nico?" I said it out loud involuntarily, barely above a whisper.

"What?" Hayley said, snapping toward me. "Where?" She turned around, looking over her shoulder.

"I–I hear him," I told her.

"Well what is he saying?!" she demanded.

"Hang on!" I shouted impatiently. *Nico, can you hear me?* I focused the thought until I was sure he would make it out.

Yeah, I hear you. I breathed out a huge sigh as relief consumed me. Nico was alive. We weren't too late. In all of the panic, I probably hadn't been able to get my thoughts across adequately. But Nico was alive. He wasn't dead. He was alive.

Where are you? It took him another second to reply.

The hospital's chapel. I crinkled my eyebrows. The chapel. My drawing. That's the chapel it meant.

What are you doing there?

Just meet me in here. And hurry. He's coming. I tried to argue, but I felt him sever the connection.

"He wants us to meet him in the chapel," I said. "And he said, 'he's coming'."

"He?" Natalie said. "He, as in…"

"I think so," I answered. "We should go." They nodded. We started through the door to our right. I vaguely wondered why we hadn't gone through this door before. Part of me didn't remember seeing it before. It led into a hallway, which led into several different sections of the hospital. Administration, reception, MRI. And the chapel. I pushed open the doors, going in ahead of the girls in case the killer had managed to find it before we did. The chapel was different from the sanctuary from our church. There were no stained glass windows. Under different circumstances, I would've been disappointed about that. But I had more important things on my mind. They still had rows of pews, though it was significantly smaller than the other one, but then, this didn't have to fit every religious person in town every Sunday. This was just for people of faith who came to pray for sick loved ones. There was a large altar at the end of the room, where Nico now sat.

"Nico!" Hayley yelled. Handing Natalie over to me, she ran down the aisle to him. Dropping to her knees next to him, she grabbed him and kissed him. Nico kissed her before pulling back to look at her with what I thought could've been sad eyes. Helping Natalie into one of the pews to sit, I went down to them. I dropped to the floor with them, giving Nico a one-armed hug.

"Are you okay?" I asked. He looked back curiously.

"What's wrong with Natalie?"

"Used too much *mana*," I said. Hayley looked at me with a confused expression.

"Too much what?"

"Later," I said. "She'll be alright, but we need to get out of here. Nico, what did you mean when you said that 'he' was coming." Nico looked at me and I knew I had been right about his eyes looking sad. He brought his eyes up to the giant cross that hung on the wall.

"Do you know how long my mom's been here?" I was taken aback by the question, since it had nothing to do with the problems at hand.

"Five years," I replied, confused.

"Five years," Nico echoed. "And she's still the same as she was five years ago." His voice sounded thick, like he was trying to hold back tears. "You know, when I was a kid, I asked one of the doctor's here if coma patients dreamed. I wanted to know what she was dreaming about. I was just a little kid, and my dad told me that she was asleep, so I wondered what she dreamed about."

"Nico," Hayley said. "Why are you telling us this?"

"When I started learning how to use my powers," he continued, as if Hayley had said nothing. "I decided to figure out what she was dreaming about. If she was thinking, if she actually could hear me like my dad told me she could. So I went into her mind, and do you know what I heard?" He looked at us, like he expected one of us to give him an answer. We both remained silent. "Exactly," he said. "Nothing. Absolute silence. That was when I knew my mom was gone." I had never heard Nico talk like that, or sound like that. Usually, he was so collected and so put together, but he looked a mess. His dark blond hair was ragged and messy, several rebellious strands falling down into his face. He looked so sad.

"I'm sorry," I said finally. "I'm really sorry, but we need to leave. We can't stay here." He looked at me with those silver eyes that I had come to know so well; I had memorized every ray, every speck of color in them.

"I'm so sorry," he said. "I wish it wasn't you."

"Wish what wasn't me?" I asked, confused. He shook his head sadly, and I recognized the look on his face. It was the same look that my father had worn when we'd gone to my grandfather's funeral when I was three. The look he'd worn when he looked down at the open casket.

"I want you to remember the movies," he said.

"What? Nico, you're not making any sense."

"The movies. The zoo." I remembered what he was talking about. The day that he had brought me horror movies after the horrific giraffe incident.

"What about them?"

"The movie, Daniel. I need you to remember the movie we watched." I thought back to that day, struggling to remember what movie we had watched. I couldn't remember the title, but it had been something where this lady came to teach at this run-down all-girls school and found that all the girls there were witches. I remembered being terrified as the witches conjured a demon to sacrifice the teacher to, but I also remembered laughing at the atrocious special effects. And there had been this one really terrible scene where the girls stared down the teacher and tried to intimidate her, and the lights flickered really lamely...the lights.... I brought my eyes back to Nico's. He gave me a solemn nod.

"Nico..." I said. "What happened?"

"How long?" I heard Natalie call out from the back, still seated in her pew. We all turned back toward her. "How long?" she repeated.

"I'm sorry," Nico answered.

"You bastard," she spat.

"Hey!" Hayley shouted. "Back off!"

"You don't get it?" she said shrilly.

"Get what?" I looked up at Hayley. Defiant, rebellious Hayley, who barely trusted anybody since her dad left. Who had only ever trusted Nico. Like I had. I felt like I was falling all over again. Like I could never possibly get enough oxygen. Like I would pass out if the world wouldn't stop spinning. I knew that the flickering in the hallway had freaked me out. It had shined a light on something I hadn't wanted to see. That I didn't want to believe.

"You're so blind," Natalie said, pulling herself out of the pew and walking shakily down the aisle. "Look at him! 'I'm sorry'? You should be sorry."

"Okay, you need to shut up, right now," Hayley warned, stalking up to Natalie and staring her down. Natalie held her gaze, hazel eyes narrowed at her.

"I can't believe you can't see it. 'He' knew that if there was anyone who Daniel would rush to save, it would be Nico. And someone powerful enough to conjure up what we saw probably wouldn't have any trouble healing someone who's sick. Even comatose." She looked past Hayley to Nico. "Isn't that right?"

"What are you trying to say? That Nico lured us here to be slaughtered? You're crazy!"

"Oh really?"

"Hell yes! Daniel, tell her." I was silent, having lost my ability to form words. "Daniel!" She turned around and motioned for me to talk some sense into Natalie. I looked up at her, uncomprehendingly, then looked back to Nico. He was refusing to meet my eyes. "Daniel?" Hayley's voice sounded incredulous. "Don't tell me you actually believe her? Daniel! Think! This is Nico we're talking about." I was thinking. I thought about Nico's reaction when I mentioned my dad having powers. That would've made me different, because none of their parents had powers. 'He' wanted me because I was different, and that was Nico figuring out that I was different. Nico's rage at Mr. McCall's death; as if he had been betrayed somehow. He really hadn't wanted Mr. McCall to die. He hadn't been expecting him to die. Little things started clicking into place, whether I wanted them to or not. I wanted this to sound crazy and insane. I wanted to stand up and say that Natalie was crazy, like Hayley. That there was no way Nico could ever do something like that to us. Not Nico. Not the same Nico that had been there for me my entire life. But looking up at him, I saw that the person before me was not that same Nico. This Nico was someone entirely different. This Nico was a complete stranger to me.

"Even Daniel believes it," Natalie sneered. She looked at Nico with loathing.

"No," Hayley said. "Daniel. Daniel, come on! How can you even think this? Nico say something!" She was starting to sound desperate rather than angry now. I saw a wall come down and there was a part of Hayley I had never seen before. She looked scared and desperate, and she was begging Nico to tell us that we were wrong. I looked over at him, silently begging the same. For him to tell us that it was a lie. That he was, and would always be, on our side. That there was no way he could ever betray us. But he stayed silent, averting all of our eyes. "Nico..." Hayley pled quietly. He looked up at her, but he stared at the top of her head, rather than look her in the eyes.

"I do love you," he said. I was numbly shocked to see tears starting to form in Hayley's eyes. Hayley never cried. She always said she would sooner join the cheerleading squad than cry. And Hayley really despised cheerleaders. Nico looked down at me, again unable to look me in the eyes. "I'm so sorry," he said, barely above a whisper. "I really wish it wasn't you." I pulled my eyes up to look *him* in the eyes, but something was wrong. He had closed them. "Goodbye," he said quietly. A tear slid down his cheek, and I felt the terrible chill tickle my neck again. Nico opened his eyes, but they weren't Nico's anymore. His eyes had gone entirely black. No iris, no pupil, just entirely black. My breath hitched in my throat. Hayley gave a gasp of shock, and Natalie let out a whimper of fright. A twisted grin spread across his face, a grin that distorted Nico's kind features into something unearthly.

"Hello, Daniel," said a voice that wasn't Nico's. "It's nice to finally meet you."

Chapter XXII
Evil Speaks

"Nico?" my voice came out frightened and shaky. He gave a chuckle that sounded nothing like Nico. It was cold and amused, a chuckle of twisted entertainment.

"Not quite," the voice coming out of his mouth was raspy and chilled. I realized with a start that if I could've put a voice to the darkness, this would've been it. I found myself on my feet now, backing slowly away from the dark figure that was Nico and yet wasn't. "Oh come now. Don't do that." He pointed at me, and my arms snapped to my side, my legs snapped together, and I couldn't move.

The killer strolled leisurely toward me. I tried to move away from him, but I was completely paralyzed. Behind me, I heard Hayley start toward him, but he waved his arm in her direction, and I heard a thud on the floor. I panicked and I wanted to ask if she was okay, but I couldn't open my mouth. He walked forward as if Hayley had been nothing more than a gnat he had successfully swatted aside. He pointed at me playfully. "You," he mused, "have been quite a problem, haven't you?" He was looking me over like someone might appraise a high-priced gem they wished to purchase. "Hiding away your aura from me so I couldn't find you, forcing me to look all over town, trial-and-error, sifting for the one. All those bodies left behind in an attempt to find the right one." He smiled triumphantly. "And here you are." My gut knotted at the sight of him. Of the face and hair and body that were Nico's, but at the same time…it wasn't him at all. I tried to move anything, to get away from him, but I couldn't even blink. "And when I finally found you, you always had them." He jerked his chin at where I assumed Hayley and Natalie were. "Surrounding you. Eventually, I had to do away with subtlety and decided that if I wanted you, I would have to go through them."

He bent his head down to my neck and did something that made me wretch. He smelled me, breathed in my scent, like a connoisseur sampling a wine at peak. He pulled back wearing a look of pure intoxication. "So much power," he said. "So much potential. It's almost a tragedy." He circled me, examining me from every angle. I again got that feeling of being a high-priced piece at auction. When he completed his circle, he was back in front of me, with a look of satisfaction. "You're everything I hoped you'd be. Almost."

The killer tilted his head, as if examining a little imperfection, like a zit or blemish. "If not for that annoying tint of magenta." Magenta? It made no sense to me. "Oh it's quite simple," he said, as if having read my mind. "Auras give off light and radiance. Certain colors represent a person's aura and can give good indicators to the soul underneath." He tapped his fingers on my chest, right over my heart. I felt my heart constrict, as if pulling away from his touch. "Given time," he continued, "you probably could've grown to see them as well. But you see, the magenta that shimmers in you..." he shook his head like it was a shame. "It represents loneliness, misery...fear." He brought those pitch black eyes up to mine and smirked on the word *fear*.

Okay, that was enough. I did not want this creep looking into my soul. "Oh, the rest of you are brilliant reds and violets! True radiance! You truly have greatness inside of you. And..." he paused, narrowing his eyes at something he saw in my aura. "Mmm. Somebody's in love," he trilled. "She must be some girl. Am I to assume that it's a pretty little painter girl? Nico said you had a fancy for her."

"Shut up!" I shouted, momentarily regaining control of my voice. I hadn't meant to, but hearing him talk about Annabelle birthed a fury in me that I had no idea I was even capable of. I snapped. He looked at me, shocked at my outburst. He raised a hand, and my head fell back into place.

"Well," he said. "You are a feisty one, aren't you?" I realized with a jolt of surprise that I was. Through this whole conversation, all I had felt was anger. Not fear. Not fear of this killer's power, or what he had done to Nico, but rage at what he had done with that power. "Now where was I? Oh yes. The girl. She's pretty. And talented. Her aura is marvelous." He was teasing me now, talking about Annabelle because he knew it bothered me. I wondered why he didn't kill me and get it over with, but I realized that he wanted to play with me before he finished me off. I also realized that my outburst had thrown him off. He hadn't been expecting me to be able to break free, even if only for a moment, and seemed unsettled by it. I could use that to my advantage.

"She has such a brilliance about her. Powerful golds, oranges, with some intermittent blue. A passion for the arts, a kind heart. And a little hint of the lightest violet. Small, but growing. Like a blossoming flower." I had no idea what that meant, but I got an idea. Trying to do like I had with Nico, I reached my mind out to pull the answers from his mind. He laughed out loud, a sound full of mirth that echoed evilly through the chapel. "You really think you can take things from my mind? You're nowhere near developed enough for that yet." He looked at me with condescension. "But if you really want to know that badly, that color is the same thing I saw in you. The one that told me, whispered to me, that you had fallen victim to the snares of romance." He said it poetically, clutching his chest as though he were a tortured artist. He was trying to get another reaction out of me. Or rather, he was enjoying that I couldn't really react. "She could love you, Daniel. Someday very soon, she could love you."

What, so you're *psychic now?* I pushed the thought in his direction, and from the look that crossed his face, I knew he had gotten it. He wanted me for my power, and that was my power. I saw the future, and he couldn't, and that made him mad. If I was going to get out of here, I needed to do whatever I could to make him mad, to make him slip on his control.

"I will be soon," he said. "You know you're friend's auras are a mess. The blonde one," he nodded at where Natalie must've been. He shook his head with a disapproving *tsk*. "She has some light red, but it's marred by her dark orange. And that dark green." He shuddered in disgust. "Shame. And the other one." He moved out of my sight and I heard a kicking noise behind me. Had he kicked Hayley? The anger rose even further. If he touched either one of them... "She's radiant, I'll give her that. All that red and yellow. But the yellow-green is disgusting." Still, I had no clue what any of it meant. "Plus neither one of them has anything close to your power. Even Nico." So he was going to talk about Nico. "His aura is... it's just an absolute mess. Murky and fractured colors." He came back into my field of vision. "Broken." I stared at him with contempt and loathing. "Just like young Camden's."

At the mention of Cam, my blood went colder than it already was. What did he know about Cam?

"It's sad," he continued. "Just a little boy, and an empath. All of those emotions, running rampant, scarcely any of them his own. Drove the poor boy mad. It probably started off as just a faint glowing of emotion at the edge of his consciousness. Like a fly buzzing just at the edge of your vision. Sound familiar?"

If I could've moved, I would've froze. The glowing. How I had felt Annabelle's desire to believe me, Leo's rage, Nico's despair. It had all just seemed to glow off of them. No, it couldn't be...

"But then it got stronger," the killer said. "Their emotions started confusing themselves with his, he couldn't decipher his emotions from everyone else's. He was a nine year-old feeling all the emotions of a hundred full-grown adults. Stress, regret, unfulfilled dreams, anger, despair, rage. That's all waiting for you, Daniel." He smiled at me. "Seer, empath, painter; you certainly are multi-talented, aren't you?"

I tried my best to block out what he was saying and focus on throwing him off. *And if I could see auras, what do you think I'd see in you?* The killer chuckled again.

"One can never really know themselves as others know them. Like you. You see nothing but weakness and ineptitude in yourself, but you see none of the brilliance, the wit, the generosity and strength that's seen by those you let close enough to see."

I think I'd see black in you. Nothing but blackness. Just like the shadow monster you conjured to do your dirty work. He glared at me. I had no idea where this gut was coming from, but it was certainly working to get at him.

"Well, it's too bad you'll never get the chance." He extended his arm toward me, reaching for my forehead. This was it. It was exactly as it had happened with Fairchild in my dream. The touch of his hand, and all life would be drained out of me.

How did you die? I shoved the question at him with a frantic push. His face fell and he cocked his head at me in curiosity.

"What?"

How did you die? I know what y–y–you a–are. Y–Y–Y–You're dead. My thoughts were falling apart, stumbling over my fear, but I tried my best to pull myself together. *Dead. You're dead. You died, but because you were Earth Bound, you can still do these things.*

"Ah," he said, nodding. "Someone's been doing his homework. How'd you figure that out? Or did your daddy cheat by asking his friends on the other side for answers?"

Does it matter? You still died.

"That's right," he said. "No point in denying it, I did die. But, a little known secret in your world; for people like us, that's not the end."

How'd it happen? I asked. *How did you die?*

He chuckled, as if my desperate attempts to prolong my life were amusing to him. "I'm afraid that's classified. Maybe you can ask the spirits. When you join them."

He reached his hand forward again. A spark of panic flared up.

Was there blood? I threw the question out. *Is that why that happens to people? All the blood, all the pain. Is it like how you died?*

His lip curled into a snarl. "You ask too many questions. Curiosity killed the cat."

Did it kill you? Is that why you died? You were curious about something?

"You know," he said, spite gleaming in those pitch black eyes. "I'm tired of you."

The eyes! I mentally shouted as his hand drew closer. *The black eyes. They appeared on Fairchild, and McCall, and I bet if I'd looked at Angie it would've happened to her too. It's because of you, right? Your soul, it's black.*

"Goodbye, Daniel."

But you didn't have black eyes, did you? They were g–g–g–green! That's why I saw green eyes in that dream, where I saw you killing Fairchild. You tried to t–trick me by turning them black so I'd think it was L–L–Leo, but it w–wasn't, it was you! They were your eyes!

"Having trouble, Daniel?" he sneered. "Trying to put two thoughts together, it's difficult isn't it? Don't worry. You won't be scared much longer."

His hand was inches from my forehead. I wondered dimly if I would see my entire life flash before my eyes, like they say happens when you're about to die. Not much to see, I realized. Just a lifetime of hiding in fear. I wondered what would happen afterwards. What's the Spirit Realm like? Will I walk around like ghosts in movies, with nobody but other Earth Bound able to see me? If so, I was so going to haunt this guy. However that would work. Or would I live with the spirits? In that place I remembered from my dream. Living everywhere and nowhere at once, existing in every fold of space and time. Maybe I would be able to talk to my dad. Maybe it wasn't the end. I could still see my friends if I was in the Spirit Realm. They're Earth Bound, so maybe it wasn't goodbye.

As his cold fingers brushed my forehead, I closed my eyes, bidding a silent farewell to the world. Goodbye to Hayley. To Mom,

Dad, to whatever was left of Nico. Goodbye to Natalie, goodbye to Leo, goodbye to Annabelle…Annabelle. She's not Earth Bound. She doesn't exist in both places like we do. She wouldn't be able to see me. Ever. I felt my body go numb at the killer's touch, just as Fairchild's had, but the thought of Annabelle stayed in my head. The thought that we would never see each other again, that I would never smell the strawberry scent of her hair or feel the touch of her soft, sun-bronzed skin. That I would never again make her laugh or look into those deep, chocolate brown eyes and see them looking back at me. Never see her smile at me. Never again feel her perfect lips that felt even more perfect against mine as I'd kissed her. I remembered kissing her, feeling like there was nowhere else in the world I needed to be. I remembered the way I had felt when I first saw her. Like nobody in the world could possibly compare to her. I remembered the sound of her laugh and the feeling of knowing that I caused it. I remembered the taste of coconut ice cream and the sunset and…and I remembered loving her. I remembered falling so madly, insanely in love with her that even the sight of her made my heart jump, whether I wanted to see her or not.

Then I was somewhere else. A tiny portion of my brain split off and I was in my living room, staring down at my hands. Not my hands. Her hands.

I felt the fear, the anxiety, the sheer terror coursing through her. I felt her remember everything I remembered.

That twinkle in his eyes when he looks at me, that adorable way he stumbles over his words, the way he makes me laugh and makes me feel like the most beautiful special girl in the world.

Her eyes turned to a picture that sat on the coffee table next to her. It was me, a snapshot of me from when I was six. I sat at a picnic table in the park with a box of crayons and a sketchpad in front of me. My mom sat next to me, beaming down at me, and my dad had his arm around both of us, his arm outstretched to take the photo.

She smiled at the picture and felt a choke in her throat. She didn't know me back then, and she wasn't sure she completely knew me now. But she knew she wanted to, and she knew she wanted me to come back.

Please come back, Daniel, she thought. *Please just be okay. Please. I know I don't know you, but I...I...*

I brought myself back to the church, to the killer's fingers on my forehead, draining me. I had to get back. I had to get back to her. Whatever happened, there was no way on this earth I was never going to see her again.

"It's so beautiful..." he said, his eyes closed. "So much power."

My power, I thought. *Not yours.*

Defiant and determined, I mustered up all the strength I could and pushed against his hold on my body. I was met with surprise and anger. He pushed back at me, but I was not going to let him beat me. I would get out of here, and I would see Annabelle again, and I would see my parents again, and Hayley and Natalie too. No matter what. So I pushed against his power, ignoring the chill that his power gave me. I shoved against my bonds, pouring every ounce of my power into breaking free. His face was surprised, as he pushed harder on my forehead, trying to drain me so I couldn't fight any more. But I fought that too. I summoned up all the energy I had, all the love I had for my friends and for Annabelle and used it as fuel. He whipped his hand back with a shout, as if it had been burned, and just like that, my arms and legs were free. The bonds that had kept me prisoner had vanished. There were startled gasps from behind me. I looked back to see that Hayley and Natalie had regained consciousness. He screamed in rage at this. Then Hayley was on her feet, beside me, and Natalie was there too, still wobbly from all the *mana* she had used, but there nonetheless. The killer stared at us with disbelief, unable to accept that we had broken free of his power.

"Get out of here," I said, shocked at the authority coming from my own voice. "Get out of Nico, get out of this town, and get out of our lives." His lip curled in loathing as he stared at me, but I gave him as much hatred as he was giving me.

"You think you're more powerful than me? I am all-powerful!"

He screamed it out as loud as he could. In a wave of power, all three of us were sent flying about five feet down. I was in the middle of the aisle, so I only felt the impact of the floor, but looking to the side, I saw Natalie knock her head on the side of a pew.

"Nat!" Hayley yelled. She scrambled over and tried to pull her up, but she seemed to be out cold. I looked back at him, and he was stalking over in our direction, looking murderous.

"If I have to kill all of you, so be it! More power for me." He took another step, but a bright flame erupted in front of him. It sent him stumbling backwards as it spread in a line across the length of the chapel, a wall of fire separating him from us. I sensed the source of the *mana* behind us, and saw Leo standing in the chapel door. He ran down the aisle toward us.

"Come on," he growled. "We need to go!"

"Get Natalie!" Hayley and I each took one of Natalie's arms, wrapped them around our shoulders, and pulled her up. "Come on," I said, as we pulled her toward the door.

"NO!" I looked back at him and saw the wall of fire that Leo had started separate in the middle. My jaw dropped in awe as it split and the killer walked straight on through, like Moses parting the Red Sea.

"Take Natalie," I said to Hayley. "Get her out of here."

"Daniel, I'm not leaving you here alone."

"He's not alone," Leo said.

"I can't—"

"Take Natalie! Get her some help." Hayley tried to argue some more, but she knew that Natalie was hurt, and she also knew that Leo had just created a wall of fire, so she decided she could leave me with him. She carried Natalie out of the door, casting a last glance back at me. I met her gaze and nodded at her as Leo and I turned to face the killer. He was almost to us now. Since I literally had no clue what I was doing, I looked to Leo for guidance. In answer, he raised his arm and the flames that had split open moved forward to form a block around him. But the killer just waved his hand and they receded. He waved it again and Leo was sent flying. He hit the wall and was pinned there, unable to move. I looked back at the killer as he did the same to me. The impact of the wall knocked the breath out of me. He stalked up close; I could feel his cold breath on my face. His *mana* was suffocating.

"You should've burned those drawings."

"Couldn't agree with you more," I said. He practically slammed his palm to my forehead, but the power that had made him let go of me before just wasn't there anymore. I felt the life being sucked out of me, similar to a blood pressure machine squeezing too tightly. My thoughts started to go fuzzy. I tried my best to turn my head away from him, to look at Leo, but Leo was still pinned to the wall. I saw him turn his head towards us and I felt him focus his *mana*, and a bright light to the left cut through my vision. It made the killer jerk back, and I fell to my feet. It was all I could do to keep from crumpling to my knees. I looked to my left and saw another flame had erupted at Leo's command. The surprise had thrown off the killer's control over us, freeing us from his psychic chokehold.

"You can't stop me!" he shouted at me.

"Nico," I found myself saying. "Nico don't do this. Don't let him do this." I didn't know why I was doing it. I was so fuzzy, I wasn't even meaning to say those things. "Please don't let him kill me."

"Nico isn't here right now!" he shouted. "He left you when he realized I could do more for him. What can you do? Provide him someone to pity and protect."

"Please Nico," I muttered. "Please don't. Please stop him." The killer scowled in disdain.

"Now this is just sad. Your last dying wish will go unfulfilled. Quick, there's still time if you want to make a new one." He grinned wickedly and moved forward, but then Leo was there.

Leo clasped my shoulder, his *mana* radiating off of him and into me from the point where we touched. I knew what he wanted me to do, and though I knew what could happen, I did it anyway. I opened my own *mana* to his and felt the two forces collide and unify. It was like having his hand infused with my shoulder exactly where they touched. Like we were Siamese twins with joined control of one limb. And we used that limb to strike out at the disgusting thing in front of us. The one that had taken my best friend and used his body to try and kill me. The one that wanted to snuff out my life and had already snuffed out the lives of so many innocent people. I struck out at him with all I had, and when I felt it collide with him, he screamed out loud. His face contorted in agony, and I pushed harder. We met resistance. He was fighting hard against us, but I pushed him with everything I had in me.

Suddenly there was a rush of power through the room. A wave of electric darkness crackled through the room, and the shadowy fog began to close in on us. It swirled and coalesced like a vicious storm, surrounding Leo and me like the walls of a tornado. The darkness formed a ring around the two of us and began to close in. I could feel the evil on all sides of us, suffocating me as if it drew all the air away. Distantly I heard the killer's triumphant laugh, sounding so much like Nico and yet so much not.

You haven't won yet, I thought, and I sent the power against the wall of black circling us. I felt the touch of its *mana*, cold and evil, and I thought of the nightmares I had had of this darkness, the horrible premonitions that it was evil personified. But I knew better now. This thing was nothing but a manifestation of his power, just something he conjured to do his own dirty work. And I refused to be afraid of something like that.

Gathering all the *mana* I could, I shoved at it with all my might. I felt the aura of pure evil around us waver and I pushed again, shoving it back at where it came from.

"GET OUT!" I shouted, straining my voice to be heard over the rush of blood in my ears.

Out of nowhere, I felt an inflow of mana join us. I couldn't see the source, but I could feel it, deep down mingling with my own soul.

Hayley. Wherever she was, I felt her giving us her energy,

contributing her mana. And I didn't argue. I took it into my hands and heaved out in all directions, envisioning a shockwave of energy radiating from me.

And then everything snapped.

Just like snapping a rubber band, everything exploded. The darkness burst into ribbons of shadows, and a massive cold moved through the room, like a blizzard passing through and leaving in seconds. I felt a giant *boom*, like the air itself had just shattered, and I felt the shrapnel fly in all directions. I heard a scream. I felt the impact of the explosion. In the same moment, all of the energy that had kept me running fled from me. Every bone and muscle in my body shut down. Nico's body fell to the ground at the same time mine did. The last thing I remember seeing were Nico's silver eyes staring back at me.

Chapter XXIII
Everything is Different

When I came to, all I could see was darkness. I thought for a second that the darkness had come back, that we hadn't really killed it. Then I realized that my eyes were closed.

I pulled one eyelid open and was immediately met by a harsh white. I blinked until spots were no longer dancing in front of my eyes, and I realized that I was in a place I was rapidly becoming familiar with; the hospital.

"Hey there, sunshine," came a voice to the side. I opened my other eye and turned my head to see Hayley standing next to my bed, Leo on the other side of her. My dad sat at the foot of the bed, and in a chair near the door sat Natalie. She had a bandage wrapped around her head and she looked a little pale, but other than that she looked fine. I breathed out a sigh of relief.

Hayley was the one who had spoken.

"Hey," I said weakly.

"How you feeling?" Dad asked.

"Alright," I answered. "Tired." I don't actually feel any pain, just this terrible stiffness in my bones and this sort of drained feeling.

"That would be from the battle," Dad said. "You used a lot of *mana* in there. It's gonna take a while for you to recharge."

It still seemed weird to me to hear my dad talking about those things, but I just nodded along. "What about you guys? How are you feeling, Natalie?"

"I'm fine," she said. "Little bruised up but the doctors say I'm gonna be fine."

"And you?" I asked Hayley.

"You know me," she said, shrugging. "Keep on, keepin' on."

"Hayley," I said seriously. Her smile fell a little bit, but she just nodded.

"I'm fine."

"Okay," I said. Then something hit me. I shot up to a sitting position. "What happened to the spirit, did he escape?"

"Easy, easy," Leo said. "He's gone."

"Gone," I repeated. "Gone as in…"

"As in we won't be dealing with him, again," Hayley said with a smirk.

"How can you be sure?"

All heads turned to my dad. I looked at him questioningly, hoping for an explanation.

"There was a massive explosion of *mana* at the hospital. It was so powerful I felt the shockwave from it from back at the house. I knew only one thing could've given off that much power; an Earth Bound spirit being destroyed."

I didn't say anything. I just stared at him for a long moment.

"It's over?"

My dad smiled at me and gave my leg a squeeze. "It's over."

"Just call us the Ghost Busters," Hayley joked.

I began to smile, to feel a terrible weight being lifted. But then a different thought came to mind.

"What about Nico?"

Immediately, every smile fell. The air suddenly felt thick and heavy again until finally, Leo's voice cut through it like a blade.

"Nico's gone," he said. "They couldn't find him."

I stared at him for a second, sure that I must've misheard him.

"They…how could they have not found him?"

"They searched the wrecked chapel and they couldn't find any trace of him."

"But...but where did he go?"

***

When you wake up in the hospital twice in one week, it's probably time to rethink your life choices. My mom definitely agreed. She kept demanding to know exactly what happened at the hospital. We gave her the same story we gave the police; that Nico called us from the hospital, saying the killer was there, so we came running to help him, but didn't have time to call the police.

"But why?" Mom kept asking. "Why on Earth would you go there, knowing that this person has already killed three people? Why would you put yourselves at risk like that?"

"Because mom, Nico needed help." I felt a stab at talking about Nico, and I didn't bother covering it up. As far as my mom knew, Nico disappeared after the battle and no one knew where he was. That much is the truth, we just left out the crucial bit about him being an accomplice to a killer.

When my mom saw the look on my face at talking about Nico, her face twisted into sympathy and she pulled me into a hug. I let her, burying my face in her shoulder.

"I'm so sorry, baby," she whispered. "I'm sure they'll find him."

"I don't know about that," I murmured back.

"No, of course they will," she said, pulling back to look me in the eyes. "I know they will. He's gonna be okay."

Looking into her eyes, I hated myself for lying to her so much. Through all of this, all she tried to do was help and make things easier and she'd been shut out for it.

"I love you, Mom," I told her, not breaking eye contact. "I just want you to know that, I love you so much. And thank you, thank you so much for everything you've done for me. I know I give you a hard time, but—"

"Hey, hey," she stopped me. "It's okay. I love *you* so much. I'm your mother. I just want you to be okay."

There were tears glistening in her eyes and, lost for words, I just hugged her again. I stayed in her embrace for several minutes, wishing more than anything that I could be seven years old again and just stay in my mommy's arms forever. But I'm not seven years old. If this whole thing taught me anything, it's that.

So I took a deep breath and pulled back from her.

"I'm gonna go find Hayley," I told her, giving her a smile. She smiled back and kissed my forehead before I stood up, ignoring my stiff joints, and walked out of the room.

I saw Natalie walking down the hall and stopped her.

"Hey," I said. "Are you heading out?"

"Yep," she answered. "My parents decided to grace me with their presence long enough to check me out."

"So you're feeling alright then?"

"I'm fine. Though my dad did tell me off for 'playing crusader with that nothing school boy and that little piece of trailer trash.'"

"Yikes," I said. "Harsh."

"Yeah well, he's a dick," she said. "And I've never done what my dad says before so why should I start now?"

"So," I said. "You're *not* going to 'stay away from us?'"

"Easy buddy," she said, pointing a finger at me. "It's not like we're gonna be BFF's. I'm not gonna eat lunch with you, or invite you to parties…well…maybe a pity invite here and there."

"I feel so privileged," I said sarcastically.

"Down boy," she said. "Any mouthing off and you won't even get that."

I laughed, and for a moment, it felt really, really good. It made my chest feel light and airy and free, even if just for a moment.

"Bye Natalie," I said, smiling.

She gave me a reluctant grin before saying, "See you later, loser," then flipping her hair behind her and strutting down the hallway toward the exit.

"Hey wait!" I called after her. She turned back to me with eyebrow raised. "Do you know where Hayley is?"

"Where do you think?" she replied before disappearing around the corner.

I wondered vaguely if she'd ever speak to us again. Shrugging, I set off down the opposite hallway towards where I knew Hayley was.

When I ducked underneath the plastic tape and walked through the blackened doors of the chapel, I could feel her presence. I reached out my hand and extended a sliver of my *mana* to her. I felt an overwhelming sadness come over me. But it wasn't my sadness. I knew that.

When I blinked, Hayley had suddenly materialized in front of me, made solid by channeling my energy. She stood with her back to me, staring down at the altar.

"Hayley?" I said.

"They wouldn't let me down here," she said. "So I came by other methods. How'd you get in?"

I shrugged. "The guards didn't seem to notice me."

"Good for you," she said, turning around to face me. I could see tear streaks down her face but pretended I couldn't see them.

"So how you holding up?" I asked her.

"Aren't I supposed to be asking you that question?"

"Hayley."

She was silent for a moment. "What if he didn't do it?"

"What?" I asked.

"What if Nico didn't do any of this? What if that ghost, what if it was possessing him the whole time? What if none of it was the real Nico, what if he's just as much of a victim as us?"

"Do you really believe that?" I ask her.

"Well why not? I mean, this is *Nico* we're talking about. We know him."

"Do we?" I asked, more to myself than her.

"What are you talking about?"

"Hayley...I'm not sure if we ever really did know him." I thought back to what the killer had told me about Nico's aura. *Murky. Broken.* Obviously I had no reason to believe him, but when I had seen Nico there, at the altar. That lost, fractured look in his eyes. I didn't think the killer could have faked that. "I think...I think that Nico we saw in here. I think that was the first time we've seen the real Nico in a long time."

"No," she said, shaking her head. "No. That wasn't him."

"Hayley, you saw him. Nobody could've faked that."

"But it *wasn't him*."

"Hayley—"

"Dammit Daniel!" she screamed, grabbing her hair in frustration.

"I'm sorry," I said. "I'm sorry..."

"He was my boyfriend."

"And he was my best friend." We just stood there in silence. The two closest people in Nico's life, and I don't even know if either of us ever knew who he was.

After a while, the silence became too much to bear. I needed to say something, anything to fill the excruciating void.

"The...the killer said that...someday I might become an empath. Like Cam."

Hayley seemed grateful for the change of subject. First time I've ever known her to shy away from an uncomfortable topic. "And why would you put any stock in anything he said? He tried to kill us all."

"I wouldn't," I said. "Except...lately, it's like I can...sense people. From their mana, to their feelings, to if they're being genuine about something. It's faint but...what if I end up...like Cam?"

"Daniel," she said. "That's not gonna happen."

"How do you know? I mean...Cam is—"

"He's messed up, I know. But that's not his fault and it's not his power's fault either. He was just a kid when he developed his powers, he didn't know how to handle it."

"What, and I *do*?" I said incredulously. "Hayley, I'm messed up already, all by myself."

"Hey," she said, the ghost of a smile appearing on her lips. "Did I or did I not give you a speech on how tough you are?"

My face breaks into a smile and I let out a laugh. "Yeah well, let's hope I'm tough enough."

"We can only hope," she said, smiling.

I smiled at her and realized that I was wrong. I thought Hayley wasn't really my friend, but she is. She'd been a better friend to me than Nico ever was.

"I think we're gonna be okay, Hayley," I said.

"Yeah," she said after a minute. "Maybe we will."

***

Once we were out of the chapel, we barely slipped past the police who were questioning the staff. Or, I did. Hayley just vanished into thin air, gone back into wherever her body was. Once I found her waiting in the reception area, we decided to head back to my room. She took off down the hall to get herself a snack and told me she'd meet me there. When I got to my room, I saw that my parents sat there. They seemed to be talking about something or another. Whatever it was, my dad was smiling. My mom seemed like she wanted to smile, but seemed to think better of it. Nevertheless, that didn't stop Dad from trying.

The sight stopped me at the doorway. I didn't want to disrupt whatever was going on. Whatever it was, it was obvious Mom was trying not to smile, but still, it had promise. At least Dad was putting forth some effort. I guess, and I hoped, that since the whole ordeal was over, he could finally turn his attention from helping his monster-fighting son to salvaging his marriage. Who knows?

Careful not to distract them, I took a soft step back into the hallway, bumping backwards into a body I didn't even know was there before.

I whirled around, an apology flying to my lips, and I saw that it was Craig, the youth minister from church.

"Craig," I said. "Hi."

"Hello, Daniel," he said with that spick-and-span white smile. "How are you?"

"Fine, fine. What are you doing here?"

"Well I came to see you."

"Really?" I asked.

"Yes. I heard what happened here with you and your friends and I wanted to see how you were doing."

"Oh right," I said, realizing that by this time the whole town will have known about it. I could only imagine the stares I would be getting once I finally went back to school.

At least people know who I am now, I thought.

"Hm." Craig leaned around me, looking into my room. "Your parents seem comfortable."

"Uh yeah," I said, astounded. "They really do."

"You sound surprised," he observed.

"Yeah," I said. "That's just um...it's not the usual attitude, you could say."

"Ah," he said, smiling. "See, I told you. Just have faith."

"Yeah...maybe you're right." I looked back again at my parents and a smile came to my lips.

"Well, I can't stay," Craig said. "I just wanted to check up on you. And remember Daniel; just have faith. There are always people looking out for you."

I nodded, and he walked away just as Hayley came back, munching on some animal crackers.

"Who was that?" Hayley asked.

"Oh um...nobody. Just a friend of mine."

"He looked familiar," she said, staring after him. "Have I seen him before?"

"Uh...you saw him at the church that day I ran out," I offered.

"Right," she said. "That must be it."

I stood with her for a moment, staring after where he had already disappeared.

"You know…I get this feeling about him. I don't know, it's just…"

"Well," she said. "You'd better get used to it."

"What do you mean?" I asked.

"Helloooo?" she joked, tapping a finger on my forehead. "Anyone home? You're psychic, Daniel. You're gonna get feelings like that about people your whole life. Even if you don't know them now, you might someday."

"I never thought about it that way."

"You might get a flash off of any old nameless face on the street."

"That's…disturbing," I decided. "But maybe next time I'll be able to *tell* if someone is a ghostly murderer out to kill me."

Hayley laughed. "Yeah well, lucky for us there won't be a next time. It's all over now."

"Is it?" I asked as a thought came to mind. I stopped in the middle of the hallway.

"What do you mean?" she asked. "The killer is gone."

"Right," I said, pulling Hayley into an empty room. "*This* killer. But…I mean, it's not like he's the only one out there. There are other spirits, other Earth Bound, and they might come here too. I mean, *this* killer came after me for what I have. What's to stop others from doing the same?"

I could tell by the look on Hayley's face that she didn't like what I was saying. She wanted to believe that it was all finished and we could just go back to our lives, and I wanted to believe that too. But we couldn't know that.

After a moment Hayley wiped the concern off her face and flashed me a smile.

"Well then," she said. "We'll deal with it as it comes. But let's not worry about it right now. Right now let's just…*live*. Live our lives and move on. Sound good?"

I let out a sigh. "Sounds fantastic."

"Good," she said. "And hey, even if more hell monsters start gunning for you, you've got a crack team to watch your back."

I let myself smile. *She's right. I'm not alone. I have her; I've got Leo, my dad, probably Natalie. And...*

"What's wrong?" Hayley asked. "You look weird."

"It's uh...it's just...Craig, the youth pastor, he...he said something similar. About having somebody watching over me."

"Yeah..." Hayley prodded. "And?"

"Well..." I went and sat down on the vacant bed and Hayley moved to sit next to me. "There are still a lot of questions, you know? Who was the killer? Why did he choose here and now to show up? How do the stones tie into any of it?"

"Yeah," she said. "But it doesn't matter anymore. The killer's gone. But why do you look like everything isn't so over and done?"

"Hayley..." I started. "The thing is...I've been seeing this...figure for a while now."

"What kind of 'figure'?" she asked.

"Just...it's this guy, and I keep seeing him in random places, and he always has his back to me so I never see his face."

"Creepy," she said.

"Yeah, only it doesn't feel that way. When I see him, I get this overpowering sense of familiarity like I know him from somewhere. But I don't see how, since I've never even seen anything but the back of his head."

"Well what do you think this figure is? Some kind of omen, or spirit?"

"That's just it. When my dad told me that the killer was the spirit of an Earth Bound, I thought maybe that this figure I was seeing *was* the killer. And I mean, I haven't seen him at all since the battle—"

"Well then how do you know it wasn't him?" she asked.

I thought about it for a minute, trying to figure out how to explain it.

"I honestly don't know," I eventually said. "I just get this feeling from him like...like he's not stalking me, it's more like he's *guiding* me."

"Guiding you?"

"Yeah. I mean, it just doesn't feel like he wants to hurt me. It feels like he's protecting me."

"Well how has he 'protected' you? Where was he when we were fighting for our lives or when you almost died in that fire?"

I thought back to the fire, to the moments before I got out. I was on the floor, and everything was blurry, then I got the door open...no. I didn't open the door. It was opened from the outside.

"I think he got me out of that fire. He got the door open so I could escape. And...at the café, the night McCall was murdered." I thought about the wall that had bled out a message to me.

"He tried to warn me," I muttered. "About Nico. He left me a message that said 'Lies plague the beaten path, but rivers hold clear truth. Your trust is misplaced.' He was trying to warn me."

"How...how does that have anything to do with Nico?"

"Lies plague the beaten path," I repeated. "The beaten path is what's familiar, what you know. Nico was familiar to me. And rivers hold clear truth. Rivers, as in comma Leo. He was telling me that instead of trusting Nico, I should've been trusting Leo."

"Wow," Hayley muttered. "I hate poetry. You can never figure out the meaning until it's too late."

"Yeah..." I muttered. "God, he even showed me where to find Nico's floor safe, he showed up right after I drew the first murder! He's been helping me all along."

"Must be nice..." Hayley said. "Having someone looking out for you like that." She was looking down at her shoes with poorly hidden sadness.

"Hey," I said, putting a hand on her shoulder. She brought her eyes up to mine. Neither of us said a word, and while I may not be the best at reading people, I think the message got across. *You have me.*

"Okay," she said. "Well, I'd better be taking off." She pulled my hand off her shoulder and hopped up.

"Why?"

"I've gotta go see my mom and brothers, plus when I was downstairs I saw a visitor coming to see you."

She turned to head out, but I called after her. "Wait, what visitor?"

She just grinned and winked at me and then she was gone.

Shaking my head at her with a smile, I stood up and decided to see if my parents were still in my room.

When I got back, I saw my mom was talking to someone, but from her expression I didn't think it was my dad. When I moved around the corner, my heart nearly exploded out of my chest when I saw who she was talking to.

Annabelle.

Of course. Why else would Hayley be so smug?

I hadn't seen her yet since leaving for the hospital, and when I saw her there, I was reminded that we had yet to talk about the killer, the visions, and...other things that happened.

"Daniel," she said when she spotted me. I smiled in spite of myself. "Hey."

"Hey," I replied. We just kind of stood there awkwardly for a minute before my mom decided to speak up.

"Well, um...Annabelle and I were just talking."

"Yeah, I can see that."

Annabelle started. "I wanted to come see you, you know, make sure you're okay."

"I'll just leave you two alone," my mom said.

As she walked out the door, I wasn't sure if I was relieved or not.

"Sorry about that," I muttered.

"Oh no," she said. "It's fine. Your mom's really nice. Both your parents are."

"Oh right, how was it with my dad?"

"It was alright," she said. "He was worried about you." A beat. "We both were."

"You...you were?"

She paused for a moment, then nodded.

"So then, you're not like...terrified of me?"

"Why would I be terrified of you?" she asked.

"Well...I don't know. Because I'm...you know. I can..."

"Paint the future and find people by taking a nap?" she offered.

"Yeah," I said. "That."

"I'm definitely adjusting."

"Yeah..." I said. "Believe me, so am I."

She gave a small half-smile. "It's crazy."

"Tell me about it," I said, though I was referring to more than just what I can do. "It's like, nothing is the same anymore. Everything's changed."

"I know," she said, taking a hesitant step closer. "A lot has changed."

"Yeah..." I said, aware of the fact that there was less than a foot between us. "I just don't know if everything has changed for the better. Has it?"

She took a moment to answer. "I don't know. I mean, I know that things are pretty messed up right now. I heard about your friend, Nico."

"Oh," I said, taking a subconscious step back. "I um...I don't really want to talk about that."

"Right, of course," she said. "I'm sorry. I just meant to say...I know that things are complicated."

"Yeah they are." I paused for a moment, having a silent debate inside my head. "Can I tell you something though?"

"Okay," she said.

"I'm glad that you know," I said hesitantly. "I didn't like having to lie to you."

Something in her eyes shifted when I said that and she took another step forward. *"Really?"*

"Really," I said.

"Then why did you?"

"Because I didn't want you to get hurt." She was closer now, so close I could smell her, could feel the heat of her body and it drove me insane.

"You shouldn't do that," she whispered. "I want to help you."

I didn't know what to say. All I was aware of, was the fact that she was very close to me. Something snapped and my body acted of its own accord.

I lunged forward and caught her lips in mine, savoring the sweet electricity that arched through me at her touch. She pulled her arms around my neck and I ran my hand through her silky black hair, feeling the sensation rage inside of me. It was like an explosion of a million vibrant colors.

When she broke away, my lips tried to pull her in again, but my brain held them back.

"Yeah," she said, her breath shallow and rapid. "Things are definitely complicated."

After taking a moment to catch my breath, I opened my eyes to her and saw a furious blush in her cheeks. I wanted so badly to kiss her again.

"Yeah," I said. "They are."

"I think that maybe...we're both a little bit messed up right now."

"Yeah," I said. "So, where do we go from here?"

"I don't know," she said. "I guess maybe we should wait until the dust clears from all of this. See how we feel then?"

I wasn't even sure if I wanted that, but I knew she was probably right. I needed time to feel okay about what happened with Nico, and to be there for Hayley and my parents. So instead of grabbing her and kissing her like I wanted to, I said, "Okay. What do we say? Goodbye?"

"No," she said. "Not goodbye. Just...see you at school."

I smiled a little. That sounded better than goodbye. Goodbye is sad. See you at school is hopeful. A hope that tomorrow will be better. And it will.

Slowly, she disentangled herself from me and gave me a smile.

"See you at school?"

"See you at school," I responded.

I watched her go, thinking that I had never been so looking forward to going to school.

The air shifted, and I suddenly felt something all too familiar behind me. My smile fell and I knew what I was going to see before I even turned around.

Him.

The figure, standing erect with his back to me, as always.

"Who are you?" I asked. "I don't want to ask this again. I've seen you do things, lead me, guide me, warn me, protect me. I know that you got me out of that fire and tried to warn me about Nico, you've been trying to help me this entire time."

He gave no answer, just kept staring away.

"Just turn around!" I shouted. "Show me who you are!"

I didn't expect him to do it. I expected him to continue standing there and disappear as soon as I looked away, just like always. But this time he surprised me. Slowly, he began to turn, and he continued to turn until he was staring me right in the face.

My jaw dropped to the floor.

"You..." Everything suddenly connected. The familiarity, the warnings, the trying to protect me. It all made sense. It was like when I came up with the word *mana*, it was like a giant tree connecting itself. Roots and branches and leaves, painted with names and faces and dates. A wall of faces, all dotted with bright blue eyes. I was a child again looking up at that family tree, my eyes falling on the one that drew me in.

You know, they still watch over us. They're watching over us right now.

"The one with a part of me...that's how you knew, wasn't it? How you knew all of that about Nico. I have a part of you. My gift, my power. My blood..."

As I looked at him, my eyes scanned over his major features and they went straight to his eyes. Eyes that were pale and bright at the same time. Eyes that shone bright against dark hair. Eyes that were a piercing, opalescent blue. Cohen Family eyes.

My eyes.

About the Author

Luke Evans completed his first draft of *The Earth Bound* at age fifteen. Luke has been involved in theatre since he was a young child and has performed in educational and regional venues throughout Georgia. His period play *A Newsie's Tale* was produced at Stiles Auditorium by Act One Theatre. He has several short stories and novels in development.

Credits

T. Denise Clary | *Editor-in-Chief*
Fiona Jayde | *Artist*
Star Foos | *Designer*
Benjamin Grundy | *Typesetter*
Rachel Garcia | *Reader*
Sarah Landauer | *Copy Editor*
Allison Oesterle | *Proofreader*
Andrew Call | *Reviewer*
Erin Sinclair | *Managing Editor*
Travis Robert Grundy | *Publisher*
May 2016 | *The Zharmae Publishing Press*